A SPELL IS CAST

We ourselves are the true link between the world of the spirit and the world of matter, Nyctasia mused, *and thus the gateway where the two realms meet is rightly to be sought within ourselves and not otherwhere. . . .*

Nyctasia drew her dagger, and slowly closed her hand around the blade. The edge bit deep into her palm and fingers, but she barely felt the pain.

> "Approach, I am near you,
> Speak, for I hear you . . ."

Nyctasia chanted as the throbbing swelled in her wounded hand. Behind her closed eyes she thought she saw the reflections of fallen stars, or of stars which had never been. Finally she pressed her hand against the stained floorboards and waited, silent, while the living blood mingled with the dead. . . .

Ace Books by J. F. Rivkin

SILVERGLASS
WEB OF WIND
WITCH OF RHOSTSHYL

WITCH OF RHOSTSHYL

J. F. RIVKIN

ACE BOOKS, NEW YORK

PROLOGUE

A STRANGER LOOKED in the back door of The Jugged Hare and tried, with scant success, to catch the attention of someone in the kitchen. "Eh, is there anyone here called Steifann?" he shouted finally.

"*I'm* Steifann," declared a thin, grimy youth named Trask, who was slicing a pile of potatoes. He drew himself up to his full, rather unimposing height, thrust out his narrow chest, and swaggered across the room to address the traveler. His mimicry was undeniably accurate. Somehow, by the tilt of his smooth chin, he even managed to suggest Steifann's thick black beard. "What's your business with me?" he demanded, in his deepest voice.

The cooks exchanged amused glances, and a serving-girl giggled. The messenger looked doubtfully at them. "I've a letter here...."

Trask gestured peremptorily at Walden, the head cook. "Pay the fellow," he ordered, snatching up the sealed paper and perching on the table among the potato peelings. Walden obeyed, and the man withdrew, shaking his head in confusion.

"Trask, Steifann'll tear you to shreds if you open that," scolded the girl, looking over his shoulder eagerly. "It must be from Corson."

Walden shoved her toward the taproom. "Go fetch him, Giniver, you goose—neither of you brats can read anyway."

"Oh, I can make *this* out well enough," said Trask. "Listen!" He broke the seal at once and held the letter at arm's length, peering at it shrewdly, though it was upside down. "My darling, sweet lambkin," he recited, loudly. "I think of you every moment, for I have an ache that gives me no rest, and no one else can ease it. Every night I toss and tumble about, dreaming of your broad shoulders and thick, mighty arms, your wide, warm chest, your manly hips and long, powerful thighs, your—"

"Give me that, you stinking little turd, before I tear your

1

tongue out!" roared Steifann, charging in from the taproom and grabbing Trask by the collar. He seized the letter, and Trask wriggled from his grasp, ducked a blow, and scampered out the back door, snickering.

Steifann glared around at the others, but they made no attempt to hide their laughter. "Well, read it, lambkin," said Walden. "What's that worthless layabout Corson got to say?"

"That's my affair—and I don't pay you lot good wages to stand about gaping like half-wits! There's work to do." Steifann hastily scanned the letter, and everyone gathered around to hear the news, ignoring his bluster. "Nothing but a lot of lies and boasting, as usual. . . . Her handwriting's a bit better, though," he said, surprised. As he read further he reddened, cleared his throat, pushed the hair back from his forehead, and finally grinned. "She'll be home by first frost!" he announced.

1

BY THE TIME her ship docked at Chiastelm, Corson was already in a rage of impatience. She was bored by the confinement and monotony of shipboard life, which left her all too much leisure to imagine how Steifann was spending his time—and with whom.

"Rutting stud-bull," she muttered. "Probably been to bed with everyone on the coast since I've been gone, especially that dirty hag Destiver." And when she saw that Destiver's cargo ship, the *Windhover*, was in port, her suspicions seemed all but confirmed.

There was not much work for a skilled mercenary in the peaceful port town of Chiastelm, and Corson was more often away than at home. During her travels she was no more faithful to Steifann than he was to her, but this did not allay her jealousy in the slightest. However she might carry on, in the distant lands where her sword took her, she felt that Steifann ought to be passing the time thinking of her and longing for her return. She knew this was foolishness, and in her more reasonable moments she laughed at herself for it, but Corson's reasonable moments were few, where Steifann was concerned. And Steifann, a most sensible man as a rule, was just as unreasonable about Corson. Both furiously resented anyone whom they suspected of sharing the other's bed.

But Corson despised Destiver, the cargo-runner and petty smuggler, more than all the rest. Destiver had known Steifann longer than Corson had, which was an unforgivable offense in Corson's eyes. Furthermore, she'd recently charged Corson an outrageous fee to smuggle her out of Chiastelm when there was a fat price on her head. That bloodsucking bitch was probably at the Hare with Steifann right now, Corson thought grimly, the both of them drunk and randy as rabbits. . . .

But once she left the wharves behind, her ill humor soon gave way to eager anticipation of her welcome. Whenever she returned to the Hare, her friends made much of her and even pampered her a bit, plying her with food and ale and questions about her ad-

3

ventures. Well, she had tales aplenty for them this time, and the loot to bear them out. When she showed them the gold and the large, uncut diamond she'd earned by her sword, they'd see that she was no common fighter-for-hire. She, Corson brenn Torisk, was a fit companion for gentlefolk.

The jewel, and her fine red-gold earrings, were the gifts of a grateful noblewoman, a lady of the lofty rank of Rhaicime. And there was a gown of gold silk as well, a token of hospitality from a family of wealthy vintners in the Midlands—folk of noble descent they were, too. She would let Steifann know that she'd been wooed by the handsome heir of a distinguished line, while *he'd* been bedding down with that scrofulous smuggler. And if Destiver was there to hear it, so much the better!

It had been too long since Corson had enjoyed a proper homecoming. The last time she'd come back, she'd hardly been home a day before she had to sneak out of the city in the hold of the *Windhover*. It had all been monstrously unfair, Corson thought. True, she had cut the throat of a powerful nobleman from Rhostshyl, but that was his own fault, she considered, for abducting the Lady Nyctasia while Corson was her bodyguard.

But now that Rhostshyl was involved in civil war, the rulers of the city had no time to concern themselves with a mere hireling killer. Corson could safely pass the winter with Steifann and his people, who were more of a family to her than any she'd known before.

When she caught sight of Steifann's tavern her pace quickened, and she thought she could smell the savory stew, roasting meats and baking loaves. As always, she went straight to the kitchen door.

"I'm back!" she announced. "And I'm hungry as a hunter. I've been living on ship's swill for weeks."

But instead of crowding around to exclaim over her and hear her news, the others went on with their work, barely sparing her a greeting. They seemed busier and more rushed than usual. Steifann was nowhere to be seen—and neither was Destiver.

"Oh, good, Corson's here," said Trask. "She can keep an eye on the drunks out front." He blew her a kiss and went on scrubbing a pot with unwonted industry.

"Corson, my pet, just in time. Here, carry this." Annin, the head serving-woman, held out a heavy tray laden with mugs of ale.

"Never mind that," Walden ordered. "Someone has to chop more firewood. We haven't much left."

"Where's Steifann, then?" wailed Corson. "Why hasn't he cut the wood?"

"He's sick, we put him to bed. The man's no use at all."

"Sick? Steifann's never sick. He's healthy as an ox," Corson said uneasily. "What ails him?"

"Grippe. Fever. Go see for yourself—but don't tarry. I need that firewood *now*."

"Firewood . . . ?" Steifann said hoarsely, as he lumbered into the kitchen. His face was flushed with fever, his eyes red and swollen. "I'm going out to chop the wood—" He broke into a rasping cough and collapsed heavily onto a bench. "Soon," he added, and sneezed.

"I'll do it," Corson said reluctantly, "and it's more than Destiver would do, mark my word."

"First help me drag this diseased dog back to bed, before he gives us all the grippe," sighed Walden.

Steifann sneezed again. "Destiver? Is that lazy leech here again? She wouldn't lift a finger if the lot of us were dying. She only comes by to drink my ale and tell lies about her past as a ferocious pirate."

Annin bustled in carrying the empty tray. "What's he doing in here? We've enough to do without looking after him."

"I'm fine," Steifann protested. "No need to fuss. . . ." He leaned back against the wall and looked up at Corson, bleary-eyed. "So you're back, are you? It's about time. Where have you been?"

"Come along, love," Corson said resignedly, pulling him up by the arm. "I'll tell you all about it."

He staggered against her and mumbled, "I don't need any help. It's just a chill—" and started to cough again.

Corson removed an accounts-ledger and a stray boot from the bed, then gathered up the tangled quilts and shook out each one. She laid them out smoothly, as Nyctasia had done for her only a few months before, when she'd been desperately ill herself. Corson remembered how curiously comforting it had been to have the bedclothes properly arranged for her, though Nyctasia had received little thanks for her attentions.

Steifann was no more cooperative than Corson had been. "I don't want blankets," he said, kicking at them. "It's hot in here."

"It's not. The fire's gone out. And when you have a fever, you ought to stay warm. I know all about such things."

Steifann snorted. "And when did you become so learned a physician?"

"I know what Nyc did for me when I was sick—in Lhestreq it was. And I didn't have just a touch of grippe, I tell you, I was *poisoned*. I nearly died, I was too weak to move, for days and days—"

"Who's this Nick," Steifann interrupted, "and what else did he do for you?"

Corson looked smug. "She's an old friend. A lady of quality, from the aristocracy. You needn't think that I spend all my time in the company of louts like you." She picked up some of his clothes from the floor and threw them over a chest. "This place looks like a kennel."

"You've known plenty worse! When I met you, you were glad of any roof over your head—" He broke into another fit of coughing before he could give full expression to his indignation.

"There! You should be quiet, you see? You're supposed to rest, and . . ." Corson thought for a moment. "And drink something hot. I'll mull some ale," she decided.

"Corson!" Trask shouted through the door. "Walden says if you don't cut that firewood now, he'll come in after you with the axe."

Corson sighed. "I might as well. I have to make up the fire in here too."

"You might fetch in more water while you're about it, Your Highness," Steifann suggested.

Corson slammed the door on her way out.

"Corson!" Steifann called after her.

"What now? Do you want me to clean the stable too?"

"I'm glad to have you back," said Steifann.

2

ANNIN CAME DOWNSTAIRS briskly and looked around the kitchen. "Where's Corson? Isn't she up yet? It's time she was off to market."

"She left at first light and came back an hour ago with our supplies," Walden said without looking up from his bread-dough. "Then she went off on some business of her own. She brought in wood and water enough, though. First time we've had everything we need since Lambkin's been abed."

Trask wandered in, tousled and yawning. "Poor Corson! She came all this way to get Steifann into bed, and instead she can't get him out of it. I'm surprised she stayed this long."

"Wash your hands and get to work on this kneading. Corson's just gone on an errand, a letter to deliver, or some such thing. She said she'd be back before anyone in the taproom had time to get too drunk."

Annin shook her head in wonder. "That one's earning her keep, and no mistake. I've never known her so hard-working. She's been doing all Steifann's work, and everything else she can lay her hand to."

"And waiting on him hand and foot like a nursemaid," Trask put in. "He'd be a fool to get better. I wouldn't, in his place."

"She brought him his breakfast this morning too," Giniver reported, with a smirk.

"I'll tell you what's even stranger than all that," said Walden. "She's hardly been complaining lately."

Trask gave an exaggerated gasp. "By the Hlann, you're right —and she hasn't been drunk even once, or started a fight." He pounded both fists into the mass of dough on the table. "It must be love!"

There was plenty of sickness in the town, as there always was at the turning of the seasons, and Maegor the herbalist was busy.

She was not pleased when a tall, armed stranger entered the apothecary and asked for her by name.

She thought at once of Nyctasia. 'Tasia's allies from Rhostshyl had come already, asking for news of her, but were her enemies still seeking her as well? Had they learned that Maegor still heard from her, from time to time? If so, this visit could mean danger. The others had accepted her word that she did not know where Nyctasia could be found, but the minions of the ruthless Lady Mhairestri would not be so easily satisfied. . . .

Maegor was fairly tall herself, but she had to look up to meet the eyes of the unknown swordswoman. "I am Maegor," she said calmly. "How may I serve you? You don't look to be in need of healing herbs."

But the woman smiled disarmingly. "Not for myself, to be sure, but my man's down with a hard cough, and a fever. I was told you might have some remedy." Corson had little use for potions and medicaments, for she was rarely ill, and wouldn't admit to it when she was. But since the commission from Nyctasia brought her here, she might as well see about some cure for Steifann.

"I can prepare an effective cordial for that," said Maegor, somewhat reassured, "but there are others before you, as you see."

"Oh, I can come back later," Corson said pleasantly. With her back to Maegor's other customers, she drew Nyctasia's letter partway from her shirt, far enough for Maegor to see.

"Yes, that will be best. I've no doubt I can help you. I'll be ready for you, then—just after sunset," Maegor suggested.

Corson had recognized Maegor at once from Nyctasia's description. "A woman of polished walnut wood," Nyctasia had called her, and so she was. Her hair and eyes and skin were all of a deep, burnished brown, and she had something of the vital, unyielding nature of living wood as well. There were few people Nyctasia trusted so unreservedly.

As Corson expected, Maegor was alone in the shop when she returned. She handed her the letter without explanation, and Maegor quickly broke the seal, assuring herself that the writing was in Nyctasia's hand. She glanced through it hastily while Corson walked about the apothecary peering into the clay jars that lined the shelves.

"She doesn't know . . . ?" Maegor said, frowning.

"About Rhostshyl? Not when I left her. She may have heard something by now."

Maegor sighed. "I hope not. She'll think she should come back, if she learns how things stand in the city. And there are those who . . . well, no matter." She seemed sorry to have said even so much as that. "I once tried to persuade her to stay, but now I'm glad she's clear of the place."

"I promised to let her have news of the city."

So you know where she is, Maegor thought, but she said only, "If she returns, she may very well be assassinated."

"She knows that," Corson said evenly. "I've no right to make such a decision for her." She did not add, "and neither have you," but Maegor understood her well enough, and she turned back to Nyctasia's letter, silent.

"Is it true that ground hartshorn excites the passions?" Corson asked, examining a small pot of greyish powder.

Maegor looked up, startled, then laughed. " 'Tasia told you to ask me that, as a sign, didn't she? Those were the first words she ever spoke to me. Are you satisfied?"

Corson shrugged. "I was sure of you. But I thought perhaps you weren't so sure of me."

"I wasn't, at first—but it's not likely that anyone else would match 'Tasia's description of her courier. Listen: 'She who delivers this to you should be a veritable giantess, a magnificent creature a furlong high and as beautiful as a dream, with great blue eyes, skin like dark honey, and a long bronze braid crowning her proud head.' " Maegor paused to look Corson up and down, nodded, and continued, " 'If some lesser being stands before you, then this message has been intercepted, but I have no fear of that. My messenger is as deadly as she is comely, and her equal with a sword has not been born.' You seem to have made quite an impression on the Lady Nyctasia, friend."

Corson blushed and said stiffly, "That one wallows in words like a sow in muck. I don't pay any heed to her nonsense. And I can't wait about here all night, for that matter—I've work to do. If you want to send her an answer, you can find me at The Jugged Hare. But what of that remedy you promised me, eh? That wasn't a ruse, I do need it. Do you know Steifann brenn Azhes at the Hare?"

"I know him by reputation," said Maegor, discreetly, without mentioning what Steifann's reputation was like. "Is he the one taken sick?"

Corson nodded. "First time since I've known him. He's coughed himself hoarse. His throat's swollen up and he wheezes like a bellows. Can you really heal that?"

"Well, I can ease it a good bit. Keep water on the boil in his room day and night. The steam will soothe his breathing. Is he sneezing too?"

"Constantly."

"Mmmm, with a fever, you said?"

"I think so. He has the chills."

Maegor disappeared into the back of the shop and returned with her hands full of fragrant dried fruit rinds, which she tied up in a square of cloth. "Boil these in water or wine till the mixture's thick, then have him drink all of it at once, as hot as he can bear it. That's for the cough. But these"—she measured out a selection of herbs—"are for fever and catarrh. Steep them in a tea and give him a cupful at night and in the morning, with plenty of honey. Honey's good for the throat."

Maegor gave Corson further instructions on caring for a chill and cough, and sent her away laden with admonitions and medicinal preparations. Only when Corson was gone did she give her full attention to Nyctasia's letter.

As usual, Nyctasia did not say where she was. Raised among the schemes and intrigues of the court at Rhostshyl, she considered such information a weapon that might fall into the wrong hands and be used against her. The feuds and rivalries of the nobility of the city had often taken a deadly turn, and Nyctasia ar'n Edonaris had made more enemies than most. Her attempts to settle the ancient enmity between the Houses of Edonaris and Teiryn had not been welcomed by either party. Powerful factions of each family were determined that the feud should end only with the destruction of the other. Nyctasia had been forced to flee the city, and with Corson as bodyguard she had escaped the coast with her life. But even safe in exile she found it hard to abandon the caution bred by a lifetime of secrecy. The letter said that she was among friends, but gave no clue to her whereabouts.

When Maegor had last seen her, Nyctasia had revealed that she meant to join her lover, Erystalben ar'n Shiastred, but where he had settled after leaving Rhostshyl, Maegor had no idea. The Edonaris had driven him from the city years before, to end his influence over Nyctasia. He had not only threatened their plans to marry her to her kinsman Thierran, but had also abetted her in the study of magic—a study which had won her an undesirable (and largely undeserved) reputation as a dangerous sorceress.

Maegor had met Lord Erystalben, and found him overly proud and ambitious. Not a man, she thought, who ought to study magic. But his love for Nyctasia she could not doubt, and it had been comforting to know that her friend would not be alone in exile.

Yet Maegor was not truly sorry to learn that Nyctasia was not with him after all. Perhaps now she would turn from her pursuit of the magic arts. "He is lost to me," Nyctasia had written, "through a spell of Perilous Threshold, which he used in desperation to defend his stronghold against a more powerful mage. Such a spell exacts its own price, and I know not where it has taken 'Ben, nor what it has taken from him. I have 'sought in spirit, that the flesh might find,'"—a quote Maegor recognized from the *Isperian Precepts*—"but I have learned little. That he lives is certain, but he might be anywhere in this world, or in another. He may be so changed that my spirit can no longer reach out to his. I have dreamed dreams that do not lead me to hope."

Though Maegor was no magician, she knew how dangerous and unpredictable a spell of Perilous Threshold was said to be. Surely even Shiastred, with all his hunger for power, would not take such a mad risk. There was much, she realized, that Nyctasia had not chosen to tell her.

"But I have found a family who treat me as one of their own," the letter continued, "and I shall try to be content with that for the present. I have work to console me as well, for a great collection of books has recently been discovered in these parts—an entire library of rare and precious works, which are all that remain of a sect of scholars known as the Cymvelan Circle. All seven volumes of *The Manifold Ills of the Flesh* are here in full, and Rosander's treatise *On the Curative Properties of Wildroots*. I shall send you the latter as soon as I have taken a fair copy."

Maegor smiled. Nyctasia had not changed. However grave her plight, she never lost her passion for learning of all kinds—nor her readiness to display her erudition. If anything could reconcile her to exile from Rhostshyl and separation from Lord Erystalben, it would be the lost lore of an obscure lot of scholars somewhere in the hinterlands.

"No one hereabouts takes an interest in the books, and I have them altogether at my will," Nyctasia exulted. "I ought to summon scholars from the university in Liruvath to share in this discovery, but I mean to take its measure myself, first. There are certain works here on the secrets of the spirit, which may be of some use to me."

Nyctasia was unchanged indeed. Sighing, Maegor read on, but what followed was even less to her liking.

"I rely on you to let me know how matters fare in the city"— to Nyctasia there was no city but Rhostshyl—"for travelers from the coast are rarely met with here. You may safely entrust any message to my fair courier, Corson brenn Torisk by name, who can be found betimes at the ale-house called The Jugged Hare."

Nyctasia concluded her missive formally, with a traditional Vahnite blessing. "May the Indwelling Spirit guide you in all things, my dear Maeg," she had written in closing, with a characteristic flourish, "and for the *vahn*'s sake, don't forget to burn this!"

3

CORSON LAY AWAKE listening to Steifann snore, and trying to decide how to begin a letter to Nyctasia. She rarely wrote to anyone but Steifann, and her letters to him were not altogether different from Trask's idea of them—but something more formal seemed to be called for now. What form of address would be proper between persons of such widely disparate rank as herself and the Rhaicime Nyctasia? Corson hated to reveal her ignorance of such matters by using the wrong terms, but she could hardly consult a public scrivener about this letter. It was commonly believed that Nyctasia ar'n Edonaris was dead, and it would be safest to let it stay that way. For secrecy's sake, the letter would have to be sent on the *Windhover* as far as Lhestreq, but there was no help for that. Destiver at least knew how to keep her own counsel, though she had no other good qualities, in Corson's opinion.

But Destiver would soon be on her way north—this letter must be taken in hand. Knowing that nothing short of an earthquake would wake Steifann, Corson got up, wrapped herself in a blanket, and lit a candle from the hearthfire. She pushed Steifann's account-books to one side of the table and sat with her head on her hand, nibbling thoughtfully at the tip of a quill. "Corson brenn Torisk, to the Lady Nyctasia ar'n Edonaris, Rhaicime of Rhostshyl, Greetings," she murmured. That sounded impressive, but was it correct? Should Nyctasia's name come first? It would take forever to write it, either way. . . .

Corson was proud of her ability to read and write, rare skills in one of her station, but her hands were trained to the sword, not to the quill. Under Nyctasia's direction, she had practiced her penmanship, but she still found it slow, uncomfortable work.

Perhaps she ought not to reveal Nyctasia's full name in the letter at all. It would pass through many hands before it reached her, after all, and it might be wiser to be cautious. The letter could be directed to the estate in the Midlands where Nyctasia

13

was staying with a distant, disowned branch of her family. They'd see that she received it. That would be best.

With a sigh of relief, Corson flexed her fingers and carefully wrote, "Dear Nyc,

"It's happened in Rhostshyl as you said it would. It's over now, and your kin hold the city, whatever's left of the place. You're well out of it, from all that I hear. Plenty of folk fled to Chiastelm for refuge, and they say half the city's in ashes, and many killed on both sides. Maegor can tell you more of it than I, she says she's spoken with your friends from Rhostshyl. I didn't think you had any friends in Rhostshyl, but I suppose she knows what she's about. She's a fine healer, that's certain. Steifann was half dead with the grippe when I got here, and she told me how to look after him. Now he's as well as ever."

Corson paused to shake her cramped hand. She'd have liked to boast to Nyctasia about all she'd done to care for Steifann, and how much she'd learned about nursing a fever, but writing all that would be more of a chore than doing it had been. She decided to let it keep, and pass on to something more important. "I could even say that he's better than ever," she wrote, grinning to herself. "I used that comb you gave me, the wooden one, not the silver one, and it was all you claimed, I confess. I had my doubts, but I guess even you have to tell the truth now and then." Corson chuckled, remembering the evening she'd tried out the charmed comb that Nyctasia had made for her as a parting gift.

Steifann had recovered his health quickly under her ministrations, and had taken up the heavy work about the place again, bringing in supplies, throwing out troublemakers and seeing to everything else that needed doing. Corson had decided to take a well-earned rest that night, and left the others to close up the tavern while she soaked lazily in a hot bath. She had taken to washing more often of late, to prove to the fastidious Nyctasia that she was not the unkempt sloven Nyctasia had called her at their first meeting—though she would have died in agony before admitting that she cared for Nyc's opinion.

And tonight she particularly wanted to be clean, since she meant to wear her gold silk gown for Steifann, for the first time. She washed her waist-length, chestnut hair till it shone in the firelight, and went to a chest to fetch her fine silver brush and comb. Let Steifann see those too, she thought with satisfaction.

But then she noticed the wooden comb among the heaped mess of her belongings in the chest, and picked it out instead, examining it thoughtfully. It looked ordinary enough, just such a poor piece of frippery as any peasant girl might buy at market for a copper. But Nyctasia claimed to have bewitched it with a certain mysterious perfume that drove men wild with desire. Only men could smell it, according to Nyctasia, and then only when the comb was drawn through a woman's hair. It sounded suspiciously like one of her strangely convincing lies, but what reason could she have to make up such a thing?

Even if the comb did what Nyctasia promised, though, Corson wondered whether she'd be able to tell the difference. It was hard to imagine Steifann any lustier than he already was. But he might be more tired than usual tonight, working so hard after just recovering his strength . . . and it could do no harm to try the thing, after all. . . .

Steifann *was* rather tired by the time he finished securing the tavern for the night, but he forgot his fatigue when he pushed open the door to his room and saw Corson waiting for him. She half lay on the sheepskin hearthrug, sheathed in heavy cream-gold silk that caught the firelight and cast its sunset radiance over her honey-gold skin and glowing, burnished-bronze hair. Steifann caught his breath at the sight. He had always thought Corson a fine-looking woman, though he never saw fit to tell her so, but she was usually bedraggled and dirty (as he never failed to tell her) and rarely looked respectable—much less glorious.

Corson looked up and smiled a welcome as she pulled the comb slowly through her damp, shining hair. "What do you think of my gown? A rich vintner in the Midlands gave it to me."

"Very pretty," Steifann said gruffly. "What did you do to earn it, eh?" He took the comb and rapped her on the head with it, then began to comb her long hair for her.

Corson sighed contentedly. "I was a guest of the house, I'll have you know. They even named a new wine for me."

"Did they call it Shameless Slut?" Steifann suggested. "And when did you start perfuming yourself like a strumpet?" He suddenly buried his face in her scented hair, intoxicated by its sweet, heady fragrance. "You smell like a whore," he lied, his voice thick, his breath quickening. His hands had begun to shake slightly, and the comb fell from his fingers. Dizzy with desire, he pulled Corson against him, kissing her hair and her throat, sliding his hands hungrily over her breasts and belly.

A rush of passion cascaded through Corson till it seemed to pool in her hips, but she elbowed him away and said tartly, "You should know how a whore smells. You bed down with enough of them while I'm away." Let him smolder a bit—he'd burn all the brighter for it soon.

Steifann meant to retort, "And I suppose you weren't whoring all over the Midlands with that vintner of yours?" but he didn't seem to have breath enough to speak. That didn't matter, though. Nothing mattered but obeying the command of that compelling, overmastering fragrance, which no longer seemed to him a mere scent, but an irresistible power in his very blood. Without thought, he seized Corson and pulled her down onto the hearthrug, searching fiercely with hands and mouth for the elusive, maddening secret she had somehow hidden everywhere at once.

Corson gasped in delight. At that moment she forgave Nyctasia for every deception and insult. "Have a care, love," she laughed, "this is Liruvathe silk!"

Now Corson stretched and yawned, smiling sleepily to herself. Well, she couldn't write all *that* to Nyc either, more's the pity. She'd have to wait to thank her properly someday, face to face. For the present, she contented herself with writing, "Many thanks. I wouldn't trade that comb for the whole Imperial treasury!"

Corson shamefacedly confessed the trick to Steifann some days afterward, but he merely roared with laughter and called her a number of very colorful names, some of which she'd never heard before, even in the army.

"And me worrying that I'd gotten as drunk as that on so little ale," he added. "I was afraid I'd lost my stomach for drink! I can't remember half of what we did that night—but I wouldn't mind doing it again, I know that." He picked up the comb and sniffed it cautiously. "I don't smell anything now."

"Nyc says the perfume can only be smelt in a woman's hair."

"Nick, eh? The more I hear of that one, the less I like her. So she combed your hair for you too, did she?"

Corson grinned, relishing his jealousy. "It only works on men. Nyc just made the comb for me to remember her by. And she gave me these gold earrings too, when my old ones were stolen. She gave me a lot of fine things," Corson said provokingly, "because she enjoys my company. She's *very* fond of me."

"I'll give you a fine lot of broken bones to remember *me* by, one of these days, you slattern," Steifann said, swatting her affectionately.

Though he'd done nothing but complain while he was ill, Steifann had secretly been delighted to have Corson caring for him and fretting over him. He'd never seen her behave so responsibly before, and he liked what he saw. Had he heard her tell Maegor that "her man" was sick, he would have been even better pleased. And the incident of the comb had done nothing to detract from her charms.

Finding that he took such an indulgent view of the charmed comb, Corson decided to unburden her conscience of another matter as well. "Nyc did another piece of magic for me once," she said offhandedly, "a queer spell that showed what people far off were doing. I was thinking of you just then, as it happened, and I saw you pictured in a mirror."

"Charlatan's fakery," Steifann scoffed. "A false mirror, or some such. You were hoodwinked."

Corson shrugged. "Maybe. Nyc's tricksy as a weasel. But it surely seemed to be you. You were sitting right there, in this very room, late at night, writing in your everlasting account-books. You blotted the page and had to scrape the ink off. Do you remember a night like that, late last summer?"

"Dozens. And you've lain there and watched me at it scores of times. . . ." Steifann hesitated. "All the same, Corson, there was one time, in the summer, when I'd let the accounts fall behind and I was up half the night trying to right them. I remember it specially because I had the strangest feeling that you were here, even though I knew it was impossible. I couldn't help looking over at the bed, time and again, to see if you were there. I was only half awake, I suppose. Then I did fall asleep over the ledger, and I thought you shook me and said, 'Get to bed, leave that for tomorrow,' and I suddenly woke up. It was just a dream, of course, but I was so sure you were there, it was uncanny."

"That was Nyc's witchery," Corson said decidedly. "I know spellcraft when I meet it. I have an unusual affinity for magic, Nyc says. Or something like that."

"Witches, winemakers . . . was there anyone in the Midlands you *didn't* sleep with?"

"I don't think so," Corson teased. "I might have overlooked a few shepherds or laborers, though. I was only with the gentry, you see. Even Raphe, my vintner, comes of good family—his own sister's heir to the title of Jhaice. And Nyc's not some mountebank trickster, she's a scholar and a noblewoman. A Rhaicime, if you want to know."

"I don't. What are you doing under my humble roof, if Rhaicimes are so fond of your company?"

"Well . . . I came back for your sake. You looked so wretched without me, in the mirror-spell, I felt sorry for you."

Even Steifann's good nature balked at this outrageous bluff. "Then you can go right back to your fine friends!" he shouted. "Not that I believe a word of it—"

"Peace, peace," cried Corson, throwing her arms around him. "Very well, then, I was missing you—didn't I write and tell you so? I was so lonely for you, I asked Nyc to do that spell for me, just so I could see you. Are you satisfied?"

As Corson intended, Steifann was flattered to hear her admit to missing him, and he forgot to accuse her of spying on him. Despite herself, Corson had learned some of Nyctasia's subtle wiles.

"Well, I trust you've seen the last of this witch," Steifann said, mollified. He pulled her closer.

"I daresay. But she has a way of turning up again, just when I think I'm rid of her." And Corson couldn't resist adding, "I rather miss her too. She's a charming little thing, in her way."

"Bitch. I know you're just trying to nettle me."

Corson chuckled. "Nyc says my insolence is insupportable," she said proudly. "I learn the most outlandish words from that one."

"You've learned too much from her to suit me. I'll just take charge of this comb myself. You're not going to play that trick on anyone but me."

"It's mine! Give it here!"

"Not if I know it."

They tussled over the comb until they had both forgotten about it. It was some time later before Steifann rolled over and felt it jabbing him in the back. He seized it and flourished it triumphantly at Corson.

"Oh, all right, I make you a present of it," she said. "I can drive men mad with desire without any help. But you'll have to give it to Annin if she asks. I said I'd lend it to her."

Steifann glared. "Did you tell everyone about it, you—"

"No, no, only Annin. I'd no choice! You see, I had to wash the perfume out of my hair, that morning, while you were still sleeping, and I called Annin to bring me hot water. I didn't dare to fetch it myself—I'd have had to fight off half a dozen fellows, and maybe kill a few of them, through no fault of their own."

Corson laughed, remembering her whispered conversation with Annin through the door. "Annin said, 'What did you *do* to him? They must have heard him howling all the way to Ochram!' And I said, 'Never mind that! Believe me, I need to wash my hair *now*, and don't send Trask with the water, bring it yourself!'"

By now, Steifann too was laughing. "What did she say to that?"

"Plenty. She was furious. Both of us sleeping half the morning away, leaving her with all the work, and then asking her to fetch hot water, if you please! When she finished cursing me, she said, 'You just washed your hair last night! Do you think I'm your rutting lady's maid?' So I had to explain. But she wouldn't help me unless I promised to let her use the comb some time."

Steifann shook his head. "Asye! No man on the coast will be safe!"

4

CORSON'S LETTER WAS duly dispatched on the *Windhover*, along
with another from Maegor containing urgent messages from Nyctasia's allies in Rhostshyl. Some weeks later, Destiver turned
over the lot to a trustworthy courier in Lhestreq who was bound
for the Midlands, but nearly two months passed before he had
completed the journey inland, around the Yth Forest, and arrived
in Osela. By that time the winter had struck in force, and early
blizzards had already buried the Southern Trade Road under im-
penetrable banks and barricades of snow and ice. Communication
with the Valleylands to the south would be cut off until the way
was clear again. Nyctasia's letters remained in Osela to await the
spring thaw.

Winter was a time of some leisure for the farmers of the Midlands. With the crops harvested, the fields cleared, and the winter
wheat planted, there was time for a measure of rest, for mending
and making, and instructing the children.

On the estate of the Edonaris of Vale, the work of the vintnery
went on at a slower pace, now that the pressing was completed
and the new vintage sealed in casks. The barrels in their caves
had to be inspected daily against damage or spoilage, the vine-
stakes and trellises had to be kept in repair, and the plants themselves needed constant pruning, even during their barren season.
But still winter was the least toilsome time of the year, and the
family took full advantage of the respite. There were gatherings
of the local gentry, feasting and flirting, and long evenings of
gossip and storytelling about the hearth.

The labors of the estate did not much concern Nyctasia.
Though she was willing enough to learn the art of vintnery, she
did not share her kinsfolks' passion for the profession, and she
saw all too clearly that they needed no help from her to make and
market their celebrated wines.

She did contribute a useful skill to the household, however, by taking upon herself the education of the youngsters. Even the practical Mesthelde ar'n Edonaris, who ran the manor-house with a firm hand and had little use for scholars, was grateful for Nyctasia's learning, now that she herself was relieved of the unwelcome task of teaching the children their letters. "And you can give some lessons to the older ones as well," she ordered Nyctasia. "That will cure them of their notions of running off to the Imperial University!"

Nyctasia rather sympathized with her young cousins' desire to attend the university in Liruvath, but she could see the sense in Mesthelde's suggestion. Once they'd had a taste of the hard work that true scholarship demanded, most of her pupils did find the prospect of the university less inviting.

She had better success with the children, who were fascinated by her foreign accent and her exciting past. It was far more interesting to take their lessons from an exiled Rhaicime and sorceress than from Mesthelde, who'd been caring for them and scolding them all their lives.

But most of Nyctasia's time was devoted to her own studies, researching the volumes of the Cymvelan library, copying and translating rare and ancient texts, discovering works unknown to her. She took part, from time to time, in the family's winter pastimes, but she could usually be found in the tower room where the books had been housed when they were removed from the abandoned temple of the Cymvelan Circle. She pored over their pages day and night, often forgetting meals and sleep, driven by the desire to possess their secrets, as if the knowledge gained could fill the emptiness left by her losses.

Her newfound kin still hardly knew what to make of her. She had arrived in their midst suddenly, unexpected, a stranger from far-off Rhostshyl, the home of their remote ancestors, and a place known to them through tradition and rumor as a city of splendor and of danger. They had been wary of her at first, suspecting that she had come to enlist their aid in the warfare between the Houses of Edonaris and Teiryn in Rhostshyl. But much to the disappointment of the younger, more adventurous members of the family, Nyctasia had implored them to have nothing to do with the feud. She had sought only to live in peace among them, a request it would be churlish to refuse; the laws of hospitality forbade them to turn her away.

She looked like one of themselves, after all. She was nearly identical to Frondescine ar'n Edonaris, resembling her more

closely than did her own twin brother, Raphistain. And though
the Edonaris of Vale were hard-working folk who dealt in trade,
they were mindful of their noble descent nonetheless, and Nyctasia's lofty rank made her all the more welcome to the family.
They were flattered that a Rhaicime should acknowledge them as
kin, and they could not but be impressed by her elegance and her
aristocratic ways. Not a few of her distant cousins were half
enamored of her already, and when Lady Nocharis suggested one
evening, "Let someone fetch Nyc to give us a song," several
voices promptly answered, "I'll go!" and the others laughed.

Frondescine winked at her younger brother Jenisorn. "You go,
Jheine. You can talk the birds out of their nests when you've a
mind to. I daresay you can lure our little lone owl down from her
tower." Frondescine, who was always called 'Deisha, had been
Nyctasia's most ardent admirer from the first, but her feelings
had since cooled to a somewhat more sisterly affection. Dear as
Nyctasia was to her, 'Deisha could not help finding her brooding
visions and dark spells a little frightening. She had seen more
than the others of Nyctasia's strange humors and forbodings.

Jenisorn got up from the bench, grinning. "At least Nyc has
the wit to appreciate my charm and talents, unlike my nearer
relations and my loutish siblings," he declared. With his thick
brown curls and laughing blue eyes, Jenisorn gave promise of
becoming the handsomest of a handsome family, in time. He was
used to being a favorite, but was too clever to be truly conceited.

"Get along with you, you strutting cockerel," said Mesthelde.
"Tell Nyc she's not to blind herself, reading all night by candlelight."

"At once, Aunt. She'll not dare to disobey *you*."

Mesthelde glanced up from her sewing and gave him one look
that sent him hastening from the hall.

"We ourselves are the true link between the world of the spirit
and the world of matter," Nyctasia read. "For humankind is
equally composed of flesh and spirit, of earth and air, of fire and
water, and thus the gateway where the two realms meet is rightly
to be sought within ourselves and not otherwhere."

She looked up from the page when the great hound sleeping by
the fire stirred and sat up, thumping its heavy tail on the hearth-
stones. Before long, Nyctasia too heard footsteps on the tower
stairs. She quickly closed her book and returned it to the chest
beside the table, locking it and pocketing the key. Some of

her young kinfolk had already been pestering her to teach them about spells and spirits, and she dared not leave such a thing to chance. By the time Jenisorn knocked and looked around the door, a different treatise lay open on the table before her.

"Ah, Jheine, have a look at this," she invited. Jenisorn was the only one of her older pupils who showed a true gift and inclination for scholarship. He was already making good progress at learning Ancient Eswraine. "It's a collection of the Isperian Maxims. How would you translate this one? The words are all simple ones."

Jenisorn joined her and bent over the manuscript. "*Veshayin heocht...*" he pondered. "To speak to a dog? Oh, I see—'Speak to the dog at your hand.' That makes some sense, but why 'Speak to the bird at the bread'?"

"That's not quite right, though it's not quite wrong either. That form of the word can mean 'at' or 'by' or 'with,' you know. And 'hound' will match the pattern of consonance better than 'dog': 'Speak to a hound with your hands. Speak to a bird with bread.'"

"'Deisha will like that.'" The livestock of the estate were his sister's particular concern.

Nyctasia smiled. "Well, it doesn't really have to do only with animals. It means that one should deal with everyone according to each one's ability to understand. Here, now try this next one—it's rather more difficult."

Jenisorn puzzled over the unfamiliar passage for a time. "How can stars have echoes?" he said doubtfully.

"They used the same word for 'echo' and 'reflection,'" Nyctasia explained. "That's why you often see mirrors called 'echo-glass' in old translations. It's usually easy to tell which meaning is intended, though there's sometimes a deliberate ambiguity, I think. Here it's clear enough."

"Hmm..." He tried again. "'Long after those... *perhelid*'?"

"Ancient."

"'Long after those ancient stars had fallen, their reflections could still be seen on the still, dark water below.' Is that right?"

"Yes, well done!"

"But what does it mean?" he demanded.

Nyctasia laughed. "No one knows, but scores of disquisitions have been written to interpret it. None of them satisfies me, but I don't claim that I can explain it any better myself."

"Is it about ghosts, do you think?" Jenisorn asked, lowering his voice instinctively. It might be unwise to ask such a question in this isolated, ill-lit tower room, with the snowstorm howling at the windows.

"That has been suggested. Or it might simply mean that we ought always to consider the consequences of our actions. It seems to mean something different to everyone who reads it."

"No wonder she was called Isper the Mad," sighed Jenisorn.

Nyctasia rumpled his hair. "All poets are a bit mad, no?" She knew that Jenisorn had tried his hand at writing verses himself.

Suddenly the dog gave a short bark and trotted out to the stairway to greet another hound as huge as itself. It was followed by the twins, who'd come in search of Nyctasia and Jenisorn both.

"There, Raphe, just as I told you—Nyc's netted him," 'Deisha exclaimed. "We'd have waited all night while the two of them discussed philosophy."

Nyctasia looked bewildered, and Jenisorn guilty. Raphistain laughed and swept a low bow to Nyctasia. "My dear Nyc, this scatterwit was supposed to fetch you to sing for us, at Mother 'Charis's desire—and Aunt Mesthelde's command."

Raphe too was fond of Nyctasia, and he knew that the family still had hopes of a marriage between them. He had indeed considered the advantages of the match, for it would enhance the family's prestige a good deal if the title of Rhaicime should descend to a child of their line. Still, though it was most agreeable to have a mysterious, solitary scholar for a cousin, Nyctasia was hardly what Raphe needed in a wife. Someone with more stamina, less reserve, and, especially, a far greater interest in grape-farming and winemaking would be the only practical mate for him, he had concluded.

But what had in truth decided him, in the end, was that he found he simply could not court a woman who was the very image of his own sister. Nyctasia's slender frame and fine features, her long, slim throat, high cheekbones and wide brow were all mirrored exactly in 'Deisha. Both had the grey Edonaris eyes and smooth black hair, as did Raphe himself. But the Edonaris of Rhostshyl were fair-skinned, the Edonaris of Vale dark from years of working in the sun. And Nyctasia had a scholar's sloping shoulders, while 'Deisha stood straight as a young tree.

During the harvest season, Nyctasia had grown so brown in the sun that it was sometimes difficult to tell her from 'Deisha, and even now that the winter had restored her pale complexion, the resemblance was still uncanny. Raphe and Nyctasia had become excellent friends, but both knew that they would never be more.

"If you would consent to honor us with your company," he said, offering his arm to Nyctasia, "allow me to serve as escort, since Jheine has shown himself unworthy."

"I'd have brought her!" Jenisorn protested. "I was just—"

"Oh, come along, both of you," laughed 'Deisha. "Send a goose to fetch a goose, and neither you'll see again," she chanted.

5

AS THE WINTER wore on, Corson grew increasingly bored with her lot in Chiastelm. She never tired of Steifann's company, but the endless routine of chores that ordered life at The Jugged Hare always began to wear on her restless spirit after a time. The work itself was not so burdensome as the tedium of doing the same tasks day after day, like an ox at a treadmill, always plodding over the same circle of ground. There was the occasional fight with a truculent customer to relieve the monotony, but that did nothing to satisfy Corson's wanderlust.

When the captain of the city guard heard that she was in town, he offered her a position on the night watch—a post she'd held before, from time to time. Patrolling the streets and wharves looking for trouble was work more congenial to Corson's nature than marketing, or chopping wood, but serving in a garrison of guards reminded her of her years in the army—years she would rather forget. And she far preferred Steifann's bed to the municipal warders' barracks.

Corson decided to forego the job, but she let it be known that she was for hire as a courier or armed escort in the vicinity of Chiastelm. Most coastal trading was carried on by ship, but there were merchants enough on the roads—and bandits enough—to ensure regular employment for such as Corson. The pay was not of the best, but the brief journeys eased Corson's sense of confinement, and the harsh weather through which she had to ride made her appreciate the comforts of the Hare all the more, each time she returned. At every homecoming she swore she wanted no more of riding all day in the winter wind and standing watch in the snow at night, with her feet freezing in her boots; she'd be happy to sit by the fire peeling potatoes till spring.

But as the weeks passed, and spring seemed as far away as ever, Corson would feel again that the walls of the tavern were closing in around her. She wanted to be in the open, where there was room for her long limbs to move freely, where the very air she breathed wasn't shared with a dozen other people. Everyone and everything seemed to be in her way, and she found it hard to control her quick temper. She knew, at such times, that there would be trouble if she didn't get away soon.

At the close of the day, when the last customers were gone, and the tavern scrubbed and secured, Steifann and the others often sat in the warm kitchen for a while, drinking ale, quarreling amiably, and eating any food that was left in the place. Corson usually enjoyed these times, but it had been several weeks since she'd last been away, and tonight the room seemed unbearably close and stifling to her. Everything her friends said she'd heard them say many times before, on nights exactly like this one, and she suddenly felt that she couldn't bear to hear them said again. Only by maintaining a sullen silence did she keep herself from snapping angrily at the others for no reason.

If only, for this one night, she could be traveling with Nyc again, through some wild, lonely place where anything might happen.... I never knew what that one would say next, she thought wistfully, the addlepated chit! Nyc was unpredictable, always changing—like quicksilver, the mirrorlike living metal Corson had once seen an alchemist use at a fair. And she could be as dangerous as that pretty poison as well, Corson reminded herself. Nyctasia was by turns sorceress and scholar, noblewoman and vagabond, benefactor and deceiver, stranger and friend. Corson had known her as an arrogant aristocrat and as a humble healer. She had thought nothing of letting Corson risk life and liberty in her service, yet she'd nursed Corson through a desperate illness with patience and selfless devotion. She might be flattering and affectionate one moment, then sharp-tongued and mocking the next. She was capable of quite convincingly impersonating a pickpocket, a penniless student, a common tavern-singer, a pert messenger-boy, or any other guise that would suit her purpose. Nyctasia was the will-of-the-wisp that could never be clearly seen, that disappeared when you thought you'd caught it. She was sly and perplexing and altogether exasperating. She was an insufferable vexation, and Corson missed her.

There was no mystery about Steifann, but Corson did not want to discover any. His frank, forthright nature and steady reliability were the very qualities that made Corson trust him as she trusted no one else, and made her return to the Hare as often as she could. If she ever found Steifann changed, she'd feel that the earth had given way beneath her, that she was falling helplessly, with nothing to catch hold of. There would be no stability or certainty in all the world.

Corson knew that if she chose to settle down in Chiastelm she'd have a secure home, and a steadfast friend in Steifann, yet she could not bring herself to make that choice, for all of Steifann's urging. That same unchanging dependability that she valued in him was also what drove her away from him to seek the unknown and untried. "And when I was with Lady Quicksilver, I was missing Steifann all the while," she thought glumly. "What ails me? I must be under a curse, that I can never be content."

It did not improve her mood when Destiver came by to pass the time and cadge a late meal. Corson had seen a good deal more of Destiver than she liked, over the winter, and she made no secret of her displeasure, but she could see for herself that Destiver was no rival for Steifann's affections. Indeed, Destiver seemed far more interested in carrying on a long-standing flirtation with Annin.

"We're closed to custom for the night," said Corson. "Go away."

Destiver ignored her and poured herself some ale. Pushing Trask out of the way, she sat down next to Annin and kissed her hand.

"Don't mind Corson," said Annin, grinning. "She's just jealous of all my swains, aren't you, pet?"

Corson was in no humor for games, but she did her best. "Of course I am," she said heavily. "Who wouldn't be?" She drank deeply of her ale and tried to look less wretched than she felt.

"So am I," Destiver declared. "Wildly, desperately jealous. It drives me mad." She pulled Annin closer and nuzzled her bare shoulder.

"So am I!" Trask mimicked. He threw himself at Annin's feet, exclaiming, "Annin, my beloved, let me carry you away from—"

Annin kicked him. "Spurned!" he cried, crawling hastily out of reach. "I die." He collapsed with his head in Giniver's lap. "Console me, fair maid," he suggested.

Corson suddenly strode to the door and threw it open. She stood in the doorway with her back to the others, drawing deep breaths of the cold night air and staring out over the roofs of the town at the limitless black sky. Trask's antics usually amused her, but now she was heartily sick of them, and of all the rest. She felt trapped by everything familiar.

"Corson, you rutting idiot, close that door! You'll freeze us all." Steifann came over and kicked the door shut himself. "You'll catch a chill," he said, wrapping his arms around her. "And then you'll have to drink that foul, scalding brew you gave me. Here, I'll keep you warm."

"There's not air enough for a sparrow in here," Corson complained, pushing him away and immediately regretting it.

"Ah, you're just looking for a fight," said Steifann. "What you need is a job. She's bored," he explained to the others. "She hasn't killed anyone for weeks."

Destiver looked up. "I could take you on for a few days. I'm shorthanded just now."

"What did you do, keelhaul someone?" Corson sneered.

"Not yet—but I will, as soon as I get my hands on that drunken bastard Hrawn. It's not the first time he's played us this trick. I warned him I'd have the skin from his back if he let us down again."

No one asked why Destiver did not simply rid herself of such an unreliable crewman. They all knew that her evasion of the trade laws left her little choice as to the sailors she hired. The wonder was that she managed to control her crew of outlaws and outcasts at all. "What do you say?" she asked Corson. "It's only a short run up the coast to Eske, to pick up some cargo." Destiver considered Corson a demented and dangerous animal, but she thought the same of most of her crew, so this did not deter her.

Corson so desperately wanted a change that she was almost tempted by the offer, but the prospect of being under Destiver's command for even a few days was intolerable to her. "Try at the Crow's Nest, why don't you? Isn't that where you get most of the scum you sail with?" The Crow's Nest was a cheap dockside inn which was not choosy about its guests. Criminals and fugitives of every sort could usually be found there.

"High and mighty, aren't you? You were glad enough to get onto my ship, not so long ago."

"And gladder still to get off of it! I don't need—"

"Oh, our Corson's a favorite with the gentry nowadays, didn't you know?" Annin interrupted. "She hasn't much time for common rabble like us. Rhaicimes and wealthy Midlanders seek her out, to hear her tell it."

Corson flushed angrily. "It's true! I could better myself if I chose."

"And what's wrong with that?" said Trask. "I was meant for better things myself than serving in an ale-house. Why don't you get me a position in a noble household, Corson, since you consort with gentlefolk? I could be a page, a squire, a herald!" He pictured himself in silk doublet and hose, a jeweled dagger swinging at his hip as he hurried—in a dignified way—through halls of pale marble, bearing an important message from His Lordship to the chamberlain.

"You!" snorted Steifann. "You'd still be selling your skin on the docks if I hadn't taken you in. You don't even know your parents, you misbegotten foundling."

"Well then, I might be an earl's son for all you know," Trask pointed out. "You should treat me with more respect."

"Asye, first it's Corson getting above herself, and now this ungrateful little guttersnipe," Steifann said indignantly. He turned to Annin. "I suppose you think you should be lady-in-waiting to the Empress now."

"Not I. I should be Empress myself."

"You're *my* Empress," said Destiver. "And I your slave."

"Fool," said Annin complacently.

Steifann drained his tankard and poured himself another. "I know how people better themselves, and it's hard work that tells, not currying favor with a lot of Rhaicimes. Who," he added, glaring at Corson, "probably don't exist anyway."

Corson only shrugged disdainfully, somehow resisting the temptation to hit Steifann with a chair. It was almost as if she could hear Nyctasia admonishing her, "Now, Corson, don't be so hasty."

Warming to his subject, Steifann took a long swig of ale, sat back, and began to tell everyone for the thousandth time how he, a lowly sailor, had become the owner of a prosperous tavern, all thanks to his own wits and sweat. But before he was very far into the tale, he was interrupted by a loud, insistent knocking at the back door.

Trask, who was already half asleep, roused himself and sat up. "Shall I—?"

Steifann shook his head. "It's some drunk, that's all."

"The house is closed," called Annin. "Try at the Flagon and Embers."

The knocking grew to a pounding, and they heard someone

shouting against the wind, something about a message. Steifann cursed and got up to unbar the door. "Come in, then, and be quick about it. What's your business at this Hlann-forsaken hour?" His manner grew more courteous, however, when he saw that their visitor was sober and well dressed, and that he wore the livery of the Ondra, the most influential of the powerful merchant families of Chiastelm. "Er . . . will you have a drink?" Steifann offered. "Did you say you've a message for me?"

"No," said the man curtly, glancing around the kitchen. When he saw Corson he advanced and made her a bow. "Do I address Corson brenn Torisk?"

Corson hesitated. She was either in a great deal of trouble, she thought, or she was about to make a great deal of money. But since there was only one messenger the prospects were favorable, so she stood and returned his bow. "At your service, sir."

"I have the honor, madame, to serve Ioseth, son of Ondra. He desires an interview with you, Mistress Corson, on a matter of some importance, which will not admit of delay. I'm to bring you at once, if you would be so obliging. You will find him most appreciative, I assure you."

Definitely money, Corson decided. "I shall be with you directly, sir," she said grandly. "Fetch my cloak, Trask."

"At once, milady," Trask muttered, but he did as he was bid. With a triumphant look back at the others, Corson swept out of The Jugged Hare, at the invitation of the head of the house of Ondra.

6

"WELCOME BACK, WE'D almost despaired of you," said Diastor, teasing Jenisorn, his younger son. An Edonaris by marriage, Diastor had become one of the heads of the family, and between them he and Raphe bore much of the responsibility of managing the estate and vintnery.

"The both of them were buried in their books, Father—Nyc's gone for her harp," 'Deisha explained, settling herself on the hearth between her two dogs. They belonged in the kennels by rights—as Mesthelde frequently reminded her—but these were 'Deisha's favorites and rather spoiled. They were fine watchdogs, nevertheless, and Nyctasia encouraged the one which seemed to have taken her under its special protection. Accustomed to the company of an armed escort, Nyctasia felt safer with the massive wolf-hound following her about the house by day and guarding her chamber by night. Mesthelde disapproved, but tacitly allowed it after 'Deisha confided to her something of Nyctasia's nightmares.

Mesthelde judged that Nyctasia was growing easier with her new life and her new family's ways. She no longer went about armed, after all. No doubt she would leave behind her fears at last. She ought to be discouraged, of course, from shutting herself up with those bothersome books—it was such a bad example to set the youngsters. Mesthelde smiled with satisfaction when Nyctasia came in with her harp.

Nyctasia returned her smile, taking it for a welcome. Mesthelde must be warming to her at last, she thought, and she was not far wrong.

She next greeted the matriarch, Lady Nocharis, a frail, white-haired woman seated in a warm corner of the enclosed hearth, well provided with cushions and shawls. Nyctasia kissed her cheek. "Mother 'Charis, how good to see you here."

The matriarch did not often leave her own rooms, yet she was in many ways the guiding spirit of the family. Her experience and

32

her wise, gentle nature made her counsel much respected. It was she who had persuaded Nyctasia to remain with them in Vale.

"With so many of us gathered together, I couldn't stay away. Even 'Clairin home at last, and Alder, my wandering children." Diastor's wife Leclairin—the mother of five—and her brother Aldrichas were away much of the time, traveling to markets in all parts of the Midlands to deliver the wines and deal with merchants and patrons. They exchanged an amused glance, upon hearing their mother's epithet for them.

"After all, a family gathering cannot be complete without the two of us, my dear Nyctasia," Lady Nocharis continued. "Are we not the oldest and newest members of the family?"

Nesanye looked up from the half-finished toy cart he was carving. "A family gathering's not complete without song, that's certain. Nyc, give us 'The Queen of Barre.'"

Nyctasia sang every ballad and catch the others asked for, and a few of her own as well, when they called for more. Trained at court, she was at her ease playing or singing or composing verses—all necessary accomplishments for a person of her breeding. Her voice was high, clear and confident, and she accompanied herself deftly enough on her small lap-harp.

But to the others music was a rare luxury, especially in the winter, when traveling players and songsters could not visit the ice-bound valleylands. They could not have enough of Nyctasia's minstrelsy.

"Sing something from the coast," begged Tepicacia, "something we've never heard before."

"You must always have novelty, 'Cacia," Nyctasia chided her young cousin. "Very well, here's a wayfarer's song for you, a song of those who are far from home, of those who have no home to return to. I learned it in Chiastelm, a town full of travelers:

> Paved roads lead us to the city,
> Earthen roads lead us away.
> To the north are roads of diamond,
>   So they say.
>
> Village roads are dirt and ditches,
> Mud by night and dust by day.
> Kings once rode on roads of silver,
>   So they say.

> Roads of water are the rivers,
> Flowing between roads of clay.
> Pearl roads run beneath the ocean,
> > So they say.
>
> Forest roads are plagued with dangers,
> Beasts and bandits haunt the way.
> Roads of sorrow are the stranger's,
> > So they say.
>
> Freedom is for those who journey,
> Safety is for those who stay.
> Border roads are most uncertain,
> > So they say.
>
> Pathways in the wilderness
> Have I traveled, lost and lone,
> And unyielding, twisting, treacherous
> City streets of cobblestone.
> Roads of clover, roads of favor
> Follow ever, you who may.
> Homeward roads are neverending,
> > So they say."

When she finished, there was a solemn silence, except for the whispering of the children, and the snowstorm raging against the high, narrow windows. Nyctasia busied herself at retuning her harpstrings with the silver key. Finally she raised her head and said lightly, "Hark to the wind. I have a good song for such a night, and it should please you, 'Cacia—no one's ever heard it before." Smiling, she sang,

> "Harvest is over,
> The fields are shorn.
> No longer the wind
> May court the corn
> Where lovers shelter
> Among the grain,
> Where you and I
> Have often lain.

Not in the season
Of wintry weather
May the wind and I
Go a-wooing together,
But he shakes the shutters
To let me know
Of his new romancing
With the dancing snow.

Though the wind be fickle,
You'll find me true
In every season,
My love, to you.
And in the springtime
Let him carouse
With the beckoning, blossoming
Apple-boughs,
For the spring shall see us
Renew our vows.

Harvest is over,
The year complete.
No longer the wind
May woo the wheat
Where lovers sheltered
Among the grain,
Where you and I
Shall lie again."

This merry love-song met with a murmur of approval from the company. "Why has no one heard that before?" asked 'Cacia. "Did you just make it up now?"

Nyctasia grinned. "Do you like it?"

"Surely," said 'Cacia politely.

"Quite charming," Raphe assured her, and the others agreed.

"I'm most gratified by your favorable opinion," said Nyctasia, "but I didn't write this one. It's one of Jheine's."

Her announcement caused a sensation, especially among the youngsters, who lost no time in taunting Jenisorn about his secret love.

"Tell, Jheine, who's it for?"

"No one," he protested, blushing. "It's just a song."

"Who is it, boy or girl?"

"Desskara? Nolinde?"

"Eivar brenn Glaos?"

"No!"

Nyctasia intervened on his behalf. "It's an exercise in composition, on a seasonal theme," she explained. "But it's incomplete, Jheine. You've left out the summertime."

"Well, I had another verse, but I'm not sure it will do. Can 'faithless' be rhymed with 'natheless'?"

"Not on a dare," said 'Cacia, who felt that she'd been tricked into admiring her cousin's handiwork.

"I didn't ask *you*. You couldn't *spell* 'natheless.'"

"What about 'scatheless'?" someone suggested, setting off another round of debate.

'Deisha got up from the hearth and stretched. "The song's well enough, little brother, but I don't care for the way your friend the wind is carrying on tonight. I'm going out to see that the horses are well bedded."

The dogs jumped up too, eager for any activity, and one of them looked back at Nyctasia expectantly. "Wait for me," she laughed. "Grey thinks I should stretch my legs, and he's right. I've been sitting all the day."

"Be careful!" Mesthelde called after them. "That storm could swallow the two of you like pebbles down a well."

"Don't worry, I won't let the mooncalf wander off," said 'Deisha. At the door, she took two long fur cloaks from their pegs and draped one over Nyctasia's shoulders. "We'll take lanterns, but they won't be of much use. Just remember, don't take your hand from the guide-rope for a moment. Aunt Mesthelde's right about these storms—folk have frozen to death just a few paces from shelter because they couldn't see what was before them. We don't have many blizzards as bad as this in the valley, but we do have to be prepared for them."

Nyctasia had never known such weather. The climate of the coast was a good deal more temperate. Her cloak was whipped about her legs, and the blowing snow was so dense that she could hardly see 'Deisha walking just ahead of her. When she looked back toward the house, it had already vanished in the blinding white darkness that surrounded her. Without the rope that had been stretched tight across the yard, she'd have had no idea which way the stables lay. The dogs stayed close beside them all the way.

Not until they could feel the door beneath their hands did they release their grip on the rope. 'Deisha laughed, fighting the wind to push the door fast behind them. "That's better! We might have been at the bottom of the sea, out there!"

"Neither earth nor air," said Nyctasia absently. "Neither shore nor star." She stood motionless and intent, as if trying to listen to some distant sound.

"What did you say?" asked 'Deisha, pushing back her hood and brushing snow from her cloak. "Nyc, what is it? Don't stand there dripping like a candle."

"Nothing, only . . . an echo," Nyctasia murmured. "A memory of something that perhaps never happened."

'Deisha stared.

Abruptly, Nyctasia shook herself from her abstraction. "Holding to the rope for guidance," she explained. "It was a Manifestation of the Principle of Recognition. In just such a way must one follow, blindly, to seek what is within."

"Oh, I see," said 'Deisha, who didn't. Like most professed believers in the Indwelling Spirit, 'Deisha did not spend a great deal of time pondering the mysteries of the Vahnite faith. Leaving Nyctasia to her revelations, she went to confer with the ostler.

It was the barking of the dogs that finally drew Nyctasia's attention back to the mortal world. They had been sniffing suspiciously at a stall filled with fodder, growling deep in their throats, and now they set up a clamor that brought 'Deisha and the stablehands running. Nyctasia reached instinctively for her sword, and found only the small pearl-handled knife that she used to sharpen her quills.

"It must be rats, mistress," said one of the grooms, but 'Deisha waved him aside.

"They'd not raise such a noise over a few barn rats." Addressing the heap of hay she ordered, "Come out of there, or we'll have you out with pitchforks."

Nothing stirred except the two hounds, pawing at the ground and snarling. At a sign from 'Deisha they leaped forward and dug furiously into the hay, fangs bared.

There was a shriek of pain from their quarry.

The boy looked no older than Jenisorn. He was thin and ragged, with one hand wrapped in a crude bandage, and his shoulder bleeding where one of the dogs had seized him. He crouched shivering in the straw and gazed about him desperately. 'Deisha had called the dogs off at once, but they now stood guard between him and the door. "Let me go, lady, please," he appealed to 'Deisha. "I've not stolen anything—"

"Go? Certainly not," 'Deisha said sternly, and Nyctasia smiled to hear her sound so much like Mesthelde. "Where are you to go, in this weather? Come along to the house now, and we'll give you a meal. You'll have to stay until this storm passes over, at the least."

Her words were not an invitation, but a command, and the boy saw that he had no choice. He rose to his feet stiffly and limped to the door, hugging his thin cloak around him. Nyctasia took up a horse-blanket and wrapped him in it. Looking into his grey face and bright, frightened eyes, she thought, *Fever. Perhaps frostbite*, and said, "He must have some mulled wine, 'Deisha. He's half frozen."

"I could do with some myself," 'Deisha agreed. When she pulled open the barn door, a fierce, piercing wind rushed in, making the horses stamp and whinny in protest. "We've not had a storm like this in Vale for years. Not since—"

"Vale?" gasped the boy, turning to one of the grooms. "I was nearly to Amron Therain! This can't be Vale?"

"You must have circled back in the snow, lad. This is Edonaris land."

"No—no, it can't be," he cried. For a moment he stared wildly out at the storm, then suddenly he pushed past 'Deisha and disappeared into the swirling snow.

.

7

CORSON WAS IN a much better temper when she returned from her meeting with Ioseth ash Ondra. Soon she'd be on the road again, and this time for a fee that would make it worthwhile to brave the winter weather. Her new employer had revealed very little about the job he offered, but he had been particularly clear about the price the Merchants' Guild was willing to pay her for her services. Corson, who knew better than to ask too many questions, was quite satisfied with what she'd been told.

One of the young scullions, who slept in the kitchen, recognized the familiar sound of her cursing and kicking at the door, and rose reluctantly to let her in. When Corson not only thanked him, but actually gave him a silver penny for his trouble, he thought he must still be asleep and dreaming.

Corson stood in the doorway of Steifann's room for a few moments, watching him sleep. He lay to one side of the large bed, as if to leave room for her, and one arm was stretched out over the space where she usually lay. The sight of him was so inviting and reassuring that she felt a pang at the thought of leaving him again so soon. "Asye, I've not gone yet, and already I miss him," she sighed.

Making no attempt to be quiet, she shut the door behind her and sat down on the bed to pull off her boots. Steifann stopped in the middle of a snore, mumbled something, started to snore again, then changed his mind and woke up instead. He rolled onto his side and lay watching with drowsy approval as Corson undressed by candlelight. "So her ladyship honors me with her company, eh?" he rumbled. "What do the Ondra want with you?"

"I don't know," Corson admitted, "and I don't much care—it means fifty crescents in gold, and they paid half in advance." She leaned over and jingled her money-pouch in his face.

At this, Steifann woke more fully. "Fifty—! Corson, they'll want murder done."

"Nothing so simple as that, I fancy. My mission's sanctioned

39

by the Guild." Though Chiastelm was ostensibly governed by a council of its nobility, it was no secret that the powerful Merchants' Guild really made the town's laws and saw to their enforcement. Members of the Guild represented Chiastelm in the Maritime Alliance, while maintaining a purely formal fiction that they were acting in the name of the aristocracy.

"They're paying for my silence as much as for my sword," Corson continued. "The matter's so secret that I don't yet know where I'm bound, much less what I'm to do when I get there. A few days' ride to the south was all he said—and that was probably a lie. I expect I'll be guarding something precious, or accompanying someone important—an imperial emissary to the Alliance, I shouldn't wonder. They're worth a fortune in ransom, so I've heard."

"Well, if you don't know where you're going or why, do you at least know when?"

Corson hung her sword-belt over the bedpost. "Tomorrow morning," she said ruefully, "but I'll be back within the week."

"Tomorrow? Then why in the Hlann's name didn't they give you your instructions tonight?"

"They don't mean to let me have time to sell the secret. They'll not give the game away till we've started out. Every bandit between here and Ochram would be watching the roads, if word of this business got out, and the Guild's taking no chances that I'm in league with them—that's my guess. They even made sure that I wouldn't be seen going to this meeting by summoning me in the dead of night." Corson unpinned her long braid and shook out her hair, taking up her fine silver brush. "I thought I'd come back tonight and find you in bed with Destiver—with *my* comb."

Steifann chuckled sleepily. "Not likely, when Annin's in the mood. Those two are old flames. But how she could prefer anyone else to me I'll never understand."

Corson couldn't understand it either, though she wasn't sure which woman he meant. She quickly finished brushing her hair and admired her reflection in a basin of water. "Well, anyone who'd want that scarecrow harridan Destiver deserves her. I'm worth three of her."

Steifann yawned. "You're three times as big, to be sure."

"Nyc says I'm beautiful as a dream," Corson said smugly, and blew out the candles.

Steifann pulled the blankets up around his ears and turned away. "Speaking of dreams, I need some sleep."

Corson grinned vengefully as she climbed into the warm bed. Turn his back on her, would he! She was still quite cold from the out of doors, and when she slid in beside him she suddenly clamped one icy hand to the back of his neck, and clutched at his stomach with the other.

"Arrh! Get away, you're freezing! Rutting bitch!"

Steifann rolled over and tried to push her out of the bed, but Corson clung to him, laughing. "I thought you didn't want me to catch a chill."

"Let go—"

"You said you'd keep me warm," Corson reminded him, dragging him over on top of her.

Once she had his attention, she soon changed his mind about sleeping. "Well, since you're going away so soon . . ." he said.

8

"NOTHING TO CONCERN you, Father," 'Deisha said briskly. "Just a stray, hiding in the stables—a thief, I daresay. The little fool bolted off into the storm as soon as we discovered him. But he can't have gone far, his legs would hardly carry him. 'Cacia and the boys will find him. He'll still be in the yard somewhere."

Jenisorn, Tepicacia and Nicorin had already taken the dogs out on field-chains, long chains used for measuring plots of land. With one end fastened securely to a pillar of the porch, they could search the length and breadth of a field in safety. By this time, they were thoroughly tangled up with the chains and the dogs, and enjoying themselves immensely.

'Deisha led Nyctasia off to the kitchen. "Come, Nyc, we'll see to that mulled wine. They'll all be wanting some."

As she predicted, it was not long before the three returned, snow-covered and sneezing, carrying with them the still form of the dazed boy. They came down the low passage leading from a back door to the scullery, then up a short flight of stairs to the kitchen, preceded by the dogs, who bounded in and enthusiastically shook snow and ice on everyone. Greymantle, much relieved to find that Nyctasia had survived an hour without his protection, leaped up to greet her, knocking her against the table. On his hind legs, he was a good deal taller than she.

'Deisha swatted him. "*Down*, you brute. It's your own fault, Nyc, you encourage him. He'll be unmanageable soon. Ah, here they are," she said, as the others came in with their burden. "Lay him down by the fire, and get those frozen clothes off him."

"He was by the paddock, half buried in snow," said Nicorin. "'Deisha, I think his feet are frostbitten."

"Rub them hard, 'Corin. And Jheine, rub him all over with tallow. 'Cacia, hot poultices. Nyc, is the wine ready?"

"Yes, just." She had poured out bowls of the steaming, spiced drink for the others, but brewed the boy's portion a little longer, adding herbs to ease pain and give a healing sleep. Now she knelt beside him and raised his head gently. Greymantle crowded in beside her and licked his face to show that he was forgiven for being a prowler, nearly spilling the wine Nyctasia was trying to hold to his lips. Jenisorn pulled the hound away.

Revived by the heat of the hearth, the boy managed to drink some wine, despite his trembling, and stammered a few words of thanks.

'Deisha stood over him, frowning. "That was a fool's trick, running out into the open like that. You'd have soon frozen out there."

The youth closed his eyes again. "Yes," he whispered, "I knew that, lady. The snow is kind, but I don't know if you are . . ." As feeling began to return to his numb limbs, he gasped in pain, twisting his head helplessly from side to side.

'Deisha turned away. "We'll do what we can," she said. "Try to rest now."

"He's getting some color back," said 'Cacia.

Nicorin paused. "Is it enough, 'Deisha?"

"Soon. When the mash is hot for the poultices you can stop rubbing. Never mind if it hurts him—if he can feel it, he's lucky."

"He'll not feel it for long," Nyctasia murmured. "He'll sleep soon." She had heard and read of frostbite, but never seen it, and certainly did not know how best to treat it. It was strange to her to stand by uselessly and watch others tend to the afflicted. But she was well able to care for injuries, and she soon set herself to cleaning and dressing the boy's dogbite wounds. He hardly seemed aware of her, but when she took his hand and began to unwrap the dirty cloth bound around it, he suddenly cried out and pulled away from her, shielding the bandaged hand against his chest.

"If it's as painful as that, it must be seen to," Nyctasia said. "I'm a healer, I shan't hurt you."

He tried to ward her off with his good hand, clutching the other to him. "No, don't," he said weakly.

"Don't be afraid, child, let me see your hand. If a wound's not properly cleaned it will never heal."

She reached for him again, but 'Cacia barred her way, leaning over him protectively. "Don't, Nyc. There's no need."

"But—"

"Nyc, *let be*," 'Deisha said firmly. Taking Nyctasia by the arm, she pulled her to her feet and drew her away from the

others. "Let them tend to him. They know what they're about."
She picked up a bowl of wine and took a deep drink, then handed
it to Nyctasia. "Here, even a devoted Vahnite like you can drink
this. Hot wine's as weak as water."

Nyctasia sipped at the wine and watched as her young cousins
applied the poultices to the boy's feet and calves, then wrapped
him in furs and blankets. He seemed limp and lifeless in their
hands, and Nyctasia realized that the sleeping-draught had taken
hold of him.

"You can take it in turns to watch him tonight," 'Deisha was
saying, keeping her voice low. "If you lay a hot stone beneath his
feet you won't have to change the poultices as often. Use sacking
to wrap it in, and see it doesn't burn him."

"We know how, 'Deisha."

"Very well. And try to give him some broth later."

"Hush, you'll wake him," whispered Jenisorn. He sat with the
boy's head in his lap, lightly stroking his fair hair.

Nyctasia joined 'Deisha and made a last attempt to be of help.
"He'll not wake," she assured them. "And perhaps now that he's
asleep, I—we—could see how bad that hand is . . . ?"

The others exchanged a look, and 'Cacia shrugged. "Why
not? He won't know."

"Yes, show her," said 'Deisha. "Then we'll go."

'Cacia folded back the furs, uncovering the boy's arm. "It's
not a wound, Nyc," she explained, carefully unwinding the bandage. "This is what he didn't want you to see." She held up his
hand to show Nyctasia the dark scar of the slave-brand burned
into his palm.

9

ALL DURING THE ride back from Eske, Corson rehearsed to herself various ways of explaining what had taken place. Most of these accounts were true, but she doubted that Steifann would accept them, all the same. *It's not fair,* she thought. *Something like this always happens to me!*

When she'd set out with the Guild's agent, she still hadn't known her destination, though she had not been surprised to find her guide leading her north instead of south. But when they were joined by several other swordfighters along the way, she knew she'd been mistaken about the nature of her commission. If a small troupe of warriors was needed for the job, it was most likely a matter of clearing a nest of bandits out of the woods, to make the roads safer for parties of merchants. It would be bloody work, Corson knew, but she still hadn't suspected how much trouble lay ahead.

Talking with the others when they camped for the night, she found that they knew no more about the business than she did. Like her, they were not usually particular about their work, provided that the wages were satisfactory. Too much curiosity did not accord well with their profession. No doubt the Guild had taken such pains to be secret lest warning of the attack should reach their intended quarry. Corson took note that most of her fellow travelers were outlanders—southerners like herself or mercenaries from Liruvath—who were unlikely to have ties among the local brigandry.

Her guesswork was not far from the mark, but she only realized exactly what they were hunting when their leader called a halt on the bluffs overlooking a small, rocky inlet near the fishing village of Eske. By that time, it was too late to do anything but see the job through to the end. Hidden among the boulders on the dark shore, she had waited with the rest, silent, watching for the signal to attack, and already trying to think of an explanation that would satisfy Steifann. When the time came, she did her part and earned her wages. She had no choice. To retreat or raise an alarm would be more than her life was worth.

"Take them alive if you can," were the orders, and that had not proven difficult. The whole affair had been easy, Corson thought with distaste, like spearing penned and hobbled game. The three who'd arrived at moonrise had been hopelessly outnumbered. As soon as they'd signaled their confederates, they'd been seized with hardly a struggle, and their places taken by Corson and two of the others. It was just as simple to overcome the two who answered the signal, while they were busy hauling their boat onto shore.

When the boat returned to the waiting ship it rode low in the water, with two rowing, two lying flat on the bottom, one crouched in the prow, and two towed along, holding to the sides. Corson, who couldn't swim, stayed on shore to guard the prisoners and watch for anyone who tried to leap overboard and swim ashore. She knew that the ship would be taken quickly enough without her help. They were sailing shorthanded, after all. There could be no more than three of the crew left aboard, including Destiver.

10

"To AID A fugitive slave is theft, under the law," 'Deisha explained. "That's why it's best left to children and those in their nonage, like Jheine here, who aren't answerable to the law for their actions. If they're discovered, the rest of us can claim that we knew nothing about it, and no one can prove otherwise. You and I, Nyc, only saw this runaway in the stables, for an instant, and we took him for a thief—remember that. He escaped from us, and that's the last we saw of him. The youngsters went out to search, but they told us they couldn't find him. If we're asked, that's all we know of the matter."

The three had come to Nyctasia's tower-room to confer, where they were least likely to be overheard or interrupted. It was the most isolated corner of the great, sprawling stone mansion. Several days had passed since the boy had been found, but Nyctasia had not seen or heard anything of him since that night. Only the younger members of the Edonaris clan knew where he was hidden, and no one questioned them about it.

Jenisorn was leafing through one of Nyctasia's books without reading a word. He put it down, took up another, and set it down by the first, unopened. His usually merry, winsome face was grave and troubled, his eyes shadowed. "Perhaps you're not bound by Midland law, as you're a Maritimer," he said to Nyctasia. "I'm not sure. But it would be simplest if you and 'Deisha told the same tale, if you don't mind lying. I'm sorry to ask it of you."

"I'm quite an accomplished liar," Nyctasia assured them. "But I don't understand . . . surely even in the Midlands it's not lawful for someone so young to be branded! Children can't be enslaved for life, can they?"

"No, a child born to a slave is bound in service only till its twentieth year. The owner must feed and shelter bondschildren during their infancy—ten years, according to law—and they in turn must work for the owner for ten years as recompense for that upbringing. They can't be sold, except for the rest of their term of service, and of course they can't be branded. Once their debt to the owner is paid, they're supposed to be freed."

"But a good many disappear before that happens," Jenisorn said darkly.

"Disappear . . . ?" echoed Nyctasia.

"Sent on journeys from which they don't return, or sold for their remaining time of bondage, to someone who pays rather more than you'd expect for a few years' service."

"Someone who takes them far away," 'Deisha added, "usually over the Spine Mountains, where no one can question their history."

"And so into Liruvath," Nyctasia guessed, "where the laws governing slavery are even more barbarous."

"Yes. Anyone who's marked as a slave can be sold there, with few questions asked. You see, bondschildren can't be branded *unless they try to run away before they've fulfilled their term of labor.* It's an old game—their owners ill-use them till they're forced to flee, to save themselves. Then they're caught and branded as runaways, which makes it much easier to sell them to foreign slavers. . . ."

"And that's what happened to this one?" Nyctasia asked.

'Deisha shrugged. "Jheine?"

Jenisorn nodded. He sat staring at his own clenched fists for a time and finally said, "His name's Lorr. Lorr Saetarrinid."

'Deisha groaned. "I was afraid of that. Small wonder the poor lad was terror-stricken when he realized where he was."

The Saetarrin lands bordered on Edonaris property, but there were few dealings between the two houses. Wealthy, landed nobles who lived on the proceeds of their estates, the Saetarrin disdained the Edonaris as mere upstart merchants, despite their aristocratic ancestry. The Edonaris, for their part, knew much of Saetarrin history that was less than honorable, though they kept their suspicions to themselves. They were in no position to risk the enmity of their powerful neighbors.

A marriage-alliance of the two families had once been spoken of, but nothing had come of it. Only an Edonaris in direct line to the Jhaicery, and bringing a sizable dowry, would be considered worthy to marry into the House of Saetarrin, and thus far no heir to the title had been tempted by the prospect. Mesthelde, Lady Nocharis's eldest daughter, had never married, and had no intention of marrying. And her niece and heir, 'Deisha, had made it clear to her kin that she would rather marry a swineherd than a Saetarrin lord.

Now she cursed the Saetarrin and everything they touched. "We'll have their people here searching for him tomorrow, now that the storm's cleared," she worried.

"They'll not find him," Jenisorn said confidently. "But we'll have to get him away from here, as soon as may be, and it won't be an easy matter with the Saetarrin hunting him."

"Would they sell him to us?" Nyctasia suggested. "If it's merely a question of avarice, I can satisfy them."

'Deisha shook her head. "Not likely, Nyc. They wouldn't want him in Vale, free to bear witness to what he knows of them. And if they refused, we'd have to surrender him. There's only so much we can do for him, he'll understand that. He knew he'd be taking his chances."

"No," Jenisorn said abruptly. "He fled for his life, not for his freedom. He says he's killed Marrekind ar'n Saetarrin."

"Well," said 'Deisha, after a silence, "in that case, he does indeed deserve our help. I've often wanted to do the same. He'll have to stay in hiding a good while, then, till they've given up the search in these parts." She stood frowning at the fire, lost in thought, weighing plans and possibilities. One of the dogs nosed her hand, and she stroked his head absently. "In the spring, some of you must go with him to Amron Therain. He won't be as noticeable as one of a group of young folk. There'll be so many people flocking in and out of the city, once the Trade Road is clear, that you may avoid suspicion then."

Nyctasia was pacing about the small tower-room. "That seems so chancy. How would it be if his pursuers believed him dead? I can prepare a potion that counterfeits death for a time. If they saw his lifeless body, at least they'd call off the search, and it would be safer for him to come out of hiding."

"It's plain to see that you come from the coast, cousin," Jenisorn said. "Don't you know that they'd take him back, living or dead?"

"But why—?"

"To discourage their other slaves from trying to escape, of course. If there were no proof of his death, they might believe that he'd really gotten away, and be tempted to try it themselves." Jenisorn's voice rose. "Oh, they might just cut off his branded hand and bring that back—"

"That will do, Jheine," said 'Deisha.

"I see," Nyctasia said faintly. "Yes, we are a long way from
Rhostshyl. And if he reaches Amron Therain, what then?"

'Deisha answered. "There are those in Amron who'll help him
make his way to the coast, for a price. We know how to find
them."

The coast was the goal of all fugitive slaves, as Nyctasia well
knew, for slavery was forbidden by law in the Maritime cities. A
condemned criminal might be sentenced to a term as slave-
laborer in the service of the municipality, but a person could not
become the property of a private citizen. An escaped slave who
could reach the coast was safe from the laws of the east.

"It seems this isn't the first time you've been concerned in
such an undertaking," Nyctasia observed. "Does it happen
often?"

"No, not often. But Raphe and I had a hand in it, before we
came of age. Most of us do, once or twice, when we're young
enough."

Nyctasia understood their actions perfectly. They were Edonaris, after all. Her own ancestors had been instrumental in abol-
ishing slavery from the cities of the Maritime Alliance, and she
had been raised in a land free of its evils. She was proud of that
family heritage, and it had seemed only natural to her that the
Edonaris of Vale were not slave-holders.

But now she realized that their ways were not at all natural
here in the Midlands. She had thought of the Valley as a haven of
peace and harmony, far removed from the treachery and bloodthirsty ambition that threatened to destroy her homeland. But
now it seemed to her that she was lost in a primitive, lawless
land, unfit for civilized folk. Never in her exile had she longed so
painfully for Rhostshyl.

"I've seen little of the valley beyond this estate," she sighed.
"I knew there were slave-markets in Osela and Amron Therain,
but until this hapless creature came among us, I'd forgotten that
the lands between . . ."

"Hush," Jenisorn warned her, and they all fell silent as they
heard someone climbing the stairs to Nyctasia's tower.

The rest of the family knew, without being told, what had
happened on the first night of the storm. 'Deisha's careful words
to Diastor, "Nothing to concern you, Father. 'Cacia and the boys
will find him," had told everyone that she was speaking of a
runaway slave, and there they had let the matter lie. Now, the
sudden silence at his approach, and the air of secrecy that met

him, only confirmed Raphe's suspicions that the affair was far from finished.

Closing the door behind him, he asked, "Well, Jheine, how fares our guest?"

"I feel a fool denying what you already know, brother, but you ought not to ask, nor I to answer."

"Jheine's right, you know. Nyc and I are already compromised, but you've had no part in this," 'Deisha said, though without much conviction. She felt, as Raphe did, that anything that touched her touched her twin as well.

He did not argue the point. "Never mind. I only asked how he was, not where, or who. Or whose."

Jenisorn shrugged. If Raphe was willing to be told, it was his own choice to bear the responsibility for what he learned. "The frostbite's better, but he's still in a fever. It's his back that worries me most. He's been beaten savagely—flogged—and those weals don't look to be healing. I don't know if he'll be able to travel by spring thaw. It's only a few weeks away at the most. I don't know if he'll live until spring."

"In the *vahn*'s name!" cried Nyctasia. "What sort of mad fools abuse their own property? It's beyond reason and nature!"

"It's hard to understand," 'Deisha agreed. "People who take great care of their goods and livestock will nevertheless mistreat and neglect the people they own. Mother 'Charis says that's because it deforms the spirit, even of decent folk, to keep others in bondage. It's been family tradition with us, not to own slaves, ever since our ancestors learned that the Edonaris of Rhostshyl had banned slavery from the city. It was more a matter of pride than principle at first, I fear—aping the ways of our noble kinsfolk. In those days, they still hoped for a reconciliation, but *your* ancestors would have none of it," she teased Nyctasia.

"And slave-labor wouldn't really serve our purposes," said the ever-practical Raphe. "We need to employ a great many people at harvest time, but we couldn't afford to maintain them all the year long. We haven't the farmland for it. For most of the year we need too few laborers to make it worth our while to keep guards over them, or pursue them. It's foolishness. Much of what needs to be done, we do ourselves. We're a large family, and we're not ashamed to work."

"The Edonaris have always worked hard, wherever their duty lay," Nyctasia said, a touch of reproach in her voice. "You may believe that governing a city such as Rhostshyl is no heavy bur-

den, but I assure you that there's little rest for those who under-
take it."

"We know *you're* not too proud to work, Nyc," Raphe said
hastily. "You proved as much at the harvest. You labored far
beyond your strength."

"So I did, and all I accomplished by my efforts was a fit of
sunstroke. I was worse than useless. Still, though I wasn't raised
to bodily labor, neither was I raised to idleness."

"I only meant . . ." Raphe began, but stopped, realizing that he
had meant very much what Nyctasia thought he meant. He spread
his hands helplessly. "I meant no offense to you, cousin."

"Only to my rank and station, perhaps?" Nyctasia said, without rancor. "It's true that we're proud of our position, yet you
wrong us if you think our pride has not been earned—as yours
has. In all of you I see the pride of the Edonaris. Indeed, I
believe that you are prouder of your way of life than we of ours.
The better I know you, the more certain I am that we are in truth
one family, though now it is you who choose not to acknowledge
us as kin."

"If the rest were like you, we'd gladly welcome them," 'Deisha said diplomatically. She lifted up one of the massive tomes
that Nyctasia had been studying, and remarked, "I think you
work harder than all of us together. I'd rather toil out of doors all
day than try to read these thick, difficult books of yours. To each
her own task, say I, and I'm off to mine now. Come along,
Raphe, we're keeping Jheine from his lessons."

"We'll have one gentleman in the family, eh?" Raphe grinned.
"Nyc, I came to tell you that we've cleared a way up Honeycomb
Hill to the Esthairon vines and the temple cellars. Most of the
debris was removed before the storm, and a good bit of the crypts
and caves have been uncovered. They'll make perfect wine-
cellars. You said you wanted to see them again before they were
filled with barrels."

"Is it safe to go under there now?" Nyctasia asked doubtfully.
She had not been near the hill since the collapse of the temple had
crushed the last members of the Cymvelan Circle in the caverns
beneath. She felt keenly that they should have been left in peace,
that it was unseemly to disturb the ruins to accommodate the
vintnery's merchandise, but she kept such scruples to herself. She
understood that more room was needed to house and age the new
vintages. Now that the hollow hill had been cleansed of the
Cymvelans' curse, the Edonaris could not afford to let such valu-

able storage space go to waste. It was not for her, an outsider, to interfere in such a matter.

"It was the supports beneath the temple and the bell-tower that were unsound," Raphe assured her. "Now that those structures have fallen, there's no danger. What's left underneath is carved from solid rock. You can visit there whenever you like, now, but take care not to lose your way in the tunnels. All right, 'Deisha, I'm coming—"

"Nyc, take Grey with you, if you must go ferreting about down there," 'Deisha called from the stairway. "He could find his way out by smell."

When the twins had gone, Nyctasia turned to Jenisorn. "I don't imagine you've made much progress with the text of Raine of Tièrelon's *Travels*?"

"I've had no time for it," he admitted, "and I still haven't, I'm afraid."

"I can well believe that. We'll leave it for now. I'll give you passages from Book One of *The Manifold Ills of the Flesh* to study, dealing with the treatment of open wounds and febrile maladies. After I've seen the boy myself, of course."

"But Nyc, I—"

"Don't try to tell me that you can't take me to him, Jheine. You must. I don't doubt that you've done all you can for him, but that may not be enough. Fever may be brought on by a poison in the blood, from a morbid wound. Salves and tea of fever's-ease bark won't drive it out. If you don't want to see him die a lingering, painful death, you'll let me tend to him."

Though she was hardly the powerful sorceress her accusers claimed, Nyctasia was magician enough to call upon the healing power of the Indwelling Spirit, and Jenisorn knew it.

He sighed. "Would you, Nyc? I didn't like to ask it of you, but we'd all be grateful for your help. 'Cacia thinks that the weals should be cauterized, and none of us knows how to do it. I don't think you need fear the law—it's not only that you're a foreigner, but that you're a noblewoman. The law bows before a title, they say, and it probably grovels before the rank of Rhaicime."

"Rhaicime or no, I'm a healer—and an Edonaris. I've a duty to the afflicted, not to the law which allows such an outrage."

She did not claim that it was also her duty as a Vahnite to aid the helpless. She knew she was guilty of pride, but that would be pride of another sort, and less forgivable.

From the top of the house they descended to the very bottom, stopping to gather a few supplies and—at Jenisorn's suggestion —warm cloaks. The wine-cellars were as cold as the out of doors.

The dark, dank corridors were lined with immense barrels lying on their sides, and stacked jars of glazed clay sealed with wax. "Some of this wine's centuries old," Jenisorn told her proudly, "and very little of it spoiled. Someday I'll show you through the cellars properly. The whole history of the family is down here, if one knows how to read it."

Nyctasia followed in silence. She felt that she had already seen more than enough of the damp, chill cellars with their webbed walls, thick dust and foul air. The prospect of a more extensive tour held little appeal for her. She could see the shine of the snail-tracks in the lamplight, and she was certain that rats lurked in every shadow. Family history, she thought, was often best left buried. Pulling her cloak tighter about her, she said, "I'm sure that would be most interesting."

"That lot was laid down in the year of the drought, you see," Jenisorn explained, as they passed a row of casks smaller than the rest. But even these, Nyctasia saw, would be nearly as tall as she, if stood on end. "Nearly empty now, most of them." He tapped the fronts of a few barrels with a small wooden mallet, as they walked, to show Nyctasia how the different sounds told the quantity of wine within—which she found quite interesting, despite herself. "And these are from the year Kestrel Hill was first harvested," he continued, brushing away a layer of dust to uncover the falcon-brand.

Nyctasia sneezed. "Jheine, *where are we going*? If you've hidden our friend down here, he'll never heal, not in this damp and filth.'"

"I know. We hope to move him soon. But the room he's in isn't as bad as this. There's a fireplace, with a flue that opens into the back of the kitchen hearth above, so it's warmer there, and the air's fresher. You'll see—it's at the end of this corridor."

Nyctasia followed, but when they reached the far wall of the passage they came up against a blind end with a pyramid of barrels stacked against the stone, and no opening to either side. Nyctasia searched the floor, and soon found the outline of a round trapdoor, but there seemed to be no way of raising it.

Jenisorn tapped on one of the barrels.

"Empty," said Nyctasia promptly, recognizing the hollow sound. "Jheine, how are we to lift this?"

The empty barrel tapped back.

"That's just an old cistern, Nyc. The room is through here," Jenisorn replied, as the lid of the cask was pushed out from the inside. A wan, flickering light spilled out, and 'Cacia crawled from the barrel's mouth.

"Time enough you got back," she said, then seeing Nyctasia she remarked, "So you've come. I thought you would." She lowered her voice. "He's no better. He's shaking so hard his teeth rattle, and he's mad with fear and fever. He keeps asking me to kill him. I'm going to get some sleep. Good luck, Nyc."

Kneeling before the opening, Nyctasia saw that the wall was thick and solid except for the round hole piercing it behind this one barrel. The hidden chamber beyond was dimly lit by a small fire and a lamp hanging from a hook in the low ceiling. Once inside, she found that she could just stand upright, and she noted with approval that the little room had been swept and scrubbed clean. Fresh straw and mats of rushes covered the floor, to withstand the chill, and Lorr lay on a deep pile of pelts and coverlets by the hearth, wrapped in woolen blankets and fleecy sheepskin. His hands were hidden by warm, furred gloves.

But he looked to Nyctasia as if he were still huddled in the hay like a cornered animal. He struggled to sit upright when she approached, cringing away, until Jenisorn crawled into view behind her.

"Don't worry, this is my cousin Nyc that I told you about— the Lady Nyctasia, I ought to say—from Rhostshyl, on the coast." Jenisorn reached back through the hole and fitted both the front and back pieces of the cask into place again. Even if someone opened the lid, there'd be nothing to see but an empty barrel.

He came and knelt beside Lorr, who clutched at his hand desperately. "She's a healer, don't you remember? She'll soon have you fit again."

"Why?" Lorr whispered, trembling. "It's too late. I-I'm not afraid of death...only of d-death at the hands of the Saetarrin....Please...."

Nyctasia could imagine what sort of death would be dealt to a slave who'd killed his master. Jenisorn looked to her for help, and she too knelt by the pallet-bed and gently touched Lorr's fever-flushed face. There was only one way to comfort him. "You are safe in this house," she said firmly, "and when you're strong enough to go, I'll brew a deadly poison for you to take with you. Just a prick of it with a needle, or a drop on the tongue, will kill in mere moments. If you're taken, you'll have a swift death at your command. Your enemies shan't have you."

For the first time, relief showed in the youth's face. "You are merciful, lady," he said weakly, bowing his head to her. In Nyctasia he recognized someone who had also known despair.

"But take heart," urged Jenisorn. "They'll not hunt for you forever. You may yet escape with your life. They're sure to think you were lost in the storm and froze to death somewhere."

"Yes, perhaps," he said, as if to reassure Jenisorn.

He was clearly too exhausted for further talk, and Nyctasia bade him lie down again, while she looked over his wounded back. He gasped in pain as she uncovered the angry, swollen welts, but he made no complaint. Jenisorn turned away, and Nyctasia too was sickened at what she saw. Flogging was a common punishment in her homeland, for petty crimes of theft or brawling, but she had never seen at close hand how a really vicious beating tore the flesh. "Have you washed these wounds with vinegar?" she asked at last.

Jenisorn nodded. "Thrice in the day. And leeching-wort. We've tried ice for the swelling—"

"Don't use ice. It may ease the pain, but it can hinder healing," said Nyctasia. She gathered up the stained bandages and threw them on the fire, then cut a wide piece from one of the blankets and laid it lightly over Lorr's back. "Wool's best for this," she explained. "It may help draw out the poisons."

"Nyc, I've been bathing his face with snow, against the fever," Jenisorn said worriedly. "Was that wrong?"

"No, that can do no harm. But never keep ice on a wound for long, remember." She helped Lorr roll onto his side and wrapped the woolen bandage around him, then draped the covers over him carefully, trying not to let them press on his back. "Lie like that if you can."

Lorr looked up at her and gripped Jenisorn's hand more tightly. "If not ice, fire then?" he asked faintly, his voice shaking.

"It may come to that. But if I cauterize your wounds, I'll give you a drug first that will keep you in a deep sleep till I've finished. You needn't distress yourself over that."

He closed his eyes and drew a long, shuddering breath. "Elixir of Painshade, no? He was supposed to give me that when I was branded. I heard the smith say so. . . ."

Neither Nyctasia nor Jenisorn had to ask who it was he meant.

"Rest now," said Nyctasia quietly, "and we'll see what a bit of

Vahnite wizardry can do." With her knife she scraped a few coals from the hearth into the small brass bowl she'd brought with her. "This is only for burning a few leaves and herbs," she explained, seeing that both boys were watching her apprehensively. "You're to breathe the smoke, Lorr, and that will help us to achieve a healing-trance together. Jheine, leave us now—*someone* has to stay awake. Light an hour-candle, and when it's half-burned come back and waken me."

Lorr reluctantly released his hand, and Jenisorn bent over to kiss him. "You're safe with Nyc," he promised. "I'll soon be back. I'll sleep here tonight. Nyc, pull the cask-lids fast after me."

Nyctasia took his place beside Lorr and laid her hand on his brow, feeling the blood throbbing in his temple. His heartbeat was still strong—that was favorable. "Lean this way a little," she instructed. "Breathe deeply."

Dropping a small handful of crushed, powdery leaves over the coals, she held the bowl so that the wisps of bitter smoke drifted into his face. He choked and tried to turn away, but the fumes seemed to follow him, and he was suddenly too weak and dizzy to move. The floor was shifting dangerously beneath him, and unless he stayed perfectly still he would fall. . . .

Nyctasia could feel the rope steady beneath her hand, leading her forward on an unswerving course through the dense, surging snowstorm. It was Lorr who struggled on ahead of her now, buffeted by the fierce wind, barely able to cling to the guide-rope. Fearing that without help he'd lose his hold and be lost, she called to him to wait for her, but the wind swallowed her words at once. A curtain of snow blew between them, and she lost sight of him completely.

When she reached the shelter of the porch, the door stood open, casting a bright beacon of light out into the starless, treacherous night. Had Lorr made his way to the house, or had he been swept away into the icy darkness? Nyctasia searched all through the building for him, hastening from room to room but finding them empty, and calling his name in vain.

11

"IT'S NOT MY fault!" Corson shouted. "How was I to know it was smugglers they were after? If they'd told us, I'd have warned her—that's why they made rutting sure we didn't know. There was nothing I could do! Do you want me to give the money back? That won't help Destiver."

She had tried to tell Destiver the same thing, on the way back to Chiastelm, but Destiver, wounded and in shackles, had only spat at her.

Annin looked as if she'd like to do the same. "Then what will help? You put her into prison—"

"I didn't! She can blame herself. If she wasn't a stinking smuggler—"

"If you weren't a mercenary—!"

"They didn't teach me any other trade in the army!"

"You didn't have to take this job."

"If I hadn't, someone else would be fifty crescents the richer, and Destiver would still be in prison. I tell you, I didn't sell her to the Guild. I'd have saved her if I could."

"I don't believe you. Everyone knows you hate her."

Corson couldn't deny that. "I can't abide her. But you and Steifann like her, though only the Hlann knows why. I'd have done it for your sake, not hers, but I swear I'd have done it."

"What's to be done now, that's the question," Steifann reminded them. He had always disapproved of Corson's profession, but, upon reflection, he couldn't hold her responsible for Destiver's arrest. "Destiver would be no better off if someone else had taken her," he admitted, "but you might be better off, Corson, if someone else did the Guild's dirty work for them."

"You'd be better pleased, I daresay, if I'd taken the job Destiver offered me. Then I'd be in prison with her now."

"You needn't have taken any sort of job—there's plenty of work for you right here." It was their old argument, never resolved between them. "But never mind that now. There must be something we can do about Destiver."

"What about all those Rhaicimes and Jhaices you know, Corson? They should be able to obtain a pardon for her."

"I know *one* Rhaicime, and I met *one* heir to a Jhaicery, and I left them both in the valleys of the Midlands. I wish to the Hlann that I'd stayed there myself."

"Then they're no use to us," Steifann said reasonably. "But you do have friends on the city guard, Corson. Couldn't you arrange for them to leave her cell unlocked one night and look the other way? We'd make it worth their while."

Corson shook her head. "If she were just a thief or a common killer, it might be possible. But they wouldn't dare let a smuggler get away from them. The Guild would have their heads for it." The Maritime cities depended on trade for much of their revenues, and nothing could be permitted to interfere with their profits. The penalties for smuggling were as harsh as those for murder, and rather more likely to be enforced.

"But they might let you in to see her, on the sly," Corson offered Annin.

"Well, you could bring her some food, I suppose," said Walden.

"Or some ale," Steifann suggested. "That's what she'll really be wanting."

"Or a knife . . ." said Annin thoughtfully.

"That's too dangerous. You'd be caught."

"She'll be hung if we don't do *something*!"

"*I* have an idea," said Trask.

The others looked at him with as much annoyance as surprise. "Corson, drop this brat down the well, would you?" Annin said sharply.

"With pleasure."

"Don't spoil the water, just throttle him and I'll use him for stew-meat." Walden threatened to cook everyone, almost every day, but he always managed to sound as if he meant it.

"If you haven't swept out the taproom, Trask, you'd better do it now," Steifann ordered. "And if you have, go do it again."

Trask sighed and picked up a broom, but only stood leaning against it lazily. "If you'd listen to me for a change, I know of someone who might be of help," he insisted. "Eslace av Ondra. She has influence on the Guild."

"You don't know Eslace av Ondra! An Ondra wouldn't even use you for a footstool."

"I didn't say I knew her—there's talk about her, that's all. I've heard that she can be very generous, if one appeals to her in the right way." He stroked the broom-handle suggestively.

"That's the sort of thing you always hear," Corson said scornfully. "Why haven't you paid her a call yourself?"

"From all they say of Mistress Eslace, she has an eye for a man who's big and brawny," Trask explained, looking pointedly at Steifann. "There's no accounting for taste."

"Rot," said Steifann.

Trask shrugged. "Please yourself. Destiver's no friend of mine. But if half of what's said is true, the daughter of Ondra would be well pleased to grant a hearing to a petition from the likes of you. Or you," he added, turning to Walden. "If Mistress Omia could spare you for the night."

The broad, barrel-chested cook was shorter than Steifann but no less muscular, and he could beat Steifann at arm-wrestling three tries out of five. But the only woman who interested Walden was Omia, his stout, good-humored wife and the mother of his numerous children. "I could do very well without Destiver myself. *I'm* not her countryman and shipmate," he said, grinning at Steifann. "I must yield to you the honor of pleading her cause with Madame Ondra."

"It might be worth a try, at that," said Annin.

Steifann considered the matter for a while, scratching at his bushy beard. "It couldn't do any harm, I suppose. There's no reason I shouldn't address an Ondra. I'm a respectable householder."

Corson snorted. "You're a common taverner!"

"The Ondra may give themselves airs, but they're only traders, all in all. They're no better than the rest of us."

"Well, the worst she can do is have you thrown out," Annin reflected.

"We'll see about that," said Steifann decidedly. "More likely she'll beg me to stay. But I'd better take a bath, all the same. Heat up some water. Trask, clean my good boots."

Corson followed him into his room and watched moodily as he searched in a chest for his best shirt. "You never groom yourself for me," she complained.

"I will," Steifann promised, "when you're someone of influence and consequence, instead of a worthless vagabond."

"I always said you were a whore at heart."

Steifann laughed. "I don't blame you for being cross. You might have to make do without me tonight, poor creature. That must be hard to bear."

"I'll survive somehow," Corson said darkly. "Maybe I won't be here when you get back."

Steifann pushed the hair back from his face and frowned. "Destiver and I came over from Azhes together, you know."

"I know," said Corson, burning with jealousy. She had never even been to the island nation of Azhes. That Steifann's past did not include her was bad enough—that it did include Destiver was infuriating. "You Azhid always stand together."

"We do, but it's not just that." He closed the door, then went to stand at the hearth, beckoning Corson to join him. "What you don't know is that we can neither of us go back there, on pain of death. We've both been condemned for high treason."

Corson started. "High . . . but isn't that treason against the throne? How—?"

"Not so loud, Corson. Destiver and I were on the crew of the *Golden Feather*. You must have heard of it."

"The royal ship—the one that mutinied?"

He nodded, his face grim. "Not all of Destiver's stories are lies. We did live by piracy for a few years. There was no other way for us to live. Oh, it was nothing like the bold adventures she blathers about when she's drunk. It's a shabby trade. But we could hardly go back home after we'd set His Sovereign Highness Prince Breazhwen adrift, and made off with a royal galleon. And there were regal rewards for our capture in all the ports of the mainland." His voice was bitter. "They should have given *us* a reward for rebelling against that pestilent whelp Breazhwen! They only gave him command of the vessel to keep him away from court—everyone knew that. All very well for them at the capital, but Their Excellencies didn't concern themselves about the crew that would be trapped aboard ship with him for months, subject to his vicious whims." He spat into the fire.

Corson had suffered under some brutal commanders in the army, but she hadn't been penned up with them in the middle of the ocean, where she could not even hope to desert. "You should have killed him!"

"It wasn't for his sake that we spared him, I promise you. We hadn't much chance of mercy if we were caught, but no chance at all if we threw him overboard. Mutiny's risky enough without murder." He laughed suddenly. "And then someone did kill him, not a year after he returned to the palace. I suppose there was nothing else to be done. Asye knows we'd endured him as long as we could. We all tried to stay out of his way, but he noticed me, worse luck. I'm big even for an Azhid, though we're not all such a puny lot as you Mainlanders."

Corson smiled. It was an old joke between them. A southerner, she was fully as tall as Steifann, but she was one of the few people he'd ever met who was.

"He took a liking to me," Steifann continued, with a grimace, "which was more dangerous than his dislike, in some ways. That mutiny probably saved my life. . . ."

After a long silence, Corson asked, "Why did you never tell me all this before?"

Steifann put his arm around her shoulders. "I've never told anyone. The others only know that Destiver and I were shipmates in the Azhid navy. I hadn't the right to tell, you see—it was her secret as well as mine. She was one of the ringleaders. But it can't make much difference to her now, I fear. I want you to know that I trust you, Corson—and that I owe it to Destiver to try what I can to save her."

"Oh, of course you do, I know that. I wouldn't mind cutting her throat myself, but I don't much want to see her hang. She did sneak me out of the city last year, even if she charged me a fortune for it."

"She could have earned much more by betraying you, you know."

"All right, I don't deny it. Go pay court to the whole Guild, for all of me. I wish you success of it, because I don't think we can afford to bribe the magistrates."

"Well, as long as you understand that it's necessary," Steifann said seriously. He dragged the wooden tub out of the corner and pushed it over to the hearth. Trask came in without knocking, poured a kettle of hot water into it and went back to the kitchen for more.

Steifann pulled off his boots and began to unlace his shirt. "Of course, I have heard that Eslace av Ondra's still quite a handsome woman," he remarked, grinning. "A pity that comb of yours only works on men."

Corson threw the boots and a basin and ewer at him before she stormed out of the room, nearly knocking over Trask and his steaming kettle.

12

THE SAETARRIN LOST no time in inquiring after their fugitive bondservant. But the Edonaris household was astonished, and not a little disturbed, when Lady Avareth and her son paid them the honor of a visit themselves, instead of sending a messenger.

When informed of the noble pair's approach, Mesthelde had hurried to the barn to find 'Deisha and send her to wash and change her clothes. As heirs to the Jhaicery, the two of them would be expected to be on hand to greet their lordly guests, but 'Deisha, who was attending to an ailing sow, was in no state even to welcome a roadworn peddler. She cursed and clambered out of the pen, complaining loudly that she'd prefer to spend the morning in the company of a sick pig than with the best of the Saetarrin.

"And fetch Nyctasia at once," Mesthelde ordered. "It's her they've come to see, not us, you may be sure. They've heard that we have a Rhaicime among us. Well, she'll have to meet them sooner or later. Tell her she must be civil, for our sakes. She'll be in the nursery still, at this hour. And take off those boots before you set foot in the house, Frondescine ar'n Edonaris."

Nyctasia was reading a history lesson to Tsebrene, Melorin and Hespiara, who were rarely called anything but Bean, 'Lorin and Sparrow, respectively.

". . . all the way to Azhes and the Westernmost Isles," 'Deisha heard. "And that's why folk from the west like me and folk from the east like you, all speak the Eswraine tongue, and you and I can understand each other—most of the time."

"But not the Liruvathid," said 'Deisha, from the doorway.

Nyctasia smiled at her. "That's right. The Eswraine never settled the Inner Lands because they met with fierce warlike tribes there who drove them away. So they traveled through the north, around the mountains, and that's when they came to the valley. They called the mountain range The Spine because it seemed to them like the backbone of the world. And from here, some of their great-grandchildren went farther west until they found the coast. And what else did they find?"

"Azhes and the Westernmost Isles!" 'Lorin recited. "*You* didn't know that, 'Deisha."

"I didn't have such a good teacher," said 'Deisha. "But lessons are over for today. Nyc, I must carry you off to meet some of our neighbors."

"In a moment, love. And so the peoples of the Empire speak different languages from ours, and don't even understand each other very well. They're not children of the Eswraine, as we are. And *that*," she concluded, "is why we always call people from Eswrin *avina*, which means 'mother,' or *vaysh*, which means 'father,' even if they're quite small like you little minnows."

Her pupils thought it extremely funny that grown people should call children father or mother, and Nyctasia left them giggling together, with a promise to tell them more stories on the morrow.

Explaining as they went, 'Deisha hurried to her own rooms, dragging Nyctasia along with her. Mesthelde had already ordered hot water sent up for her. 'Deisha tossed her filthy clothes on the floor and began to scrub herself vigorously with a bath brush. When she'd dismissed the maid, she told Nyctasia, "And the worst of it is, they say Lord Marrekind is with her—Lorr didn't kill him after all. *Vahn*, what a shame!"

"But it's good news for Lorr, surely."

"Not at all. He must have fought with Marrekind and left him for dead. That's as serious as killing him, under the law. The law for slaves is not much different from the law for animals, Nyc. A dog that turns on its owner shall be put to death."

Before Nyctasia could reply, Mesthelde strode in to see that 'Deisha was making herself presentable. She wore a long russet gown with trimming of fox-fur at the sleeves and hem, and her hair was bound up neatly beneath a fine kerchief of gold lace. Around her neck was the heavy gold chain that signified her title. She had even left off the great ring of keys she always wore at her belt.

Nyctasia had never seen her in anything but plain, serviceable homespun, usually covered by a capacious apron. "How handsome you look, Lady Mesthelde," she ventured.

But her finery did nothing to sweeten Mesthelde's temper. "Lady Moonshine and Folly," she snapped. "Nothing but a lot of bothersome rubbish. 'Deisha, wear your green silk. What have you that's decent for Nyctasia to wear?"

"Any number of things, Aunt, don't fret yourself. I've fine clothes enough for a dozen. They never wear out," she explained to Nyctasia, "because I never wear them. Nyc, do take that gown with the silver stitching and the pearls on the sleeves—I've never dared put it on, but it might have been made for you."

Mesthelde approved the choice, but Nyctasia demurred. "It's lovely. I'd gladly wear it for a family celebration, but for this occasion I'll do as I am." She was dressed in plain woolen leggings and a simple tunic, both of dull brown. They were of good quality, but hardly elegant.

"You can't be presented to the Saetarrin looking like that!" Mesthelde protested.

"You'll find that I can," said Nyctasia calmly. "Are they in their best?"

"No, but, my dear Nyctasia, little as we may esteem these people, we must stay in their good graces. We can't afford to give them offense—"

Nyctasia had never before contradicted Mesthelde, but the usages of etiquette were something she understood far better than any of her kinsfolk here in Vale. "They'll not take it amiss, I promise you. On the contrary, they'd think the less of me if I showed them more honor than they show you. As a Rhaicime, I'm their superior in rank, and they won't be satisfied unless I behave accordingly. It is, as you so justly observe, great rubbish, but they'll expect it of me."

"Well, perhaps you know best," said Mesthelde doubtfully. "We'd not ask you to receive them, if it could be helped, but they'll take it as a slight if you don't. I've already had to apologize that my mother's not well enough to welcome them herself —as if I'd let her be bothered with them. You will be amiable to them, though, won't you?"

"Ah, no, not amiable—gracious," Nyctasia said with a knowing smile. She went to the door, pausing to say, "I'll be down directly. I believe I do have a few preparations to make. Don't worry, I want to meet them very much indeed—especially Lord Marrekind."

'Deisha curtsied stiffly. "Lady Avareth, Lord Marrekind," she said, "you honor our house." In her green silk kirtle, with lace at her wrists and breast, and slippers of gold kid on her feet, 'Dei-

sha looked perfectly exquisite, and felt like a perfect fool. Dainty
gloves of spiderweb tracery might hide her work-hardened hands,
but she knew that fine raiment could not make her a lady in the
eyes of the Saetarrin, and she hated to take part in such a masquerade. They were sneering at her, she was certain. The dogs,
sensing her mistrust of the visitors, regarded them balefully,
hackles raised.

Lady Avareth inclined her head slightly in greeting. She considered 'Deisha an insolent chit who had dared to decline an
alliance with the House of Sactarrin, and who ought to be put in
her place. But if it were true that a foreign Rhaicime had settled
among the Edonaris, then perhaps it was as well that no mar-
riage-accord had been made with a mere Jhaice. . . .

Much to 'Deisha's disgust, Lord Marrekind was more atten-
tive to her. When he bent to kiss her hand, she saw a large, dark
swelling over one eye that looked like a recent injury. A blow
that could raise a bruise like that, she thought, could easily knock
a man senseless.

"Mistress Frondescine, what a pleasure to see you again," he
was saying. "We ought to meet more often, neighbors as we are.
If, as rumor has it, your distinguished kinswoman from the coast
resembles you closely, she must be beautiful indeed."

"You flatter me, my lord," said 'Deisha, politely withdrawing
her hand. "My lady cousin is far more comely than I. But you
shall judge that for yourself. She will be with us directly."

"We shall be honored."

"The Lady Nyctasia is eager to make your acquaintance,"
Mesthelde assured them. "Pray sit by the fire. May I offer you
wine?" If Nyctasia kept them waiting much longer, she thought
grimly, she'd go fetch her herself and drag her downstairs by the
ear, if need be.

A servant had set a tray of silver goblets on the table, and
Diastor himself had brought a dusty jar of a very old vintage from
the cellars. When he cut the seal, an inviting, heady fragrance
filled the air for a moment.

"The wines of this household are surely a Manifestation of
Temptation," said Nyctasia, from the doorway. "Good day to
all."

'Deisha saw at once that Nyctasia had been right to refuse the
gown of silver and pearl. Her plain attire was clearly the best
complement for the rich gold chain of office she wore, crown-
like, around her head—as was traditional only for those of the

highest rank. She smiled, bowed to the company, and advanced into the room, all with an air of stateliness and queenly dignity that no fine raiment could possibly have improved. Even Mesthelde was spellbound.

To one who could command such presence, 'Deisha realized, splendid garments were not only unnecessary, but even excessive. Then, recalling herself to her duty, she recovered her wits sufficiently to say, "Lady Avareth, Lord Marrekind, allow me to present our newfound kinswoman, the Lady Nyctasia Selescq Rhaicime brenn Rhostshyl ar'n Edonaris."

"Oh, well done, milady sister," Raphe murmured in her ear. "You've been practicing."

'Deisha stifled a laugh. "A commoner like you doesn't understand these things," she whispered. Raphe pinched her.

They watched in awe while Nyctasia indulgently accepted the formal obeisances of the Saetarrin, as if this were a duty that she willingly performed for their benefit. Greymantle growled softly as Lord Marrekind approached her, and Nyctasia laughed, not in the least discomposed.

"Why, lie down and be still, you mannerless cur," she said lightly. "These are friends of the house." Her tone might have deceived a person, but certainly not a dog. Greymantle obeyed, but continued to watch the guests suspiciously.

When Lord Marrekind knelt before her, Nyctasia took his hand and seemed to study it for a moment, a faint frown creasing her brow. But then she bade him rise, with a smile of the utmost benevolence.

"Permit me," she said to Mesthelde, and poured out the wine, handing the guests their goblets herself, to do them honor. "You must not think it an insult that I refuse to drink with you. I am a healer, and so a most strict Vahnite. Even these excellent wines which bear my family name are forbidden by the Discipline, I fear. It is the price one must pay to serve the Indwelling Spirit— and to master it."

"Your servant, my lady," said Lord Marrekind, raising his goblet to her before he drank.

Her eyes met his, and again she frowned. "Forgive my impertinence, sir, but you suffer, do you not, from sleeplessness, and a throbbing pain of the temples, at times? Perhaps nosebleed?"

He stared. "And did the Indwelling Spirit tell you that?"

"The signs are plain to any healer—the beat of blood in your hand, your ruddy complexion, and the blood-web in your eyes—"

"Of what are these the signs?" he demanded, anxious.

"But surely your physicians have warned you?"

"I have little faith in physicians' ways, Lady Nyctasia. Pray let me hear your judgment of my state."

Nyctasia laughed. "Perhaps you are wise to distrust the skills of leeches. I believe they harm as often as they heal. Indeed, though you will think I boast, our court physicians often came to me for advice on such matters. It seems that scholarship may be as valuable as experience. You are surely afflicted with tempestuous blood—what is commonly called the Surge. It is often found in those of powerful will, but is more dangerous to some than to others. You should eat little meat, sir, and be bled often, especially in the winter months. If you allow me, I shall send to your physicians a copy of the pertinent texts from the writings of the great Iostyn Vahr."

"I should be very grateful, my lady." That the Saetarrin did not keep a retinue of personal physicians was something he had no intention of admitting in the present company.

Nyctasia was in fact quite aware of this already, but her words would serve to remind him of the difference in their stations. "I shall also take the liberty," she continued, "of sending you a certain preparation, a specific against the seizure known as The Red Veil. You may never need it perhaps, but if you should be stricken suddenly with a pain that dims your sight, and casts a red mist over all you see, lose no time but drink it at once. Such a wound"—she gestured at his bruised brow—"could be dangerous for one who suffers from tempestuous blood. It might bring The Red Veil upon you at any time. The color of the flesh is unwholesome, and . . . well, it is best to be prepared."

By now Lord Marrekind was thoroughly alarmed. He finished his wine and gladly allowed Nyctasia to pour him another. "You are most kind, Lady Nyctasia. I shall certainly heed your counsel. If I may ever in any wise be of service to you . . ."

Nyctasia dismissed his thanks with a smile and a graceful wave of her hand. "It is a sacred duty, sir, to put such knowledge to use. But it is my passion as well, I do confess. I cannot see an illness or an injury without desiring to know its history, and to direct its treatment." She regarded his face again, and said slowly, "A blow, I believe, raised that bruise, and not a fall. Am I correct?"

At this, Lady Avareth came forward to claim Nyctasia's attention. "Entirely correct, my lady. And it was that very matter which brought us here today—or rather, provided us with a pretext for coming here to make Your Ladyship's acquaintance."

Nyctasia admired the skillful way in which Lady Avareth disguised the truth as a flattering lie. It was a ruse she had often employed herself.

"My son was attacked by one of our own bondservants," Lady Avareth continued, "who has so far escaped capture. We came to inquire whether he'd been seen by anyone of this household."

"No one's told me about it if he has," said Mesthelde, with perfect truthfulness. She looked questioningly at the others.

Diastor shook his head. "We'll ask among our people, of course, but I doubt that we'll learn much. Still, if the man's dangerous, folk should be warned to be on their guard."

"Dangerous he may be, but hardly a man—and I daresay he never will be one," said Lord Marrekind. "He's little more than a boy, but he's given trouble before. I should have had him hamstrung the last time he ran off."

Nyctasia looked startled. "What, a fair-haired youth? 'Deisha, do you suppose it was that young thief we found in the stables, on the night the storm began?"

"I—I don't know, he might have been," 'Deisha said in consternation. She did not have Nyctasia's experience at lying, and was not aware that a half-truth was usually more effective than an evasion or an outright lie. Or even an outright truth.

"That must have been the boy Lorr," Lord Marrekind exclaimed. "He fled just a few days before the storm struck. You say you found him?"

"Oh yes, we found him, and lost him, almost at once," Nyctasia said thoughtfully. "He ran out into the snow, deliberately, as soon as he was discovered. I thought the poor wretch must be mad. If only I'd known . . ." She sighed. "We searched the yard, but he'd already vanished. I couldn't understand it at the time, but of course I see now that he didn't wish to be rescued. He preferred to perish in the storm than to return to servitude."

"To death, rather," said 'Deisha grimly. "For raising his hand to his master." She did not suppose that Nyctasia had forgotten this, but she was beginning to guess at her cousin's game.

"My dear, I'm sure you do not mean to insult our guests," Nyctasia reproached her, "but you have sadly misunderstood their intentions, unless I much mistake. Gentlefolk do not avenge

themselves on their inferiors." She sounded shocked at the very
suggestion that the Saetarrin might take such savage measures.
"The laws of your cruel country may *allow* an atrocity of that
sort, but surely they do not *demand* it?" she asked, turning to
Lord Marrekind.

"By no means, Your Ladyship," he said hastily. "But I beg to
assure you that the youth is not deserving of Your Ladyship's
concern, nor of such mercy as the law allows. I myself am witness to that."

Nyctasia smiled. "As the Principles of the philosophers tell us,
'Mercy dealt to the deserving is not mercy, but merely justice,'"
she said sweetly. She had often had occasion to reflect that the
greatest gift of Vahnite philosophy was its power to answer almost any argument.

Having silenced her audience with these lofty sentiments,
Nyctasia continued, "But I fear he is beyond our mercy or our
vengeance now. He can hardly have survived the storm." She
opened her hand in a Vahnite gesture of resignation. "I feel in
some wise responsible. . . . If he should somehow be found alive,
perhaps, sir, as you hold yourself in my debt, you will be so kind
as to let me know your decision?"

She had left Lord Marrekind no choice, and he knew it. He
bowed and said, "Upon my honor, his fate shall rest entirely in
Your Ladyship's hands." Behind his back, 'Deisha winked at her.

"You have greatly relieved my mind, Lord Marrekind," Nyctasia said warmly. "Though it may well be that the lad who concerns me is not, after all, the one you seek. I had only a glimpse
of him, but he hardly looked strong enough to overcome a grown
man."

"He's strong enough to wield a large stone—and I confess
that he took me by surprise. I knew he was wayward and disobe-
dient, but I'd no idea what a vicious little beast he was."

"Yet, as a Maritimer, I cannot condemn him. We say on the
coast that if you make beasts of people, you must not expect them
to behave better than beasts. We prefer to be served by free folk
who know their own worth."

In as cold a tone as she could bring herself to use to a Rhaicime, Lady Avareth asked, "And are the peasants on your estates
any better off than slaves?"

"Those on *my* estates are," Nyctasia said evenly. "But you are
quite right, of course—on many manors the laborers are mis-
treated, and have little recourse to justice. Unfortunately, there

are those everywhere who disregard the law with impunity."
Nothing in her face or voice was accusing, but the force of her
remark was not lost on anyone present.

The Saetarrin soon took their leave, much to the relief of their
hosts. Nyctasia accepted an invitation to hunt with them in the
spring, and reassured Lord Marrekind that she would soon send
the promised medicine. Until they were shown from the hall, she
remained as flawlessly, formally polite as when she'd entered.
Her manner was one of perfect courtesy mixed with condescen-
sion such as the Edonaris had never before seen her display. Her
treatment of the Saetarrin had made entirely clear to 'Deisha and
her aunt the vast difference between "amiable" and "gracious."

Raphe applauded her, and 'Deisha cried, "Nyc, you were
wonderful," embracing her wildly, and tearing a seam in the
green silk gown. Excited by the commotion, Greymantle jumped
up on them, sending Nyctasia's chain of office flying.

Raphe retrieved it, and returned it to her with a bow. "Tell me,
Your Ladyship, how do you manage to bow, wearing this thing,
without letting it fall off?"

"It's not at all easy," laughed Nyctasia. "Shall I give you lessons in deportment?"

"I should say not!" Mesthelde returned from escorting the
guests out. "You did very well," she conceded. "They took to it.
But if you ever behaved to me like that, I'd slap your face for
you, you conceited creature. 'Deisha, get out of that dress before
you destroy it." She paused and fixed Nyctasia with a shrewd
look. "Is Marrekind really ill?" she demanded.

"I hope so," said 'Deisha earnestly.

"'Powerful will!'" snorted Mesthelde, before Nyctasia could
answer her question. "It's folk with ungovernable tempers who
suffer from the Surge."

"That's true, but it would be less than gracious to tell him so. I
believe that he is ill, yes . . . or that he soon will be."

"Hmmm . . . and what was all that nonsense about a red mist,
or some such? I've never heard the like."

"It's rather an uncommon malady, but a very grave one. I'd
best go see to the preparation of the specific. I suspect that he'll
be needing it quite soon."

But though Nyctasia made ready the necessary remedy, she
did not yet send it to Castle Saetarrin.

13

CORSON WAS NOWHERE in sight when Steifann came back, just past dawn, looking tired and a little tipsy. Walden had gone to market for the day's supplies—usually Steifann's chore—leaving Trask and his other underlings to finish the baking. Annin was already bustling around the kitchen.

"A most charming woman," Steifann reported. "But not very encouraging, about Destiver."

"What did she say?" Annin asked anxiously. "Can she do anything to help?"

"Oh, she sympathized, said she quite understood—old shipmates and all that—"

"But . . .?"

"But there's nothing to be done at least till the Maritime Alliance meets, and she doubts that much can be expected then. She very kindly explained that this matter does not concern Chiastelm alone, but the whole enterprise of coastal shipping. The Guild means to raise its standing in the Alliance by showing the rest what Chiastelm has done to fight smuggling, and Destiver's their prize."

"She's safe till late in the spring, then, that's something gained. They won't hold such an important council until the thaw's well past, and the roads dry."

Steifann pushed the hair out of his eyes and stretched wearily. "Maybe before then we'll find a way. Where's Corson?"

"Still abed," said Trask.

"Lazy wench. I'll join her for a while. I could do with some sleep." He winked. "Being persuasive is hard work."

But he found Corson not only awake, but dressed and waiting for him. "Good," he said, "since you're up you can go help Annin. I'll be out when I've had some rest. I didn't get much sleep last night," he teased, throwing himself across the bed beside her.

"Neither did I," said Corson smugly.

Steifann sat up again. "Eh? Why not?"

"If you think I spent the night here alone, missing you, you're sadly mistaken, my friend. I was out looking for another man. I found him too."

"I don't believe that. You're just jealous."

"Ask Annin, then. She knows. Annin!" she called, "come in here, will you?"

Annin looked in. "What is it, pet?" She no longer seemed at all angry with Corson.

"Was I here last night?" Corson demanded.

"Why, of course you were. You were with me all night, if anyone asks. You never went out at all."

Steifann looked from one woman to the other in confusion. Corson laughed. "That's right, so I was, *if anyone asks*. But I shan't be here tonight, that's certain. One of the 'Vathid soldiers told me that the Border Guard of Tièrelon is hiring people to train new recruits, and they pay well in the Gemlands. I'll bring back diamond buckles for you all." She stood and shouldered her pack.

Steifann hastily got up. "But you don't have to go now," he protested. "Wait a few days, why don't you?"

"No sense in delaying. It will take a good while to get that far north, with the roads shin-deep in mud. I want to get an early start. I was only waiting to tell you good-bye, love."

A hard hug and a hearty kiss were all of Corson's farewells. She had never been one for prolonged partings.

Steifann held her back for a moment. "Corson, you're not going just because I—"

"No, no, it's not that. If I were jealous of your tryst with Eslace av Ondra—that scheming crone—I'd stay right here and see that you didn't make a habit of it. And you'd better not," she added, on her way out.

Steifann looked after her, angry and uncertain. "Then why in the Hlann's name—!"

"Let her go," Annin advised him. "It's almost spring, and you know Corson can't stay still with the spring fever in her blood. She'll be back before long, I'll warrant." She pointed imperiously to the bed. "Sleep while you can, before the house is full of folk."

Steifann sat on the bed and pulled off his boots, grumbling to himself. "Thinks she's the only woman in the world, does she?

Goes off for months at a time, never a thought for me. . . . Well, one day. . ."

Annin shut the door before remarking, "Oh, I almost forgot— you were so busy all night, you haven't heard the news, have you? Someone cut Hrawn brenn Thespaon's throat last night, in the alley behind The Crow's Nest."

Steifann looked up sharply. "Is that so?"

"Yes, it seems he'd come by a good bit of money somehow, and of course the fool got roaring drunk with it. The talk is that he started bragging how he'd sold a pack of smugglers to the Guild for a pretty penny."

"And does the talk say who killed him?"

"Not that I've heard. But they don't take kindly to informers in that quarter, you know. It could have been anyone. And I don't think the authorities will try very hard to find out, either. Hrawn was nothing but a troublemaker. The city guard will think themselves well rid of him."

Steifann sighed. "And now Corson's suddenly heard of a job in the far north. Well, I hope you're satisfied."

"She'd have gone soon anyway. She left you this in the meantime." Annin took a well-filled purse from her pocket and tossed it to him. "She says you're to hire someone to help with the heavy work here till she comes back. She suggested that someone ugly and unpleasant would be best." Annin grinned. "And preferably bald."

14

TRUE TO NYCTASIA'S prediction, it was only a matter of days before messengers from the Saetarrin arrived to entreat her help for Lord Marrekind.

'Cacia interrupted her and Jenisorn at their studies. "They say the Red Veil's come upon him, whatever that may be, and that you have a cure for it, Nyc, which His Lordship begs you'll send at once."

"I shall do better than that. I'll go myself to tend to him, and bring the remedy with me. I have it right here."

"Don't you do it!" 'Cacia protested. "Let the bastard suffer. Let him die!"

"I know what I'm about, girl. Trust me. Run and tell them that I'll set out at once."

"What *are* you about, Nyc?" Jenisorn demanded, as soon as 'Cacia had left them. "Why should you help him?"

"Why, Jheine, I'm surprised at you. It's my manifest duty to heal Lord Marrekind." Nyctasia grinned, and held up a small silver flask. "And when I've given him this, he'll be so exceedingly grateful he may even keep his word to me about Lorr. One who's been cured of The Red Veil doesn't soon forget it."

"You're quite sure you can cure it, then? If you go there yourself, and fail—"

"Don't worry, my lad. I cannot fail. I have only to give him this antidote to the poison I put in his wine. You'll agree, surely, that it's my duty to do so."

Jenisorn dropped the vellum scroll he was holding. "Sweet *vahn*, Nyc!"

Greymantle watched in surprise as the scroll rolled across the floor toward him. He stalked it suspiciously, sniffed it, then decided that it was unfit to eat, and sneezed disdainfully. Nyctasia took it away from him before he could change his mind.

"You're not to tell the others, mind you, Jheine. I don't know that Mother 'Charis would approve—and I think young 'Cacia would approve too much."

"As you will, of course. But I'd not rely on Marrekind's promises, even if he believes that he owes you his life. I think we'd best try to get Lorr away in secret, nonetheless."

"By all means. It's not only his promises I wanted, but his pain as well. Oh, not for spite's sake—much as the prospect pleases—no, rather to create a certain Symmetry. Understand, Jheine, that Balance is the Principle that must be satisfied in order to bring about healing. To invoke any Influence, a sacrifice must be made, never forget it. I tried to give of my own strength to heal Lorr, but I feel that I was unsuccessful."

Jenisorn nodded. "He's been a little better since you saw him, but he's still far from well."

"That's because he doesn't *want* to live, you see. But it may be that I can find the power to overcome that Resistance, through the suffering of Lord Marrekind. The *vahn* forbids, in the natural order of things, that one should win such power from the sacrifice of another—but, in this matter, Balance will be served because Lord Marrekind was the one responsible for Lorr's suffering. Do you follow?"

"I think so. Is that why you must go to him now?"

Nyctasia hesitated. "No. Not for this Influence, but for another spell I mean to try. An older spell, and far more powerful. Perhaps the oldest spell of all—the blood of the guilty to heal the wounds of the victim. I shall order Lord Marrekind to be bled— which will do him good, in truth, though that's by the way—and bring back with me a measure of his blood, to bathe Lorr's back. It's a primitive magic, and wild and wicked, according to some. It certainly has nothing to do with the Indwelling Spirit."

"Let me come with you, Nyc. I can help. You could say you're teaching me to be a healer."

"So I am, but there's something I want you to do here while I'm gone. Do you know of the hot spring that was found in the great crystal cavern of the Cymvelans? It should be possible to reach it now, through the tunnels, to fetch some of the water. Such springs often possess healing waters, or so it's said. We may as well try. Wash Lorr's wounds with it, and give him some to drink."

"I've done that already," said Jenisorn proudly.

"Indeed? Then I shall take you along with me, if your elders don't object. Here, put these books where they belong." She paused. "I have read, though, that it's best to partake of such waters at their source. Perhaps we could bring him to the spring one night, and keep him hidden there. It's as secret as the cellars, and—"

Jenisorn laughed. "You *are* a witch, Nyc, and no mistake. That's just where we moved him, once the way to the ruins was cleared. The air is pure there, and it's warm near the spring. I didn't mean to tell you unless it became necessary, but I see it's no use trying to keep anything from you. He's had the water in plenty, and bathed in the pool."

"Well done, by my word. With you to look after him, he'll have no choice but to mend."

"Nyc . . . could I be a healer, in truth? Will you really teach me?"

"I intend to," Nyctasia said seriously. "But you will be a far better healer than I, one day. If you can be spared from the vintnery, I'll put you to work in earnest soon. Come along, now, 'prentice, we've kept His Lordship waiting long enough."

But with the change of the seasons, her plans were changed as well. By spring thaw, Lorr was well enough to travel, and reached Amron Therain in safety. Jenisorn was now free to apply himself to his studies, and the family was willing to let Nyctasia make a scholar of him if she could. But the opening of the Trade Road brought other travelers and a courier from Osela with news and messages for the household. Nyctasia's letters from Chiastelm were finally delivered.

They were bound together in a packet, and neither bore Nyctasia's name, but Mesthelde handed them to her at once when the messenger said that they'd come all the way from the coast.

"They must be intended for our westerner," she said.

Nyctasia seemed to receive them with a certain reluctance. "Yes, I believe these are mine. This one's from an old friend, an herbalist. She always seals her letters thus." She showed the others the clear impression left by a leaf that had been pressed into the warm wax.

"Nightingale's-tongue, the minstrel's herb," said Mesthelde. "A good choice for you. A tisane brewed of it is supposed to preserve a singer's voice."

Nyctasia nodded. "And I was born with the Nightingale in the ascendant, you see." She examined the other letter, which was stamped with the seal of a crudely carved hare. "I don't know this mark, but it must be from Corson. Only she knows that I'm here." She broke open the seal and immediately recognized Corson's untrained scrawl.

"Ah, my adored Corson," sighed Raphe. "Goddess of Danger and Desire. How fares the glorious warrior, Nyc?"

"Nyc . . . ?" said 'Deisha anxiously.

Nyctasia had read the beginning of Corson's letter, gasped sharply, and suddenly turned a deathly white. In a choked voice she whispered, "Forgive me, I must—I can't—" and hurried from the hall with the letter crushed in her hand. Greymantle loped after her.

"I fear I've brought ill tidings," said the courier apologetically.

"Were those letters from Rhostshyl?" Jenisorn asked him.

"Chiastelm, I was told, though Rhostshyl's not far from there. But if it's news of Rhostshyl you want, there's plenty, and none of it good. Outright war broke out a few months ago, between the two ruling families. I forget which side won, but it was a doubtful victory either way. Fires destroyed half the city, and hunger and sickness followed, as they always do. Rhostshyl's a ruin, hadn't you heard?"

Nyctasia sat staring at Corson's letter without seeing it, as the words she had read seared her spirit and her understanding. She had known that war must come, of course she had known. Even here in the Valley folk had heard rumors from the coast, leaving little doubt that the fragile peace in Rhostshyl could not last.

Yet she was unprepared for the news, now that it faced her at last, no longer a fear for the future, not a rumor or a vision, but an inescapable fact. No warning could have prepared her to accept the reality.

Winter in Vale had been so still, so changeless, that time might have been frozen like the mountain lakes, like the wagon-ruts of the great Southern Trade Road. With news of the lands beyond the valley walled out by snow, and travelers almost unknown, it had seemed as if nothing could possibly be taking place anywhere in the world. Lost in her studies, sheltered and cherished by her newfound kinsfolk, Nyctasia had almost ceased to feel herself an exile and a stranger. But now as the land woke to spring she too was roused from her dreams to receive the thaw's tidings. Rhostshyl in ashes . . .

She had been living as if she meant to settle permanently at Vale, and she had nearly deceived herself, but now she understood that beneath all her plans had lain the belief that one day she would live again in Rhostshyl, and someday die there. Only now did she realize that she had taken this for granted, for the future suddenly seemed to stretch before her empty and meaningless. If Rhostshyl perished, she would be homeless forever. It was unthinkable.

"When feeling returns to the numbed flesh, there is pain," she thought ruefully. Did the earth too suffer when the winter ice melted away, and life seized the land again?

Shaking off such thoughts, she forced herself to reread Corson's words, but could find no comfort in them. The offhanded hopelessness of "It's over now" filled her with a sickening, chill despair. She read on, but Corson had soon lost interest in the subject and turned to her own affairs. She was enthusiastic in her thanks for the wooden comb. She complained that her life in Chiastelm was a bit dull at times. "Sometimes I even miss you, with all your endless nonsense," she had written. "Charms and chatter and rhymes and riddles. But when I'm sober I remember all the trouble you put me to. No one here believes the half of it, and I don't blame them much. I hardly believe it myself."

She ended with fond greetings to the rest of the Edonaris clan —especially to Raphe—but she had no more to say about the plight of Rhostshyl.

But from Maegor's letter Nyctasia learned all the particulars of the tragedy. Corson had not exaggerated, it seemed. "My Dear 'Tasia," Maegor began, "I have been tempted to spare you news that can only distress you, but your loyal courier shames me to the truth. It is, as she says, your right to decide for yourself what you must do. Yet if your spirit knows peace where you are, then you will bide, if you are wise. When you left, you told me that you'd be crazy to return to the city, and that worries me greatly, for you are an Edonaris, and therefore mad, as all the world knows. Consider well, 'Tasia—Emeryc and Lehannie were among the first to be slain, and not by chance, as you will well understand. Would you not be the next target, if you returned? And even if the enemies of your house are no longer a threat, can you be sure of a welcome from those of your kin who survive? You always opposed their claims to sole rule of the city, and now that they've achieved their desire at last, and done away with the only challenge to their power, will they allow you to share in that power? What will be gained by your joining the ranks of the dead?"

Nyctasia shuddered, remembering with cruel vividness her dream of Rhostshyl as the abode of the dead, a city of fallen stone and blackened timber, where only ghosts dwelt—ghosts who had invited her to become one of them. Now she recalled that her brother Emeryc and her mother's sister Lehannie had been among them, though both had been alive when she left the city. Maegor's warning seemed prudent indeed. Nyctasia read further.

"They came to me for news of you, not long ago," Maegor had written. "I could tell them nothing, of course, but I think they believe that I could send word to you if I chose, for they left this message with me nonetheless. I would that I had burned it before the doughty Corson sought me out, for now I must, in all conscience, let her send it on to you. I have not read it, and it is my hope that you will not do so either. For the good of your spirit, 'Tasia, leave it unread, and destroy it."

Nyctasia knew that she would be well-advised to heed this counsel, and knew just as surely that she wouldn't. Maegor's advice was always wise, and Nyctasia rarely followed it. She snatched at the other page and shook it open at once. It was unsealed, and bore neither salutation nor signature, but Nyctasia knew that the writer was Therisain ar'n Edonaris, one of her staunchest allies at court, who had joined with her in calling for a treaty of peace with the Teiryn. The others had not thought him a serious threat to their ambitions, since he was only of minor rank, but things had changed in the city now. . . .

Not for the salvation of her life or her spirit would Nyctasia refuse his message while the faintest hope yet remained to her. For her dream had shown her another vision of Rhostshyl as well. She had seen herself as a young bride, heralded by horns and banners, leading the living back into the heart of the city. With that image before her, she did not hesitate to read Therisain's words, and as she read she began to understand for the first time what these shadows might mean.

His letter repeated some of what she'd learned already from the others, though without referring to any person or place by name. But then, unlike Corson or Maegor, he spoke not only of the city's present state, but of its future. "We have your letters of warrant, and by their authority we have thus far prevented the execution of the heir and many other prisoners. The matriarch is persuaded that more deaths might spur further uprisings among their supporters, but she will not be satisfied to hold her hand forever. She has been weakened, and this is the time to act. You must return to claim your prerogatives soon, if our plans are ever to bear fruit. We shall have the support of the populace and much of the nobility, I believe, for this conflict has devastated the high and the low alike, and folk remember that you sought to prevent it. Even the twins now oppose further bloodshed, and agree to await your word. They are still licking their wounds and are grown less bloodthirsty, having once tasted blood.

"I tell you, reconciliation may be within our grasp, but you must make your presence felt and establish your power beyond question. Only you are in a position to impose order and stability upon this chaos, and to assure that peace and mercy prevail in the city. Your duty is manifest."

The hope he held out was a ray of light piercing the dark wilderness of Nyctasia's grief. She could bear any bereavement, she thought, if Rhostshyl might yet be saved. She hardly knew what she felt about the death of her brother. He had been a follower of the matriarch Mhairestri, devoted to keeping Rhostshyl in the hands of the Edonaris at any cost, and he had condemned Nyctasia's efforts at every turn. He had been as one dead to her for years, and she had long since ceased to mourn him. It was too late to regret their differences now. His death changed nothing between them.

But it changed the balance of power in Rhostshyl a good deal.

Neither Corson nor Maegor had realized the full significance of the news they'd sent, but Lord Therisain had understood it very well, and he knew that there was no need to explain it to Nyctasia. The titular lines of descent of the Edonaris were as familiar to her as her own name. Emeryc and Lehannie had both been of Rhaicime rank, which, as Maegor had suggested, was why they'd been marked for assassination as soon as hostilities had been openly declared. But the heir to Emeryc's title was his young son Leirven, still a child, and Lehannie was to be succeeded by Nyctasia's sister Tiambria—one of the twins—who would not come of age for another three years. With the heads of the House of Teiryn dead or defeated, there was no one at liberty who had the right to serve upon the council of the Rhaicimate. Nyctasia was entitled, quite legitimately, to declare herself the absolute ruler of the city of Rhostshyl.

15

ANXIOUS AS SHE was to depart, Nyctasia would not have considered leaving without making her formal farewell to the Lady Nocharis. Indeed, when she presented herself, the matriarch seemed to be expecting her.

"Ah, here you are, my dear." She beckoned Nyctasia closer, and looked searchingly into her face. "And so, after all, you found the treasure you came here to seek?"

"I did not know what I was seeking when I came, but I believe I did find it here. And I shall always be grateful."

"Already you have flown in spirit. When will you start out?"

"Tomorrow, at first light, by your leave. But you will give me your blessing, Mother, before I go?" She knelt by Lady Nocharis's chair.

The old woman touched Nyctasia's hair lightly with one frail hand, murmuring a ceremonial phrase, then took Nyctasia's hand in both her own. "We shall be sorry to lose you so soon, but you must not stay here. You're like an arrow shivering on the string, waiting to be released. How impatient is youth. Our poor Jheine will be a lost fledgling without you."

Nyctasia sat on the floor at her feet. "Yes, I promised to speak to you about him. I do think he should be sent to study with the scholar-physicians of the Imperial University." She sighed. "That's what I most longed for, myself, when I was Jheine's age. I even cast the lots about it once."

"And how were you answered?"

"With ambiguities, as always. 'You shall not have your desire, yet in a manner you shall'—or something of that sort. The fates never did reveal more than that to me. Perhaps it meant that Jheine would attend the university in my place. He'd do well there, I'm certain of it, and his heart's not in his work here."

"I suppose we must see to his education, now that you've spoiled him for lesser things," said Lady Nocharis, with a smile. "But I thought you did not trust the skills of leeches?" It seemed

82

that nothing was said or done in the household without Lady Nocharis's knowledge.

"So I told Lord Marrekind," Nyctasia admitted. "And it's true that a false physician is worse than a murderer. But Jheine has the makings of a true physician and healer—and they are rare. He has the gift of compassion, which never should be wasted."

"It never is wasted, my dear. It cannot be. But is compassion a gift? Or is it a responsibility?"

"'To be kind is a duty, to be kind-hearted is a gift,'" said Nyctasia. "Well, it loses something in the translation. To those who do good and are good, there seems to be no difference, perhaps, but to the rest of us kindness is a Discipline."

Lady Nocharis shook her head. "Philosophy," she said indulgently. "Don't fret too much over the heart's secret reasons. Such scrupulous distinctions may cloud the judgment, and make confusion of what is simple. Jheine is a good lad, yes, but you are not less good than he—you are simply less innocent. And that is to be expected of one who has more experience. There is no great mystery to it." She raised Nyctasia's head and met her serious, questioning gaze. "Only remember that you are a healer. Let nothing persuade you to forget that. Then all will be well."

"You have the second sight, Mother 'Charis, have you not?"

"Oh, my dear, everyone has, to a greater or lesser degree." She sighed and released Nyctasia's hand. "And now you must be gone, child. I shall rest for a while."

Nyctasia stood, and kissed her cheek. "I feel somehow that I've bid you farewell before."

"Do you, daughter? You know that means we'll meet again, so they say."

"I hope so," Nyctasia said. But she knew how very unlikely it was.

One of the most difficult lessons Nyctasia had learned in her exile was to moderate her habitual caution and suspicion. She had soon come to trust her second family as she had never trusted her first, but still it was some time before she could accustom herself to being without a weapon, or sleeping behind unbarred doors, with only Greymantle on guard. Such carelessness could have been fatal in Rhostshyl.

But now she had grown so well used to the free and open household that she was not at all alarmed—or surprised—when 'Deisha slipped into her room that night and perched on her bed, waking her. Greymantle only looked up and wagged his tail lazily, recognizing her familiar scent.

"Nyc, I know you want to make an early start in the morning, but I've had no chance to speak with you—it's been so sudden, all of this. I still can't believe that you mean to go off and leave us all heartbroken. How *can* you?"

Nyctasia chuckled and threw back the covers to allow 'Deisha to slip in beside her. "Lass, you are shameless." It was not the first time 'Deisha had stolen into her room, and her bed.

'Deisha kissed her. "Shameless I may be, but not heartless," she said reproachfully. She propped herself on one elbow and let her other hand rest gently on Nyctasia's cheek.

Nyctasia turned her head and kissed 'Deisha's palm. "'Deisha, my wanton dove, in a week's time you'll have forgotten me."

But 'Deisha, suddenly serious, regarded her sorrowfully. "Don't tease, Nyc. It's you I'm worried about, in truth. I'm afraid for you. You've told us often enough how dangerous it is in Rhostshyl."

"Sacrifices must be made," said Nyctasia. "'When a life is taken, it is lost, but when a life is given it is received.'"

"Well, it oughtn't to be given, or bought, or bartered, whatever the philosophers say! Life's not an outworn pair of boots."

"Well said," Nyctasia laughed. "But never mind—I don't intend to be killed, I promise you. The city is changed now, love. Many of my enemies are dead or defeated, and my people are in power. I've nothing to fear." Like most of Nyctasia's lies, this one was partly true. There was less to fear, now.

'Deisha sighed. "I promised you, when you first came, that I'd never let you go back, Nyc. But how am I to stop you, when even honey-tongued Jheine can't persuade you to stay?"

"You've kept your word," Nyctasia said, after a silence. "I shan't go back, not to the way things were when I left. I mean to go forward now, not back—to look to the future, and not repeat the past. It is not only Rhostshyl that is different now, but I too. And that is your doing. You've made it possible for me to return home, not because I need to be there, but because I'm needed there."

"I? I don't understand. What have I done?"

"You've set me an example—all of you, just by your way of life. Whether you're caring for the grapes, or the animals, or the children, or one another, whatever you do is done only that life may continue and flourish. Your lives are not spent in the service of ambition or fear, but only of life itself. And that's as it should be. You've taught me what peace means, and what it could mean to my city and my people. Knowing that, I could never go back to what I was."

'Deisha found all this unintelligible, like most of Nyctasia's explanations. But if Nyctasia was satisfied with matters as they stood, she would be content. "Well, I insist that you take Grey-mantle with you, at least," she said. "He'll look after you in my place."

Not long afterward she woke Nyctasia again, this time to rouse her from the nightmare that gripped her. 'Deisha had to shake her and call her name for a good while before she could make her awaken, and then Nyctasia only lay and stared into the darkness as if she saw her dreams anew with waking eyes.

'Deisha held her and tried to comfort her. "Nyc, it was only a nightmare. It's over now."

"No, no, he's dead, but it isn't over."

"Dead? Who's dead?"

"Thierran... my cousin. We were betrothed as children." Nyctasia had begun to recover herself, and she did not tell 'Deisha that Thierran had once held her prisoner, or that it was Corson who'd killed him. "I was dreaming of a time, when we were quite young, and he was wounded in the hunt—*vahn*, how he bled! They all believed that he'd die, and at first they kept me away, but he called for me all that night, and finally they had to let me stay with him and tend him."

("'Tasia, don't leave me," he had whispered, and for days she had refused to move from his bedside.)

"And so you saw him die?" 'Deisha asked sympathetically.

"No—not then. He did recover, and I was exceedingly proud. I believed that I'd healed him. Perhaps I did."

(But in her dream he was a grown man, and he whispered, "'Tasia, come back to me.")

"It doesn't matter," said Nyctasia. "I'm all right now. Come, we'll sleep a few hours more."

'Deisha was too sleepy to question her further. They nestled together, and she soon slept like any healthy, hard-working farm girl. But Nyctasia lay awake for some time, haunted by the figure in her dream. He was Thierran, and yet she had somehow recognized in him the embodiment of her afflicted city. It was Thierran who called her, and yet it was Rhostshyl.

* * *

Her journey was uneventful until she reached Larkmere, where a great many things seemed to happen to her at once. First of all she was robbed, while watching the acrobats perform in the town square. They were the same troupe she'd seen at Osela the autumn before, and she was more impressed than ever at their mastery. The rope-dancer had somehow stretched her rope between the two tall towers of the city hall, and her performance at that dangerous height drew all eyes irresistibly. The watchers gasped as she leaped and turned in the air, landing firmly on her feet on the quivering rope. Someone in one of the towers tossed gleaming gold-painted balls to her, and she juggled them deftly, capering back and forth along the rope.

Nyctasia was by no means the only spectator to have her pocket picked while gazing upward in rapt fascination. Indeed, she did not even discover the theft until the acrobats' drummer came round to collect coins from the crowd. When she reached for her money-pouch, she found that the thongs had been cleanly cut from her belt.

But she had no time to consider how best to deal with this loss, for just then Greymantle gave a great tug at his leash and suddenly bounded off across the square, dragging Nyctasia after him. Nose to the ground, he galloped through the marketplace, following a chosen scent, and Nyctasia could barely keep up with him, much less stop him. But they did not have far to go.

Greymantle, followed by Nyctasia, ran into a long, open shed roughly divided into stalls. Wagging his tail wildly, he searched through these till he found Lorr and pounced on him to lick his face. Then he pranced proudly back to Nyctasia's side, looking to her for praise.

"Lady!" said Lorr, astonished. "How did you know I was here?"

"I didn't know," gasped Nyctasia, still trying to catch her breath. "How do you come to be here?" She looked around uneasily. Lorr was not alone. There were perhaps a dozen people in the shed, linked together in small groups by chains fastened to the wall or the roof-posts. Lorr was joined to a one-armed man and a middle-aged woman, neither of whom would fetch a good price in the slave-market, Nyctasia realized. The more profitable merchandise would be on display outside.

"By ill luck," Lorr was saying. "Bandits attacked our party. They let the others go, but those who were marked they sold to bounty-hunters. We were . . . forced . . . to tell whose we were."

Suddenly he blanched and his voice rose in fear. "Lady, you said—if I was brought back—Lord Marrekind would give me over to you! But if you're not there—"

"Hush," Nyctasia warned him, as one of the guards looked in through the far door. Like everyone else, he and his cohorts were neglecting their business in order to watch the daring performance of the rope-dancer. There was little danger that the chained prisoners would escape in their absence.

But seeing Nyctasia within, he came in and swaggered unhurriedly down the length of the shed toward her, swinging his heavy whip at his side. Shrewdly appraising her patched cloak and worn boots, he assumed that she couldn't afford to buy. A minstrel, most likely, with that harp slung at her shoulder.

But plenty of folk came in just to look—or to touch—and often they were willing to part with a few coins to satisfy their curiosity. And they were most generous, he had found, when he chivvied the prisoners about for their amusement. He had to take care not to damage his employers' property, of course, for he was supposed to protect the slaves as well as guard them. He could claim that they'd attacked him, for his keys, and that he'd had to beat them off—no one would heed their denials—but that tale would wear thin with too much use. A little extra silver now was not worth a loss of pay later.

So he merely lashed out with the whip and kicked at a few of the prisoners as he passed, snarling, "On your feet! We've a customer here—look sharp." As he approached Nyctasia, he seized one of the men and thrust him to the front of the stall, ordering the rest to show themselves as well. They shuffled forward, cowed and silent, and the guard looked down at Nyctasia with a leer. "Do you see anything you like, mistress?"

She glanced around briefly and shrugged. "Not a very choice lot, are they?"

He was not deceived by her pose of indifference. "I thought this young fellow seemed to catch your fancy," he said, taking Lorr roughly by the arm and turning him this way and that for Nyctasia's inspection. "He may not look like much now, but clean him up and a pretty lad like this will fetch plenty in Celys." He grabbed a fistful of Lorr's hair and pulled his head back, the better to display his features. "If you want him, you'll have to chaffer with the traders, though. He belongs to some estate in the valley, they say, and his owner'd probably pay well to have him back. But I daresay they'd part with him for the right price."

Greymantle growled, and Nyctasia hastily quieted him. The guard pushed Lorr aside carelessly, and turned back to Nyctasia. "But perhaps you haven't that much to spend, eh?"

Nyctasia had been considering whether or not to make an offer for Lorr, and now she came to a sudden decision. She had money enough, for she carried her valuables safely hidden, and had lost only a few crescents when her pouch was stolen. But the money she had left she needed for her passage from Larkmere to Stocharnos, and if she spent it now there might be days—perhaps weeks—of delay before she could arrange for payment. She was desperate to reach Rhostshyl as soon as possible. Too much time had been lost already, and lives might depend upon haste now.

Now, as she watched the guard bully Lorr with obvious enjoyment, she made up her mind what to do, compelled as much by rash anger as by necessity.

"You're right," she told him, "I haven't much money. But I do see something I like, after all, and maybe I can afford just that much." She looked him up and down in a way that made her meaning unmistakably plain. He was tall and broad, with large hands and a muscled neck, rugged, coarsely-carved features and thick, tightly curling hair. He was probably a southerner like Corson, hired for his size and strength. But Corson, Nyctasia knew, would starve sooner than work for slave-traders.

She ran the tip of her tongue over her lips, and smiled seductively. From her shirt she drew a small leather bag and took out a shiny ring, set with a red gemstone, which she slipped on her finger and held out for the guard to see.

He grinned. Oho, so she was *that* sort, was she? That was common too—some folk couldn't resist a chance to lie with a slave-handler, and they liked a bit of rough handling themselves, he had found. He pulled Nyctasia into an empty stall and dragged her down onto the straw. The trinket she offered wasn't worth much, but then she didn't ask much in return. And she was a pretty little thing, too, now that he had a good look at her. He wouldn't mind satisfying her curiosity for free.

Nyctasia laughed and threw her arms around his neck, clasping her hands behind his head, as he rolled on top of her, tugging impatiently at her breeches. Feeling completely calm, she pressed her finger firmly against the red glass jewel in the ring, to release the tiny, curved spring-blade it concealed. Then she turned her hand and just scratched his neck with the needle-sharp crescent of steel. He gave one cry as the merciless, burning poison seized him by the throat, but he was dead within the moment. Nyctasia crawled free of his lifeless weight with some difficulty, then carefully sealed the deadly ring and put it away. It ought not to be dangerous until it was dipped in *uzanna*-venom again, but she had no intention of pricking herself with it, all the same. She straightened her clothes, grimacing with distaste, and picked up her harp before she bent to pull the keys from the guard's belt.

The slaves in the shed did not realize what she'd done until they saw her emerge from the stall alone and release Lorr and his two companions from their fetters.

"You really do have that poison!" Lorr whispered. "You said—"

"I thought you wouldn't need it. I had Marrekind in hand, and I wasn't planning to leave, then."

By then the rest were clamoring to be freed as well, calling for the keys and crowding around Nyctasia as she hastened from stall to stall. Having just committed murder, she did not hesitate to augment her crime with theft, and she was able to unlock a good many manacles and leg-irons before the other guards noticed the commotion, and remembered that they weren't paid to watch the acrobats. They ran in through the far door, whips swinging, and were set upon at once and outnumbered. In the confusion, Nyctasia tossed the keys to the last set of prisoners, grabbed Greymantle's leash with one hand and Lorr's arm with the other, and dashed out the way she'd come, hoping to disappear into the crowd.

No one paid much attention to them as they mingled with the throng of marketers and idlers gathered in the square to gape at the troupe of tumblers plying their trade in a space cleared before the town hall. Had she been less intent on escaping, Nyctasia too would have lingered, entranced by the spectacle. The rope-dancer had finished her act, but the performance on the ground was well worth watching.

Dressed in colorful costumes and fantastic masks, adorned with ribbons and feathers and crystal beads, the dark-skinned acrobats balanced on tall poles, juggled flaming clubs, and did astonishing leaps and flips to the dramatic rhythm of the drumbeat. A boy clambered up an unsupported ladder, launched himself into the air, flipped over, and landed gracefully on the upturned feet of a woman balanced on her hands on the shoulders of one of the men. A girl with a wooden flute stalked among them, embellishing their tricks with trills and flourishes of music.

Nyctasia and Lorr made their way to the edge of the crowd, but looking back they saw one of the guards from the slave-market pushing through the press toward them—a woman tall enough to see them over the heads of the crowd. She was pointing in their direction and shouting something over her shoulder.

During their travels together, Corson had given Nyctasia some practical—and often painful—lessons in swordfighting, and now a piece of Corson's advice came back to her: "When your opponent is bigger than you are, keep the fight in a tight place, where the enemy will be hampered while you can move freely. You can't help being such a little speck of a thing, but you can put your size to use." Nyctasia hurried Lorr into a narrow, cramped alleyway that led to the back of the town hall.

When they turned the corner, Nyctasia drew her shortsword and waited. "Keep going," she ordered Lorr. "Get away from here, find someplace to hide." With surprise on her side, and Greymantle at her command, she felt confident that the odds were in her favor.

But Lorr's escape was cut off. "Someone's coming the other way," he cried, panic-stricken.

Nyctasia thrust Greymantle's leash into his hand. "Take the dog, he'll defend you. Now run!"

She very rapidly revised her plans. No one could prove that she'd killed the guard, after all. There was not a mark on him to show how he'd died. Suppose she claimed that she'd run off in fright when he collapsed—who was there to contradict her? And the slaves might have stripped his body of the keys themselves. They were not likely to bear witness against her, and if they did she could deny it all. Even the word of a penniless minstrel-lass was worth more than a slave's. Why would a harmless harper commit such a crime in the first place?

And if matters came to the worst, she could always reveal her exalted rank to the magistrates. It was true, as Jheine said, that the law often gave way before a title. Perhaps it was a slim chance, but Nyctasia had talked her way out of tight straits before this. She only hoped that she wouldn't be delayed too long in Larkmere by the formalities. But Lorr was truly in danger—he must be given time to get away.

She had not long to wait till her pursuer rounded the corner, but by then she had sheathed her sword and merely stood with her hands on her hips, looking aggrieved and defiant. "Why are you chasing me?" she demanded. "It's nothing to do with me! Leave me alone—"

But the guard was in no mood to be reasoned with. Several of the slaves had escaped while she was supposed to be on duty, and if she came back empty-handed she'd be blamed, perhaps accused of theft and held accountable for the loss. She could be enslaved herself for such a debt. But if this sneaking minstrel was somehow responsible, she might redeem herself by capturing the wretch. She seized Nyctasia triumphantly, ignoring her protests, and twisted her arm painfully behind her back.

Nyctasia revised her plans again.

Swinging her feet off the ground, she made herself a dead weight and pulled her captor completely off balance, breaking her grip and allowing herself a chance to draw her blade again. The guard was armed only with her whip, and there was not room enough to swing the lash in the confining space of the alleyway. Nyctasia was able to hold her off for a time, but her skill with a sword was no match for the enemy's longer reach and superior strength. Wielding the haft of the whip like a club, she soon drove Nyctasia back against the wall of the building that loomed over them.

"It's not enough to defend yourself," Corson had taught Nyctasia. "In a fight, you must always be on the attack." Nyctasia ducked to avoid a blow, scooped up a handful of dirt and pebbles, and flung it straight into her opponent's face with all the strength of desperation.

When the woman staggered back, Nyctasia pressed her advantage, gripping her shortsword with both hands and swinging from her shoulders, forcing the strength of her whole back into the blow. Corson would have been proud to see the result of her teaching.

Nyctasia had aimed for the knees, hoping to cripple her adversary and flee, but though she strained every muscle, the wound she inflicted had little effect. The guard suddenly crumpled to the ground in a spreading puddle of blood, but it was not Nyctasia's sword that had felled her. It was a large chunk of masonry pushed from the parapet of the city hall.

16

A HEAVILY KNOTTED rope-end thudded to the ground at Nyctasia's feet, and a voice from overhead said urgently, "Catch hold, hurry! There are more of them coming."

Perhaps the most important lesson Nyctasia had learned from Corson was that there were times when action, not thought, was called for. This, unquestionably, was one of those times. She grabbed hold and began to climb.

The rope was drawn upward, and for a moment she found herself face to face with a stag with silver antlers—a sight that nearly made her fall. But then the masked acrobat dropped to the ground, landing on his feet in a practiced crouch. "Here, I'll give you a boost," he said. Taking Nyctasia by the ankles, he half-lifted, half-tossed her up to where the rope-dancer, hanging by her knees from a carved waterspout, could catch hold of her arms. For a small woman, she was surprisingly strong. She quickly pulled Nyctasia up to a ledge, somehow righted herself, and clambered over the parapet, dragging Nyctasia after her.

While Nyctasia lay hidden behind the stone battlement, the rope-dancer leaned over the crenellated wall, looking down into the alley. A moment later, Nyctasia heard her call, "They went down that way—a woman and a boy—"

"We saw them from up there," the other acrobat said excitedly. "Follow me, you might still catch them."

When the sound of running footsteps receded, the rope-dancer helped Nyctasia to her feet, and for the first time she had a good look at her rescuer. Like her confederate, she too was disguised, but her mask was painted directly onto her face, so as not to hinder her vision when she was doing her daring aerial tricks. A lacy pattern of green leaves and white blossoms adorned her dark skin, as if she were spying out from behind a screen of flowering vines, and her close-fitting leggings and vest were embroidered with the same design. It was impossible to discern what she really looked like.

She grinned, returning Nyctasia's scrutiny. "I'm Ashe," she offered, "and that was Auval who ran off just now. He'll lead them a merry chase." She spoke with an accent Nyctasia did not recognize.

"But they'll suspect you," Nyctasia worried. "That guard—"

"Not a bit of it. Auval will tell them we saw the lad attack her from behind, while you fought with her. He knocked her off her feet, and she hit her head on that fallen stonework. See for yourself."

The woman's body had been moved so that she lay on her face near the bloody masonry. Nyctasia looked down at her, then turned away. "Come," said Ashe, "we'd best not stand about here." Nyctasia followed her along the narrow stone walkway to the twisting stairs that led to the roof.

"They'll not suppose we had anything to do with it," Ashe continued cheerfully. "We'd nothing to gain by it, had we?"

"No, nothing. But you'd plenty to lose. Why in the *vahn*'s name did you take such a risk?"

"You took the greater risk, harper, setting loose half the chattel in the marketplace, all on your own. We can see quite a lot from up here. You went in alone, and came out running, with the boy in tow, and it rather looked as if you might have forgotten to pay for him, no? Then the slaves were scattering and the warders chasing about—a fine to-do you caused! I don't ask why you did it, but as for us, we don't like slave-traders, or their minions, and we have our reasons." They had reached one of the twin towers, and Ashe began to fasten her tightrope to a stout pillar. "No one will notice you up here, friend," she assured Nyctasia.

Nyctasia looked around her, feeling half-dazed, as much by the strange course of events that had brought her there as by the height and the long climb. Her companion was right, she realized. From this vantage point she could see all the chaos of the town square below, and anyone who looked up could see her— but not recognize her. In full view of the whole marketplace, she was as good as invisible.

"Forgive my ill manners," she said, "I ought to have introduced myself. I'm Nyc brenn Rhostshyl. And I've not even thanked you for your help."

"Well, we've no time for that. You'll have to help *me* now, since Auval's busy elsewhere. There's more of a crowd than ever down there, thanks to you, and that means it's time I went back to work. Wait here." She darted off across the steep roof with her

rope, and made it fast to a column of the other tower. After
testing the knots, she tightened the laces of her supple doeskin
slippers and ran nimbly across the rope back to Nyctasia. A few
people below stopped and pointed. "Now hand me the horn," she
ordered Nyctasia.

Flourishing the long, straight brass trumpet, Ashe marched
boldly to the middle of the rope and blew a few loud, clear notes
to catch the attention of her audience, then swept them a low
bow. Nyctasia held her breath, but Ashe's balance never wa-
vered. She straightened up gracefully and strutted to and fro, with
her head thrown back, playing a lively song on the horn, and not
seeming to pay any mind to where she stepped. Then she threw
the horn down to another member of the troupe on the ground,
who caught it and took up the tune, while Ashe—to Nyctasia's
horror—performed a series of cartwheels from one end of the
rope to the other. The crowd cheered lustily, and the drummer
(and the pickpockets) collected a tidy sum.

Nyctasia was kept busy tossing out wooden balls and clubs for
Ashe to juggle. When she finished with one set Ashe threw them
to her fellow tumblers below, not trusting Nyctasia to catch them.
A large hoop she used like a skipping-rope, rapidly swinging it
over her head and hopping through it, over and over again. A
dozen times Nyctasia restrained herself from crying out in alarm,
or playing the fool by begging Ashe to be careful. But much to
her relief, it was not long before the rope-dancer called a halt, at
the first fading of the daylight.

"I *could* do this in the dark," she boasted, "but if no one can
see me, there's nothing to be gained." She dropped the remaining
objects down to the waiting jugglers, including—before she
could protest—Nyctasia's harp. "You'll not want to be seen with
that," she explained. "They know it's a harper they're looking
for. We'll wait till after dark, of course, but you'll find the climb
easier if you're not hampered with a harp."

"Climb . . . ?" said Nyctasia uneasily.

They made their way across the closely crowded roofs of the
city, silently and slowly, with Ashe in the lead. When she found
that Nyctasia was fairly surefooted, and could follow her with
only occasional help, they moved more quickly from building to
building, only stopping to wait, lying flat on the slate shingles or
crouching behind a chimney, while warders of the night watch
patrolled the street below them.

"This is the place," whispered Ashe. When a sentry on his rounds had ridden past, they dropped to the top of the high wall that circled the city, and she gave a low whistle, which was answered almost at once. A tall pole was leaned up against the wall between the two of them. "I'll hold this end steady for you," she told Nyctasia. "You've only to slide down."

Nyctasia drew a deep breath, then leaned over the edge to grasp the pole, and let herself swing free of the wall, out into the night. She wrapped her legs around the pole, and it held firm, but she seemed to drop down through the darkness for a very long time before strong hands caught her and set her on the earth.

Ashe was beside her on the instant, and the three moved off together without a word. There were encampments of tinkers and gypsies and peddlers outside the city walls, but Nyctasia and the others took care to stay out of sight until they approached the wagons belonging to the troupe of acrobats. Then Ashe laughed in relief and said, "You did well, Harper Nyc. I believe we could make a tumbler of you."

"Yes, let's," agreed the other. Nyctasia could barely see him, but she recognized his voice as Auval's. "She weighs no more than a walnut—I could toss her as high as the treetops and catch her in one hand."

"I would like to learn your trade, in truth," said Nyctasia. "To me it seems a most beautiful Discipline. But I fear I cannot take it up now."

"You could, you know—I can tell. We'll first teach you to juggle. You must be good with your hands or you'd not be a harper."

"I'm not a harper," said Nyctasia, with unwonted candor. "I'm a scholar and a healer, and much as I admire your art, I cannot take to it now because I must get to the coast just as soon as I can."

"Well, don't try to take a riverboat. The city guard will be watching the waterfront for you."

"You'd best travel with us as far as Stocharnos," Ashe was saying, when they were interrupted by howling and shouting from the acrobats' camp.

"Let him loose, he'll pull over the tent!" Nyctasia heard, mixed with words of a language that was unknown to her.

"Kestrai chelno, ifca! Libos!"

"You let him loose! I'm not going near that monster."

A moment later, Greymantle came loping out of the darkness

and hurled himself on Nyctasia, whining and wriggling with delight. "Good lad," she laughed, pushing him down, and rubbing
his great head affectionately. "Be still, now!" He frisked about
her as they hurried into the encampment, and was very much
underfoot as Ashe introduced her to the rest of the troupe of
acrobats. They were sitting about the cooking-fire, most eating
bowls of stew, or mending their motley costumes.

The girl who'd been playing the flute that afternoon was now
playing Nyctasia's harp, and singing a song in the same unfamiliar tongue.

> "Bai vrenn ifca, onn mid n'arved,
> Arved, bai vrenn ifca hloe?
> Hyal, mid shahn ath ypresharved
> Nastle'im ver, ad dinascoe.
>
> Nastle'im ver, ad dinascoe,
> Cendri y'ath—"

But she broke off when she saw Nyctasia, and called out,
"Cleyas shi, merisol bircordas!"

"That's Lhosande," said Ashe, and translated, "She says,
'Welcome, sister!' She's a music-maker, like you."

From their dark skin and their strange speech, Nyctasia
guessed that the acrobats were of the Lieposi, a mountain-dwell-
ing people from the other side of The Spine. They greeted her
with the mountaineer's handshake—not a clasp of palms, but a
firm grasp about the wrist, which, after a moment's surprise, she
returned.

The Lieposi were known as much for their fierce indepen-
dence as for their strength and agility. The Empire, having failed
time and again to conquer them, had at last wisely decided to
corrupt them instead. Ambassadors had been sent, to persuade
them of the advantages of citizenship, bringing gifts of fine silk
and precious metals, jewels and rare spices, delicacies and luxu-
ries that were not to be had in the heights of Mount Liepos.

Those whose curiosity overcame their suspicion went as emissaries to the Imperial Concourse, and came back with thrilling
accounts of the splendid city of Celys and the magnificence of the
court. In time, more and more of the younger Lieposi had been
tempted to experience these marvels for themselves. With their
grace and comeliness, their musical language and their remark-

able skills of balance, they were a welcome novelty for a time, to the wealthy and noble denizens of the capital. Though they were well-nigh invincible on their own ground, the Lieposi had been ill prepared to defend themselves against the dangers of imperial civilization. The work of conquest was now well under way.

The Lieposi were rarely seen on the coast, and Nyctasia knew little about them, but her brief acquaintance with them so far had impressed her very favorably indeed. She gratefully accepted a bowl of hot stew and devoured it ravenously while she listened to the curious mixture of Eswraine dialects, Liruvathe, and Lieposi which the various acrobats were speaking. There were a great many questions she wanted to put to them, but the day's adventures had left her famished, and it was not until she'd scraped up every morsel of the savory stew that she paused to ask, "But how did my dog get here?"

One of the boys bowed to her. "He came with me, m'lady. When I ran up the alley I met with someone coming the other way—but it was one of these folk, and he brought me here."

"'Lady'. . .?" said Ashe. "Well, well!" But she asked no questions.

Nyctasia was completely taken by surprise. Had Lorr not given himself away, she would never have recognized him in this merry Lieposi youth. The acrobats had stained his skin as dark as their own, and dyed his fair hair black. In gaudy tatters, in bells and beads and ribbons, he was like one minnow in a school, among the other tumblers.

Nyctasia took his hand, examining it curiously. "Walnut-husk dye?" she guessed.

Ashe nodded. "It doesn't wash off."

The brand was still visible, though not nearly as noticeable. "I can still see it," said Nyctasia doubtfully.

"Because you know it's there, and look for it," said Ashe. "But you never saw this one, did you now?" She held out her hand to Nyctasia, as she had done often that day, and there indeed was the mark that Nyctasia had completely failed to notice every time. "We don't come close to others when we perform," she explained. "Especially not those of us who've been branded. And we keep to ourselves, of course. We stay in our tents and wagons, not at inns, and we never eat in company. But we don't hide—folk look at our masks and our finery, not at us."

"People see what they expect," Nyctasia agreed. "Are *any* of you really Lieposi, then?"

"I don't remember, *m'lady*," said Ashe, with a grin.

"Some of us are," the drummer laughed. "I think."

"All of us are," someone else insisted.

"None of us are."

"*He* is," one of the boys said, pointing to the surprised Lorr.

"I'm one," said a woman who spoke with the accent of a Midlander.

"No you're not, *I* am."

"You're a Liruvathid!"

"*You're* a—"

Ashe lit a lamp at the fire and beckoned to Nyctasia. "Whatever we are, *you'd* best be Lieposi, at least till we reach Stocharnos. Come along."

Nyctasia meekly followed her to one of the gaily painted wagons, and submitted to having her hands and face covered with a dark, oily paint. So many bizarre and unexpected things had already happened to her that day, that it seemed useless to do anything but accept what fate had in store.

"Ashe," she began, "I can never repay you and the others for all you've done, but I—"

"Close your mouth," Ashe said curtly, "or you'll get paint in it."

Nyctasia obeyed, and Ashe, smoothing the stain around her lips, could feel her smiling. She began to stroke Nyctasia's face and throat, leaving dark streaks, and gently working the coloring into Nyctasia's skin. Nyctasia closed her eyes, and felt Ashe carefully brush a layer of paint on her eyelids with one fingertip. "Don't open them yet a while," she cautioned. Taking Nyctasia's face between her hands, she softly blew on her eyelids to dry them.

Nyctasia shivered. "If you keep on like that, I'll not be responsible for what happens," she murmured.

Ashe chuckled, unlaced Nyctasia's shirt and playfully kissed the hollow of her throat before she spread the dye over her collarbone, and above her pale breasts. "You're safe enough for now, my piebald lady—this stuff tastes foul. Turn around." With tickling fingers, she stained the soft skin behind Nyctasia's ears, then rubbed the paint into the back of her neck and shoulders. "You'll never make a tumbler with such stiff sinews," she scolded. "I can well believe that you're a scholar. You need to use your limbs more."

"What I need's a hot bath," said Nyctasia wistfully.

"Well, that you can't have. This paint will wash off. The walnut really changes the skin's color, but this only hides it."

Nyctasia suddenly grew serious again. "Ah, that's what I meant to tell you, Ashe, in return for your help—you must listen. The white flowers painted on your face—wash them off, and never wear them again! None of you must wear that poisonous paint on your bare skin. Perhaps the walnut-stain offers some protection, but that's far from certain."

"But I've worn it before, and come to no harm," Ashe protested.

"The effects make themselves known only over time," Nyctasia explained. "That very pure white is made from powder of lead, and lead's a slow-working poison, but a deadly one. Paint your masks with it if you will, but don't let it touch you. And if you make the mixture yourself, bind a scarf about your face and don't breathe in the powder. I tell you, an ancestor of mine was murdered by means of a leaden goblet that turned everything he drank to poison. It took a long while to do its work, but his enemies were patient."

Ashe frowned. "It sounds like great nonsense," she said skeptically. "Probably just an old tale."

"For the *vahn*'s sake, you *must* believe me," begged Nyctasia, miserably aware that she was never less convincing than when she was telling the truth. "You came to my rescue today—let me rescue you from a worse fate. If you continue to wear lead-white, in time it will poison your very blood. At first it will make your head ache, and turn the food to bile within you. Then your hands will commence to tremble and your limbs to shake, till you no longer have the mastery of them. And when it has crippled and maddened you, *then* perhaps you will be fortunate enough to die. . . ."

Ashe had already taken up a flask of vinegar, poured some onto a rag, and begun to scrub at her face, muttering to herself in Lieposi. "It's only the white that's dangerous?" she demanded.

"So far as I know. You could still paint on the leaves."

Ashe opened a chest and rummaged through the heap of tawdry trappings within. "I can wear this instead," she said, pulling out a worn chaplet of white silk blossoms. "And here's what *you* need, my dark beauty." She held up a long, tangled black wig of human hair. It was none too clean, Nyctasia noticed with dismay, but it would disguise her cropped hair most effectively.

With Ashe's help she put it on and combed it, trying her best not to think about head-lice.

By the time they rejoined the others, Nyctasia could easily have passed for one of the troupe. A shirt sewn with glass jewels, and stitched with stars of silver thread, lent her the same air of shoddy splendor that graced the rest of the company, and her gift for masquerade and deception completed the transformation. There was nothing of the stoop-shouldered scholar or the gracious lady in her bearing now. She moved with the same free, dancing step as the tumblers, holding her head high and imitating their loose-limbed grace with seeming ease. She put on their bold manner as well, laughing at their surprise. "Did you lot think you were the only imposters on the roads?" she mocked. "They call me Mistress of Ambiguities who know me best." Greymantle sniffed her and sneezed indignantly, confused by the smell of the paint.

Ashe repeated Nyctasia's advice about the lead-white, in a variety of languages, until everyone had understood the warning. "That lady knows all about poisons and potions, according to him," one of the boys affirmed, gesturing toward Lorr. A young woman, half of whose face and one of whose hands were a stark white, got up hastily and hurried off to wash.

Auval frowned at Lorr. "Learn right now, youngster, not to tell what you know about your friends, not to anyone. You'd no call to speak to us about her, and you're not to speak to others about us, do you understand? You're a fugitive, you ought to know better."

Abashed, Lorr mumbled an apology. "I . . . I do know better. I was foolish. I may trust you with my life, but not with someone else's."

"Yes, that is a necessary lesson," said Nyctasia. "Yet I begin to think that there may be a time to give one's trust freely, to follow the promptings of the spirit alone. I too, Lorr, trust these new friends of ours." There was a time when she would have blamed herself for allowing strangers to learn anything about her, but somehow it did not alarm her now. The acrobats already knew her for a criminal, but they were hardly in a position to betray her. Her real secrets lay elsewhere, and Lorr knew nothing of them. She turned to Auval. "In truth, there is little enough he could tell you about me. He only knows that I'm a healer, and anyone may know that."

"Indeed they may not. Why would a healer be traveling with

the likes of us? You're no juggler, so you'll have to be a minstrel, or perhaps a fortuneteller. Can you sing?"

Nyctasia smiled to herself, amused that he should find it necessary to teach *her* guile and caution. Was it possible that she had changed so much as that? She must take pains to relearn her wary and mistrustful ways before she dared return to court!

"I can sing," she said. "And I can interpret dreams, and tell the secrets of the stars, though the stars be silent. I can read the future in folks' eyes and tell them just what they wish to hear. I can brew love-potions that do no one any harm. I should think I could earn my way, and be most useful to you."

"Why, let's hear what you can do, then, and we'll judge your talents for ourselves," said Ashe. "We've more use for a singer than for a charlatan!" She spoke to the girl with the harp, who reluctantly handed the instrument to Nyctasia, asking her something in a puzzled tone.

Someone translated, "Lhosande wants to know how to tune the strings. Those silver pins won't turn like the ones on her *bircorda*."

The girl took up a small, long-necked lute and pointed out the wooden tuning-pegs, then gestured at the harp, clearly demanding an explanation. As soon as Nyctasia had shown her how to use the silver key, she insisted on trying it herself, and Nyctasia understood her well enough without translation. She almost cried out, "Tell her not to tighten them too far!" but when she saw how carefully Lhosande turned the key, she held her tongue.

"She'll not be satisfied till we get her a harp like that," Ashe predicted.

"Tell her to keep it for me, till I send for it. I'd best not carry it about Stocharnos. Perhaps the magistrates will set a watch for the harper who escaped from Larkmere." The harp was beautifully crafted of polished ebonwood, its fore pillar ornamented with inlaid silver, and it had been designed as much to be looked at as listened to. It was almost small enough to seem a toy, and there were only fifteen strings, which had to be re-tuned for each new song. It was a lady's instrument, not a harper's, and Nyctasia had owned far better ones. But this harp had been Erystalben's last gift to her, and she did not want to lose it. "She'll take good care of it," she said, "and I'll send her a finer one in its place."

"How will you know where to send?" Ashe asked reasonably. "We don't know ourselves where we'll be from week to week."

"But a messenger could find you at the Osela fair next autumn, I'll be bound. Performers never miss it, so I'm told."

"So you *do* remember. I saw you there too."

"What, among all those people? Surely not."

"Oh, I told you, I can see quite a lot from my roost, and I was no higher than your head, in Osela. Auval and 'Rashti held the rope. Isael noticed you too"—she pointed to the drummer—"because you gave him two crescents in good silver, and he wondered that a harper should have such a sum to squander. He thought you must want something in return, for an offering like that. We rather expected you to visit our camp that night."

"Oh? And do folk often try to buy your favors?"

Ashe shrugged modestly. "Who could blame them? But the reason *I* remembered you was the way you gazed at me all the while, like someone lovestruck."

"So I did. I'd never seen a rope-dancer before. I thought you were a Manifestation of Grace and Balance."

"Well! I've been called a mountebank and a mudlark, but never a maffestation. I hope it's something pleasant—it sounds like a plague."

"It is a sign to the seeking spirit that there is, after all, order and significance in the world we know," Nyctasia said slowly. She seemed to weigh her words carefully, and she wore a faraway look, as though she were alone and only speaking her thoughts aloud. Had Corson been present, she would have warned the company that Nyctasia was about to embark upon one of her learned lectures, if nothing was done to stop her.

But Ashe insistently recalled her to their conversation, complaining, "I know every tongue twixt the woods and the water, and I can't make sense of that. Is it flattery or philosophy—that's all I want to know. And given my choice, I'd prefer flattery," she added.

"Why then, you shall have it," laughed Nyctasia, and reached for her harp again. She thought for a moment, fussing with the strings, and then sang:

> "Not more nimble is the spider,
> Strider on a silken strand,
> Than the web-walker, graceful glider,
> Who owns the air and scorns the land.
> Ruler of a realm no wider
> Than a maiden's velvet band
> Is her Highness the rope-rider."

"*High*ness . . .!" someone groaned, making a wry face.

> "There is the riddle, here the answer—
> Queen of the acrobats is the rope-dancer!"

sang Nyctasia.

"More!" shouted Ashe, delighted.

"Mercy, Your Highness, I haven't the strength," said Nyctasia, with a yawn. "We stiff-limbed scholars need our repose."

"One more verse," Ashe urged, "then I'll show you to a bed, my word on it."

"Only one, then."

"Hush!" Ashe commanded the others. Lhosande took her flute and played a soft harmony to Nyctasia's harping.

> "For the bird that takes its rest
> On a twig as slender as a thread,
> With one foot tucked to its downy breast,
> The while beneath one wing it hides its head,
> Is not more certain of its perch, I vow,
> Than the rope-dancer on her hempen bough."

"Enough!" cried Auval. "You'll make her vainer than she is already."

"No fear," said Nyctasia, "my rhymes are spent." Had she only landed in Larkmere that morning? It seemed that she'd been running, hiding, climbing for days without a rest. She handed the harp back to Lhosande, and hung the key around the girl's neck on its silver chain. Some of the others rose too, stretching.

"We've room for another in here," said Ashe, leading Nyctasia to her wagon. "For a little one like you, at least." She began to push aside chests and sacks and bolts of cloth, to make a bit more space on the floor. "I was disappointed that you didn't seek us out, in Osela," she remarked. "I was sure you would."

Nyctasia sat wearily on one of the chests, and watched her unroll the bedding and blankets. "Do you know, I might have come, but I couldn't. I was in prison that night, as it happens."

"Prison! What did you do, set free all the slaves for sale at Osela market?"

"Alas, no, it was quite a different matter—disturbing the peace of the fair. But it wasn't *my* fault—"

"Oh, I daresay," Ashe mocked, shaking her head. She dropped onto a pallet in the corner, and pointed out a place against the far wall, for Nyctasia. "The first abed sleep to the back, so the others needn't step over them," she explained. "Leave the lamp for them, they won't be long. You can put your boots and things on that shelf above your head."

Nyctasia was accustomed to more comfortable accommodations, but she was too tired to mind. She crept into the small space allotted to her and collapsed onto the lumpy pallet with a grateful sigh. "It wasn't," she said sleepily, "my fault . . ."

Ashe chuckled. "You must be of very high birth indeed, Lady Nyc brenn Rhostshyl."

For a moment, Nyctasia was startled to wakefulness. Calm denials and thoroughly convincing lies, inspired by a lifetime of suspicion and secrecy, immediately suggested themselves to her, but were just as quickly discarded. For one thing, it was unnecessary, she told herself. For another thing, Ashe deserved better of her. And it was also just more trouble than it was worth. . . .

With a feeling of relief that was almost luxurious, she replied simply, "Yes, I am. But how did you know that?"

"By your lawless habits, of course—only aristocrats think they can do whatever comes into their heads and get away with it."

"Aristocrats and lunatics," Nyctasia agreed. "Lunacy's not unknown in my family. But I'm not always as impetuous as I was today. Usually I'm uncommonly circumspect."

"As you will, lady," said Ashe, with unconcealed disbelief. "But I'd not be surprised to learn that you disturb the peace everywhere you go. I'll wager you're always in trouble of some sort, no?"

Nyctasia sighed. "Yes, I am," she said again.

17

WHEN MAEGOR HAD finished her morning's marketing, it was not long after dawn, but already there were plenty of people about and busy. She carried a milkjug in one hand, and her basket was heavy with cheese and bread, honeycombs, a sack of meal, marrowbones for broth, and eggs nested in straw. Before she had gone far, a gypsy girl, half her size and narrow as a needle, darted up to her and offered to carry it, to earn a few pence.

Maegor tossed her a silver penny. "Get along with you, and have something to eat. I don't believe you could carry a sprig of lavender."

The girl snatched the coin and curtseyed clumsily. "I thank you, mistress greenwoman. For your kindness, I'll tell you your fortune, if you will."

Maegor stopped. "How do you know I'm an herbalist?" she demanded.

"Nothing is hidden," said Nyctasia, "from one who knows the secrets of destiny." She grinned at Maegor's look of astonishment and recognition. "You will soon have a visit from an old friend," she predicted.

" 'Tasia, how long is it since you've eaten?" Maegor chided. "You look like a wraith."

Nyctasia was busy eating most of what Maegor had just brought home from market. "Oh, well, I'm used to fasting, you know," she said vaguely. "It took most of my money to buy a horse in Stocharnos, and Grey had to be fed, of course."

At the sound of his name, Greymantle looked up and slapped the floor with his tail, then went back to gnawing on one of the soupbones. "It's past believing how much the creature eats," Nyctasia complained, scratching his back with her foot and looking down at him with obvious pride. "I'll need some of the money I left with you for safekeeping. You told me I'd be back to claim it one day, and you were right, as you always are."

Maegor began to fry more mealcakes. "I told you you were just crazy enough to come back, as I recall it."

"I've missed your scolding, Maeg. And your cooking. Now, the one thing I need most of all—"

"A bath, of course. I knew you must be starving if you were willing to eat without bathing first. But aren't you afraid your dusky hue will wash off?"

"I only hope it will. And as for *this* filthy thing"—she pulled off the wig, holding it at arm's length with her thumb and forefinger—"it ought to be burned at once." She dropped it on Greymantle, who regarded it with surprise and shook himself.

"No, not burned, buried in the garden. Human hair's good for the soil. But is it wise, 'Tasia, for you to go about undisguised?"

"Why, Maeg, you always reproached me for being too sly and secret, and now I'm too free and forthright to suit you. I declare, there's no pleasing you."

Maegor turned the mealcakes and slid more butter into the pan. "Forthright's one thing, and foolhardy's another. And you've never been either of the two before."

"Well, I've never been sole claimant to absolute rule of the city before," Nyctasia said, through a mouthful of egg and bread. "Soon enough, everyone will know where I am. But I shan't be so very foolhardy, I promise you—I mean to have Corson brenn Torisk at my back, if she's to be found. With her, and Greymantle here, for protection, I'd defy an army of enemies. What did you make of my Corson, then?"

"She looks like a cutthroat—until she smiles."

"Oh, that's when she's most dangerous. But of course she's a cutthroat. One of the best. I couldn't have a better bodyguard."

"I can well believe it. You've cast your charm over that one, and no mistake. It's plain to see that she's devoted to you."

Nyctasia laughed. "*Corson*? That she-demon claims that she's only saved my life time and again lest she be cheated of the pleasure of killing me herself. You've never heard the like of her insolence." But she was pleased by Maegor's opinion. "I'll go to the Jugged Hare later, and see if she's in Chiastelm. I'll be sending for some of my own people from Rhostshyl too, so you needn't worry over my safety. And no one will be looking for me in these parts, not yet."

"That's not so, 'Tasia. There are rumors of your coming already, even here in Chiastelm. It must be common talk in Rhostshyl."

At this, Nyctasia grew more concerned. "But how can that be? I've not sent word to anyone." Who could possibly have betrayed her plans?

"I think it must have been Therisain who started the stories, to strengthen his own position. He hinted as much to me once. When he left the letter here, he suggested that it would help your cause if I encouraged such rumors."

"Of course," said Nyctasia, disgusted with herself for her suspicions. "My letters of warrant would carry more weight if folk believed that I'd soon return to direct my affairs myself. Therisain was quite right, but this does make matters rather more difficult. It will be just as well, perhaps, if I adopt a less conspicuous guise...."

So soon, Nyctasia brooded, before she had even set foot in Rhostshyl, she was caught up in the scheming for power, the endless intrigues of the court. She could play the game as well as anyone, if she must, but it was not for that that she'd come back to her homeland.

"I truly believed that I'd escaped, Maeg. But now it seems as though I'd never been gone at all."

"Then go back, 'Tasia, for the *vahn*'s sake!" It was not an oath Maegor used lightly.

"For the *vahn*'s sake," Nyctasia echoed, her voice bitter. "Of what use is it to appeal to me in the *vahn*'s name? I've no right to call myself a Vahnite—I've betrayed the Principles too often, and I shall do so again, I've no doubt, before many days have passed. I killed a man, on my way to the coast, only to save myself a few days' delay."

"I don't believe that of you, 'Tasia," said Maegor. Yet she knew that Nyctasia would never say something so outrageous unless there were some truth in it.

"Oh, very well, don't look so shocked—perhaps my reasons were better than that. But I can hardly claim that it was the act of a Vahnite, nor even that I've suffered true remorse. And there's no telling what measures I may have to take soon...." She looked away, not meeting Maegor's eyes, but she spoke with calm certainty. "I only know that I can't be an able ruler and a good Vahnite. Sacrifices must be made, and I care more about my city than about my spirit. This is wrong of me, I have no doubt, but sometimes it is a luxury to be right, an indulgence one must deny oneself." Nyctasia had faced this paradox before, but never had her duty seemed so clear to her. If she was to be more honest with others, she must be more honest with herself as well.

"It is not for me to judge you, 'Tasia," Maegor said gently. "What is right for one is not so for another. You bear burdens that I am thankful to be spared." She sighed. "But you were happy in the home you'd found?"

Nyctasia smiled. "I was taking root very well, so I was told. I was among a clan of vintners, you see, and they were distant kin to me as well. They regarded me as a delicate foreign scion, grafted to their hearty Midland root-stock, and they tended me with every care. You'd have liked them, Maeg. They taught me much."

"So I see. You've grown so forthcoming, I scarcely know you."

Maegor had asked Nyctasia nothing about where she'd been or what she planned to do, and she certainly had not expected to be told. Nyctasia might deny the *vahn*—or believe that she had done so—but she seemed more at peace with herself than Maegor had ever known her.

"Well, I'll prepare that bath for you now, shall I?" said Maegor.

By the time Nyctasia emerged from the apothecary, she had transformed herself yet again, into a travel-worn messenger, or a vagabond student—or, indeed, almost anything else. In her completely commonplace leggings and tunic, her old boots and patched cloak, she was ready to assume any role that was necessary, at a moment's notice. She had even reluctantly left Greymantle behind, the better to slip through the streets unnoticed. From her walk, and the set of her shoulders, she seemed a slight, carefree youth as she sauntered down Market Street, a servant-boy on some household errand.

Vroehin the Moneychanger was alone in his shop, and Nyctasia no sooner entered than he gave an exclamation of surprise and pushed past her to slam and bolt the door. Standing with his back against it, he frowned down at her fiercely and jabbed a long, bony forefinger at her face.

"So you've appeared again! You've some explaining to do, my fine young scapegrace. You're no more page to Lord Heirond than I am—whose money was it you left here, Master Rastwin, *if* that's your name? Speak up!"

Nyctasia backed away, holding out her hands placatingly.

"Just as you say, sir. Rastwin is not my name," she admitted, "but however did you find me out?"

"Very simply! When Lord Heirond died, I sent to know what his heirs' orders were, and his steward knew nothing about the sums you'd deposited with my house, nor about you. The household had never employed a messenger the likes of you. Now I'll have the truth from you, my lad—I'd be within my rights to keep that money, you know. You'd best have a reasonable tale to tell, or I'll have you up before the magistrates for theft."

"Mercy!" Nyctasia laughed, not at all contrite. "I'm a liar and a deceiver, but not a thief, I promise you. So His Lordship died at last. He'd been ill for so long that I expected him never to die, I suppose. Carelessness has ever been my greatest failing."

Suddenly she was tired of carrying on the masquerade, and galled by all the deceptions she had practiced for so long. She sat down on a bench and regarded Vroehin with composure, abruptly abandoning the manner and affectations of the impertinent rascal Rastwin. "It is not a violation of the law to arrange one's affairs under an assumed name and guise," she pointed out, "provided that one acts for one's own protection, and not for the purpose of cheating others. The money I've kept here was my own, you may be quite easy about that. It's true that I was never page-boy to Lord Heirond—"

"You were never a boy at all!" said Vroehin in an astonished whisper. "For the love of Asye, who are you, woman?" He had never before seen Nyctasia's features in repose, nor heard her so serious and softspoken. Now for the first time he saw her clearly, and he could not understand how he'd failed to perceive the truth about her before.

Nyctasia smiled. "I know you to be perfectly trustworthy, sir, but I have reasons, good reasons, to be secret in my dealings. It would not do you—or your daughter—any good to know who I am. You understand." She stood. "I only came here today to tell you that the money still in your keeping is to go for Mellis's dowry. I meant to send instructions as to that, but—"

"So it *was* you who sent Mellis that valuable gold locket," Vroehin interrupted. "She declared that it must be your doing."

"*Vahn,* so I did. I'd forgotten it. I couldn't resist the temptation to send her some little keepsake—I didn't expect to pass this way again, but my plans have changed, you see."

Vroehin was thinking hard and fast. He was a shrewd man, and by now he had begun to suspect whom he was dealing with.

Not long before Lord Heirond's death there had been much talk of the mysterious disappearance of the Witch of Rhostshyl, and Vroehin had seen the last of young Rastwin at much the same time. This woman was wealthy enough to be a Rhaicime, and witch enough to convince him for years that she was nothing but a common messenger-boy. . . . And he'd heard the rumors from war-torn Rhostshyl that folk were calling for the return of the exiled lady of the Edonaris. . . . Decidedly, it was as well not to question her further.

"Well, you've a right, I suppose, to dispose of your own goods in what way you will," he said. "But you might have made your wishes known sooner."

"Forgive me, sir—I'd have done so if I'd known of Lord Heirond's death, but I've been far away. I'm sorry to have given trouble."

Vroehin hesitated. "I thank you for your bounty on my daughter's behalf," he said uneasily, "but, meaning no offense, I'd as soon you were gone before she returns from market."

Nyctasia nodded. "That is wise." But at the door she turned back to him for a moment, with Rastwin's impudent grin. "Farewell, Vroehin. Pray give my best love to the fair Mellis, and tell her I sigh for her still."

"Get about your business," snapped Vroehin, from sheer habit.

Nyctasia bowed. "It may be that we shall not meet again," she said with mock solemnity, "and so, good luck to this house!"

Vroehin watched till she reached the market square and vanished into a sidestreet. "And to you, my lady," he murmured.

18

"SOMEONE'S ASKING FOR Corson," Trask reported to Annin, in the kitchen. "Take a look. The little one in the corner."

Annin peered through the knothole in the kitchen door, which was convenient for spying on the taproom. "Looks harmless enough," she observed. "What did you tell her?"

"Nothing," said Trask, drawing a mug of foaming cider from the cask. "Do you think Corson's in trouble again?"

"Probably. Get rid of her, and we'll lock up for the night—it's almost time. I'll start chasing the others out." There were only a few customers left in the tavern, and the kitchen had already been set to rights for the morrow. Walden had gone home not long before, and Steifann was in his own quarters, scowling over his accounts and downing a large tankard of ale.

Trask set the cider before Nyctasia and asked curtly, "Will there be anything else, mistress? We'll be closing our doors soon."

Nyctasia had told too many lies in her life to be misled by the likes of Trask. She had not for a moment believed that he could give her no news of Corson, but she knew that further questions would only make him more suspicious. She sipped at her cider and said only, "I shan't keep you, then. I'll come back another time for a meal. Corson always says you have the best cook on the coast here. Tell her Nyc's looking for her, if you happen to see her, will you?"

"You're *Nick*? Oh, well then—Corson's told us all about you. She talks about you all the time."

For someone who denied having seen Corson for months, he seemed remarkably well informed about her habits, Nyctasia thought. She saw that she would soon find out whatever she wanted to know from Trask. "Does she indeed?" she murmured encouragingly. "And what does she find to say about me?" It was gratifying, in a way, to hear that Corson had spoken about her, but exactly what had she said? Surely she knew better than to tell her friends too much . . . ?

"Corson claims that you're a great lady." Trask eyed Nycta-

111

sia's worn garments dubiously. "Not that we believed her."

"Oh, but I *am*," said Nyctasia, in a tone which could only invite disbelief.

"And I'm High Lord of Torstaine," said Trask, with a grin. "As if a great lady would take up with Corson! But she always has some fool story to tell when she comes back here."

Nyctasia smiled. "She's told me about all of you, too. You must be Trask. And *that*—" She broke off and stared as Steifann came out of his room to fetch himself more ale, slamming the door behind him. He was simply the largest person she had ever seen. "That *must* be Corson's he-bear, Steifann."

"Does she call him that?" Trask asked eagerly.

"Well, only when she's been drinking."

Trask was delighted. "Steifann!" he called. "Look here, this is Corson's friend Nick we've heard so much about."

It should be said in Steifann's defense that he *was* rather drunk. It took a great deal of ale to affect Steifann's judgment, but he'd been worrying about Corson, and when he worried he drank even more ale than usual. Corson should have been back days ago. She'd only been escorting a shipment of merchandise to Ochram, and that couldn't have taken more than a fortnight. Unless she'd tangled with robbers on the way. . . . ? The roads were most dangerous in the spring, Steifann brooded. Bandits were desperate and reckless after the scanty pickings of the winter, when travelers were few—and the coast road led through deep woodland at more than one point. He pictured Corson lying dead in the forest, hewn by swords, impaled by arrows, maybe devoured by wolves. . . . Or it might be that she was just tarrying in Ochram, spending her pay with some newfound friend, and letting him worry. By the Hlann, he'd kill her himself when she came traipsing back—!

All in all, he was in no fit frame of mind to meet Nyctasia.

So this was the one Corson had spent half the year with—the scholar, the enchantress, the high-born lady. He might have known she'd be just some vagabond in a patched cloak. All the same, she had a knowing look about her that Steifann didn't care for in the least. Corson was too rutting easily impressed by folk with a little learning, like that blasted student 'Malkin she sometimes talked about. Frowning, he strode over to Nyctasia's table and glowered down at her fiercely. "Do you sleep with Corson?" he demanded.

Nyctasia nearly choked on her cider. What had she let herself in for *now*? A man whose fist looked larger than her head was looming over her like a ferocious giant in a fable—a hungry giant who'd caught the hapless human hero trespassing on his property and meant to dispose of the intruder in a few bites. Nyctasia didn't know whether to laugh or flee for her life.

But an Edonaris ought always to maintain her dignity in the face of threats or insults. Turning to Trask, she asked coolly, "Tell me, is that the way he greets everyone?"

"Not always," said Trask. "Sometimes he's downright rude." At a look from Steifann, he scurried off back to the kitchen, where he lost no time in informing the others of the situation. They soon gathered in the doorway to watch.

"Why don't you ask Corson that?" Nyctasia was suggesting to Steifann, with a sneer in her voice.

"I'm asking you!" Steifann bellowed, hitting the table with his fist, and spilling Nyctasia's cider.

Had he been of her own station, or at least a nobleman, Nyctasia would have flung the rest of the drink in his face and challenged him to a duel. As it was, however, she struck at him instead in the way such low-bred insolence deserved.

"Who is there that Corson *doesn't* sleep with?" she said, and saw with satisfaction that her blow had hit home. With a shrug, she added, "And for my part I think it no wonder that she should prefer my company to yours." It is not easy to look *up* at someone contemptuously, but Nyctasia was one of those who know how to do it.

Steifann had reddened like a victim of the Surge. "Look here, you little slut, you may be someone important where you come from, but this is my place, and—"

Nyctasia had heard enough. She stood, and tossed down some money for her drink. "I'm a Rhaicime where I come from," she said evenly, "but if I were a fishmonger I'd not waste words with an ill-mannered boor like you."

"On your way!" shouted Steifann, throwing out one arm to point to the door.

It was this threatening gesture which brought Greymantle out from under the table, snarling and baring his fangs. He'd seen no harm in Steifann's shouting—the Edonaris were always shouting at one another—but to a dog a hand raised in anger means only one thing. His mistress was in danger. Greymantle advanced on Steifann slowly, with the obvious intention of tearing out his throat as soon as he made the slightest move in Nyctasia's direction. His fur bristled, and his every muscle was tensed to spring.

Nyctasia grabbed his collar and held him back, as Steifann slowly lowered his outflung arm.

"You heard me, take yourself off," Steifann said, though not in quite as menacing a tone as he'd used before.

Ignoring him, Nyctasia turned to Trask. "Tell Corson that she can find me where she found me before," she ordered, and took her leave without so much as a glance at the furious Steifann.

She missed Corson by only a matter of hours.

"Oh, well done," said Annin drily. "Idiot! What if that woman's really a Rhaicime? She'll have your head for talking to her like that."

Steifann knew he'd made a fool of himself, and the knowledge did not improve his ill humor. "Plague take her, brazen little bitch! She'd no call to—"

"Sit there drinking cider and minding her own business? Certainly not. Villainous of her."

"I'll go after her and offer your apologies," Trask announced, taking one of the lamps from its bracket. "If she has you thrown in a dungeon, who'll chop the wood?"

"You get back here—"

"Go!" said Annin. "Hurry up or you'll lose her." She turned on Steifann with real anger. "Don't you see, she might have done something for Destiver, and now you've set her against us!"

Steifann hadn't thought of that. And Annin was right, he realized. If this was the same woman who'd fled Chiastelm with Corson last year, as he suspected, then she did have reason to be grateful to Destiver. Fool that he was, had he not only made trouble for himself, but helped put Destiver's neck in a noose as well? "Curse Corson, this is all her doing!"

"And how do you make *that* out?"

"If she'd been here, it wouldn't have happened in the first place. And where *is* she, for that matter—answer me that. Probably dead in a ditch."

Annin shook her head, and turned back to the kitchen. Steifann followed, drew a pitcher of ale and sat down to resume his interrupted brooding. Now there was twice as much to worry about.

Nyctasia heard someone running behind her in the dark street, and she thanked the *vahn* for the second time that night that she hadn't come out after dusk without Greymantle. By the time

Trask caught up to her, she had turned to face her pursuer and was waiting for him, sword in hand.

Trask halted abruptly and fell back a step. "Er—Your Lady-ship—pardon me—" He had no idea how to make a formal bow, but he did his best.

"Well, what is it, boy?" Nyctasia said imperiously. "I left payment for my drink."

Her manner and bearing, even her voice, were so different from what they had been at the tavern, that Trask wondered for a moment if he'd followed the wrong person in the dark. "You really *are* a Rhaicime," he said stupidly.

Nyctasia sheathed her sword. "And did you chase after me to tell me that?"

"No, I—that is, Steifann—he didn't mean to offend you, lady. . . ."

"Indeed?" She sounded amused, now.

Encouraged, Trask grinned winningly, assuming his most deferential demeanor. "Well, he didn't mean any *harm*, I promise you. He's always in a temper when Corson's late coming back. He growls at everyone, but he wouldn't hurt a flea. You'll like him when you come to know him better."

"I do *not* mean to know him better."

"No, of course not," said Trask hastily, "but, you wouldn't complain of him to the City Governors, would you, m'lady?" His tone was wheedling, but Nyctasia saw that he was genuinely worried.

She had in fact dismissed Steifann from her mind almost as soon as she'd left the Hare. She had been angry, but as much with herself as with him, and it would never have occurred to her to seek to punish his loutish behavior. Nyctasia had been taught that one could not expect a commoner to behave like a gentleman. If one mixed with base-born folk, one had only oneself to blame if one encountered unpleasantness. "A lady," she said to Trask, "does not stoop to resent the ill-advised scurrility of an inferior."

Trask would have found this more reassuring if he'd understood what it meant. "As you say, my lady," he said glumly. "But really, I swear—"

Nyctasia couldn't help laughing. "Never mind, lad, you may tell the host of the Hare that he's forgiven. I wouldn't dare to make trouble for him, you see—Corson would kill me."

19

THE PLACE WHERE Corson had found Nyctasia before was an old stone house on the cliffs just outside of Chiastelm, known as the Smugglers' House. Nyctasia had bought it years ago, as a retreat from the duties and dangers of her life in Rhostshyl, but she had never passed much time in the place. Now she meant to establish her household there, for the time being, and send for those with whom she must meet—her allies first, and then the others.

It was important that she make them come to her. To obey her summons would be to acknowledge her powerful position, and only if her right to govern was recognized by all could she hope to fulfill her dream for the city's future. She must return to Rhostshyl as its ruler, or not at all.

She was not surprised to find the house standing open, the locks broken. It had been long empty and unguarded, easy for thieves and vagbonds to invade. But there was nothing left to steal, and Nyctasia found no further sign of intruders as she explored the building by lamplight. She'd heard it said that the house was haunted, and she supposed that such talk kept trespassers away, but she did not suspect that the sinister reputation of the place had grown since the mysterious murders there the year before. The killer had reportedly vanished in the very midst of a troupe of guards, leaving three dead—or six, or eight, according to the varying versions of the tale. But most folk agreed that it looked like the work of demons, and shunned the place more than ever.

Nyctasia wandered through the deserted rooms with Greymantle, searching the cellars and the scullery, then each floor above, to be certain that she was alone in the house. There was nothing to find but dust and cobwebs and the ash of long-dead hearthfires. She could have the locks seen to in the morning, and the house cleaned and readied for habitation. She would send for sentries from her own guard in Rhostshyl to garrison the premises while she dwelt there. But tonight while the house stood empty, she had one thing to do there alone.

When she reached the topmost story, Greymantle at once led the way to the one door in the corridor that was closed, and sniffed at it mistrustfully, his ears pricked for any sound within. But Nyctasia looked into all the other rooms before returning to this one, the room where Thierran had been killed, where she herself had come so close to death. Greymantle was pawing at the sill and growling softly, and Nyctasia wondered if it were true that animals possessed a special awareness of immaterial Influences. Perhaps the Smugglers' House had not been haunted before, she thought grimly, but it surely was now. "You will make me a good familiar, Grey," she said, and pushed open the door.

She half-expected to see Thierran still lying there, his throat slashed, though she knew that he must have been long since interred in the crypts beneath the palace of the Edonaris in Rhostshyl. As children they had defied their elders' orders and explored those crypts together, frightened but fascinated, knowing that they would lie there themselves one day among their ancestors—yet not really believing that they would ever die.

But the dark, dried blood staining the far wall and the floor reminded her of how wrong those children had been. Greymantle sniffed at it, and she called him away hastily. Then, when she had looked around the room, she hung her lamp in the corridor outside and came back to the chamber in darkness. The window was still open, as it had been on the night Corson clambered through it to find her, and the wan moonlight it gave the room was quite sufficient for Nyctasia's purposes.

While she knelt by the spot where Thierran had fallen, Greymantle examined every corner of the room, even resting his front paws on the windowsill to sniff the night air suspiciously. When his searching led him out to the corridor again, he looked back, waiting for Nyctasia to follow, but she remained on her knees, silent and motionless. Greymantle came back to her and nudged her chin with his nose insistently until she took heed of him.

"Talk to a hound with your hands," said Nyctasia. "Talk to the dead in your dreams." She stroked Greymantle's rough fur, then gently pushed him away. "You stand guard, Grey. Go on now." The dog gave a whining sigh and resumed his restless prowling.

We ourselves are the true link between the world of the spirit and the world of matter, Nyctasia mused, *and thus the gateway where the two realms meet is rightly to be sought within our-*

selves and not otherwise. . . . Nevertheless, in this room she had last seen Thierran in life, and here she had met him again, in her troubled dreams. The way she must take lay within, yes, but here if anywhere was the place from which to depart.

Nyctasia drew her dagger, and slowly closed her hand around the blade. The edge bit deep into her palm and fingers, but she barely felt the pain at first.

> "Approach, I am near you,
> Speak, for I hear you . . ."

Nyctasia chanted, over and over again, as the throbbing swelled in her wounded hand.

Behind her closed eyes she thought she saw the reflections of fallen stars, or of stars which had never been. Finally she pressed her hand against the stained floorboards and waited, silent, while the living blood mingled with the dead.

Corson couldn't stop laughing. Her ribs ached, she could barely breathe, and tears of laughter flooded her eyes. Every time she thought of Steifann and Nyctasia face to face, his red-hot rage facing her pale, cold fury, she collapsed in howls of helpless glee. She could picture them both perfectly.

Trask had reported every word of the quarrel to her, with a few embellishments of his own, emphasizing Steifann's folly and his own heroism in braving Nyctasia's wrath to intercede on Steifann's behalf.

Steifann had contributed an indignant denial here and there, but he was content to let Trask tell the tale while he sat by with a sheepish grin and nursed a mug of ale. Now that Corson was back safe and sound, his good humor was quite restored, and matters did not look nearly so grim. Trask claimed that Her Ladyship had graciously forgiven his behavior, and Corson clearly did not think that much harm had been done. She sat with one arm around him and leaned against him, breathless with laughter. Her hair had started to come undone, and it tickled his neck pleasantly. He was mellowly drunk by now, and feeling far too comfortable to mind her mockery and teasing.

Indeed, the whole affair now seemed nearly as funny to him as it did to Corson. He could already hear himself repeating the story over his ale in years to come, telling friends about the time he'd threatened to throw one of Corson's countless lovers out of his place. ("An insolent little minx, no bigger than your thumb, she was, with a way of looking at you as if you smelled of the cesspit. And then when I'd finished telling her just what I thought of her—not leaving out much, you understand—she simply looked me up and down as cool as you please, and said, 'I'm a Rhaicime where I come from . . .' I thought I'd be in the pillory before dawn and on the scaffold before dusk! How was I to know Corson was telling the truth about knowing a Rhaicime? It's not as if she'd ever told the truth before.") Steifann chuckled to himself. It would make a fine story—the only trouble was that he didn't yet know how it ended.

Corson wiped her streaming eyes on her sleeve. "You dolt!" she said for the twentieth time, and kissed him heartily. She didn't know which delighted her more, Steifann's jealousy, or the thought of Nyctasia being called a little slut in public. "You must have scared her half to death, you brute—a little mite like that! For shame!"

Steifann was, in truth, ashamed of that. No one who knew him would have supposed for a moment that he would strike anyone as small as Nyctasia. He might at the worst have taken her by the collar and pitched her out the door. But how was she to know that? Still, if she'd been frightened, Steifann thought, she'd certainly hidden it well. "It was that hound of hers scared *me* out of my wits," he protested. "I was nearly chewed up and swallowed, but do *you* care? Anyway, it was all your fault, Corson," he concluded with drunken complacency. "You should have been here to deal with your Rhaicime yourself—and to protect me from her."

"By Asye, I wish I *had* been here. I'd give a fortune to have seen it." She kissed Steifann again. "Well, I daresay she deserved it. She's the most vexing little gadfly ever born."

"And where *were* you while we were entertaining the nobility here? I expected you days ago."

"They kept me waiting for my pay in Ochram till a courier arrived with letters of credit. But I made them pay for the delay, and for a room at The Golden Goblet too. I had a fine time."

"I'll wager you did," Steifann said sourly. "You could have sent a message, curse you."

Corson shook her head, and her braid tumbled down the rest of the way. "No one I met with was leaving for Chiastelm any sooner than I was. *I'm* not to blame that you're too hot-tempered by half. You should try not to be so hasty."

"Hasty! If I weren't such a forbearing fellow, your ragged Rhaicime would be in shreds and splinters now."

"Why *does* she go about looking like a peddler?" said Trask suddenly—a question Steifann and Annin had known better than to ask, and which Corson knew better than to answer. She sent Trask off to the kitchen to find her something to eat.

"Nyc would try anyone's patience, it's true," she said to Steifann, "but really she's a pet when you come to know her. She doesn't mind a few rough words. You'll see."

Steifann snorted. "Know her! Rhaicime or no, if she sets foot in here again, I'll—"

"You'll beg her pardon," Annin put in sharply, "if it'll help us get Destiver back alive. What of that, Corson?"

"I don't know. . ." Corson said thoughtfully. "You see, Nyc's *met* Destiver, and I don't suppose she thinks of her very fondly. Destiver was even less respectful to milady than you were, love. Threatened to have her keelhauled, as I recall."

Annin groaned.

"But all the same, if I ask her, she might do what she can. She'd do anything for me," Corson continued, grinning at Steifann. She lowered her voice. "If she's here in secret, though, she can't very well make herself known to the Guild. I don't know what she means to do, but I'll ask her about Destiver—after I've had something to eat."

"What, tonight?" Steifann objected. "You just got here. Wait till morning."

Corson hesitated. It was late, and she'd been riding since dawn. But Maegor's words came back to her: "If she returns, she may well be assassinated." Suppose Nyctasia had sought her out because she needed her services as bodyguard? Corson knew that she wouldn't rest easy till she'd seen for herself that Nyctasia was safe. "You might have to make do without me tonight, poor creature," she told Steifann vengefully. "That must be hard to bear. But I'd better go see whether Nyc needs me. She might be in danger. Asye knows she usually is."

20

NYCTASIA WAS, AS usual, in danger. But she knew nothing of her peril till it was past, till Greymantle roused her from her stupor, licking her face and whimpering. She clutched at him, struggling to rise, and felt that his coat was wet and matted. Her hands came away dark and shiny with blood. When she saw the still figure lying near her on the floor, she believed for one dizzying moment that it was Thierran, and she cried out in confusion and denial of the sight. She seemed to have stepped outside of time itself, and returned to the night of his death, as if everything that had happened to her since had been only a strange dream.

But as she came slowly to her senses, the moonlight and the dim lamplight from the hallway revealed who it was who lay there, his throat torn open raggedly, not slashed by Corson's keen-honed dagger. She reached out a trembling hand to stroke Greymantle's massive head. "Good lad," she whispered. "Well done."

Greymantle flicked his ears, listening, then trotted back out to the corridor on some quest of his own. But this time he wagged his tail in welcome. This was a scent he recognized.

Corson laughed at the eager hound who greeted her like a skittish puppy, tugging at her cloak then running ahead of her and turning back to bark impatiently. "All right, beast, I'm coming. Get out of my way, then." But when he came back a second time to herd her along, she saw that his muzzle and ruff were caked with blood, and her laughter died in her throat. Sword in hand, she followed him at a run the rest of the way, calling, "Nyc! Where are you?" But she knew, somehow, where she would find Nyctasia.

Greymantle darted to Nyctasia's side but Corson stood frozen in the doorway, faced with the ghost of the man she'd killed, and Nyctasia standing over him with the same half-dreamy, absent look she'd worn that night.

"It's not Thierran, Corson," she said, in an unnaturally placid voice that Corson remembered.

"I didn't think it was!" Corson lied, beginning to breathe again. "He's dead and gone, and good riddance to him. The dead don't return."

"Our dead do not return to us," Nyctasia agreed, "but we may go to them betimes, if we will. It is written, 'To seek to commune with the dead is forbidden, but if the dead would commune with us, it is permitted to listen.'"

"What are you babbling about?" Corson demanded. She strode over to the dead man and shoved him with her foot, angry at him for giving her a fright. "Who's this, then?"

Nyctasia did not seem to hear. "But why should it be easier to listen to the dead than to the living? If I'd listened to Thierran while he lived, perhaps he'd not be dead now."

Corson had been with her only a few minutes, and already she was exasperated. "Nyc, talk sense! Are you hurt?"

Nyctasia looked at her blindly. "I? I'm never hurt. It's those around me who suffer . . . Corson, the night we left Rhostshyl, he came to warn me about the attack waiting outside the city gates. Oh, but he was pleased with himself, that he knew something I didn't—I with all my schemes and precautions. He'd defied Mhairestri to save me. Even Mescrisdan didn't know his plans. He believed that I'd be forced to stay in the city, under his protection . . . that I'd be *grateful* to him. *I*, grateful!" She laughed bitterly.

Corson shook her head. "He'd drawn on you, fool, don't you remember?"

"How else to make me listen, save at sword's point?"

"You're dreaming, Nyc. He was a madman, that cousin of yours, and his brother no better. Now, what—"

"Oh yes, he was mad. He had the madness of the Edonaris, and the pride, and after that night madness and pride were all that was left to him."

"If you mean to say that I shouldn't have killed him, you're crazier than he was. He was after your blood, and mine too!"

"Of course you'd no choice, Corson. He might not have killed me, but he'd certainly have killed you. Not because you wounded him in my defense, not even because you killed Mescrisdan, but because you spoke to him with scorn. You sneered at him." She seemed quite unaware that a dead man lay at her feet.

Corson wondered whether it would do any good to slap her.

Probably not, she thought glumly, but *I'd* feel the better for it.

"Let be," Nyctasia said, as if to herself. "I know now what he wanted to tell me."

Corson did not ask how she knew, and didn't want to hear more. "Perhaps, if it's not asking too much, you'd be good enough to tell me," she began, making use of expressions she had learned from Nyctasia, "what you're bloody, rutting well doing here with a corpse in the middle of the night, curse you!" she concluded, in her own words.

Nyctasia seemed to see her for the first time. "How charming to meet you again, Corson. This—" she added, gesturing toward the body as if introducing it, "is one of the Lady Mhairestri's henchmen, unless I much mistake. His name escapes me." She sighed, sounding tired and vexed. "She must have set him to watching the house some time ago. She's admirably thorough. I expected something of the sort, of course, but I searched and found no one. He must have entered afterward. I wonder that Grey let him come so close, though."

But Corson pointed to the open window. "More likely he came in that way. He might have been here all the while and climbed up to the roof to hide when he heard you coming. It's easy to do."

Nyctasia nodded thoughtfully. Corson waited for her to say something about carelessness, but she only remarked, "I suppose he didn't see Greymantle in the dark. That dog is almost as good a bodyguard as you are, Corson —and he has much better manners."

"But you enjoy my company, you know," Corson reminded her with a grin. She handed Nyctasia her lantern, then bent and pulled the would-be assassin up by one arm, hoisting him over her back. "Over the cliff with this one, I think. The gulls and fish will make short work of him."

Something fell from his hand and lay gleaming on the blood-stained floor, catching the moonlight. Nyctasia picked up her silver earring, and Corson saw her face harden with a fleeting fury, but when she spoke her voice was still calm and flatly amused. "A token for Mhairestri that the job was done," she said lightly. "I'll send her this instead." She took one of the plain brass earrings the dead man wore, and slipped it into the pouch at her hip. "She'll understand."

She turned to the door, then, and called Greymantle to her. "Thank you for disposing of the carrion, Corson. I must take

Grey down to the shore and give him a washing. I could do with one myself, come to that, I'm filthy. Seawater's as salt and sticky as blood, but cleaner at least. Cleaner..." Her clothes were bloodstained and dusty from the floor, and her hands were grimy with gore, though there was no longer a knife-wound slashed across her palm and fingers. Only the drying blood remained to show where the cuts had been.

Corson followed with her lifeless burden, wondering what could possibly happen next. She could not remember that Nyctasia had ever before thanked her for anything, in all the time she'd known her.

21

CORSON FOUND THE new arrangement much to her liking. She was once again personal bodyguard to a Rhaicime—a position of some prestige for a mercenary, and one which she could at last boast of openly. Nyctasia made no secret of her rank and station now but rather made every effort to enhance her own dignity and authority. She had a company of guards about her, as well as an entourage of servants—a steward, maids, pages, scribes, cooks, scullions and other menials, and people whom Corson classed vaguely as "courtiers," whose duties were a mystery to her, although they always seemed to be extremely busy.

And the cream of it was that, with Nyctasia in Chiastelm, Corson could watch over her by day and then spend her nights at the Hare, while sentries patrolled the Smugglers' House, and Greymantle defended his mistress's chamber.

Nyctasia's days were spent in a series of meetings with the lords and ladies who arrived from Rhostshyl to confer with her—meetings which took the form of furious disputes more often than not. Corson stood by, keeping a wary eye on these confrontations. It was plain to see that some of Nyctasia's fellow nobles would have liked to kill her there and then, and even some of those she counted as allies condemned her plans as mad and foolish. And all were afraid of her, Corson thought, and trusted her no more than she trusted them.

"You'll beggar the city, do you understand that?" one nobleman or another shouted at her, pacing angrily about Nyctasia's audience-chamber, while Corson watched his every move and kept her hand to her sword-hilt. Greymantle lay with his nose on his paws and looked on with disapproval, occasionally uttering a warning growl.

But Nyctasia merely reclined in a cushioned chair and said slowly, never raising her voice, "The city is already beggared, from all report. What you mean to say is that I'll beggar the nobility—and so I shall, for the present, so I shall. We are responsible for the condition the city is in. Would you have it said that we do not pay our debts?"

Corson did not give much heed to what was said, but even so she gathered that Nyctasia meant to expend most of her personal fortune, and that of her House, to buy grain to feed the hungry of Rhostshyl—and she expected the other noble families of the city to do the same. The countryside around Rhostshyl had been nearly as ravaged by the war as the city itself, fields and granaries put to the torch, the harvest all but lost. Foodstuffs would have to be brought in from neighboring municipalities, perhaps shipped up the coast from the fertile lands to the south, at a cost which the City Treasury alone could not begin to meet. Nyctasia had already sent out emissaries to nearby courts to ask for terms, and she had seen to it that rumors of her plans were spread through Rhostshyl to folk of every degree. There was more of an outcry than ever for her return, and prophecies arose that the Witch of Rhostshyl would work her magic to save the city. If Nyctasia's proposals failed to find favor with her peers, yet they had support enough among her people.

But it was not only her designs upon the wealth of the city that outraged her friends and foes alike. Even more contention was caused by her insistence that she would declare a general pardon when she assumed power—a pardon which was to include the enemies of the House of Edonaris.

"You're mad, sister, to consider such a thing," cried the Lady Tiambria, Nyctasia's younger sister. She and her twin, the Lord Erikasten, spoke up boldly enough to Nyctasia, but Corson thought that they had the air of angry, frightened children, who wanted to be told what to do. The sight of them had startled her at first, for they looked much like Raphe and 'Deisha, though years younger. Not yet twenty, Corson judged them.

"'Tasia, if we don't put an end to this rivalry now, our victory, and our losses, will have been in vain," argued Tiambria. "You've not seen the destruction in the city—"

"I have seen it," said Nyctasia softly. "And I tell you that all such victory is in vain. If we allow ourselves to profit from it, how are we to learn not to let it happen again? Perhaps we could destroy the rest of the Teiryn, and their followers, but in time another house would arise to challenge us. No, you need not repeat Mhairestri's arguments to me. You may tell her that I shall give her views a respectful hearing when I return to court, at any time she may consent to receive me."

The twins looked at each other, mantling, shifting their

shoulders uncomfortably. Corson half expected them to break into tears. "We may repeat the matriarch's words, 'Tasia, but she didn't send us," Tiambria said at last.

"She forbade us to come," Erikasten put in wretchedly.

Nyctasia regarded the pair thoughtfully, one eyebrow raised in mild surprise. "Could it be that you two are finally growing up?" she asked, almost smiling.

Nyctasia was playing a new role, one that was unfamiliar to Corson, though she had seen Nyctasia in many guises and many humors. Was she at last seeing Nyctasia as she really was—an autocratic ruler, responsible and duty-bound, unyielding in her resolve, wielding her authority as readily as Corson wielded her sword? If so, Corson did not find it an improvement in her character. She was rarely alone with Nyctasia now, and when she was, Nyctasia hardly seemed aware of her presence. But Corson was not the sort to put up with that for long.

"I'm leaving now," she announced one evening. "Do you hear, Nyc?"

It was much earlier than Corson usually left for the night, but Nyctasia only nodded, without looking up from the document she was studying. It had been delivered by messenger that morning, but she'd had no time for it all day. "Tell Ioras to post another guard at the door, then," she said absently, frowning at the papers.

"No," said Corson.

That drew Nyctasia's attention.

"You won't need another guard," Corson explained, "because you're coming with me to the Hare."

"I haven't the time for an outing now, I'm afraid."

"You'll find time. You've not set foot out of this cursed house in a fortnight. The place is haunted, right enough, and you're the ghost."

Nyctasia drew a sharp breath and remained silent for a time, but then said, "Corson, no doubt you mean well, but—"

Corson paid no attention. "You can have a decent meal at the Hare, at least, and not fear that it's poisoned. You don't eat enough to nourish a gnat, when you remember to take a meal at all. You look like a half-starved beggar-brat, and you act like a queen, and I've had my fill of it!"

In spite of herself, Nyctasia started to laugh, and Corson knew that she'd won. "But, Corson, I daren't go there—what of that jealous giant of yours? He'll tear me to pieces."

Corson grinned triumphantly. "He'll be most pleased to make

you welcome. Steifann's no fool—he's thought of the distinction it would bring his place to have the patronage of a Rhaicime. He never ceases to plague me about it. And Walden wants a chance to cook for the nobility, too, and Annin wants a better look at you, and Trask's simply in love with you. I'll have no peace till I've presented you to them."

"Well, I should hate to disappoint them. Perhaps another time."

"Now," said Corson firmly. "Nyc, do you remember when we were in Yth Forest, and you all but changed into an Ythling yourself?" Giving Nyctasia no chance to answer, she continued, "Well, you're even stranger now than you were then. It'll do you good to get away from here. Here's your cloak." She whistled for Greymantle, who trotted to the door at once and looked back at Nyctasia expectantly.

"Are you coming?" said Corson, "or must I throw you over my shoulder and carry you off?"

"Greymantle wouldn't let you lay hands on me."

"Oh, wouldn't he though? Did he go for Raphe's throat every time he and 'Deisha got to swatting each other? We'll just see." She started toward Nyctasia.

Nyctasia hastily rose and grabbed her cloak. "Very well, we'll go! Perhaps you're right." When Corson insisted on having her way, she was usually right, as Nyctasia had discovered—and it was always less trouble to give in to her.

Nyctasia's second visit to The Jugged Hare was less eventful, but more successful, than her first, and it was by no means to be her last. She found it a relief to escape her retinue for a while, and be again Nyc of the roads, the harper and minstrel. Her harp was the first thing she'd had sent to her from Rhostshyl, and she often brought it to the tavern and sang for the entertainment of the house. Had Steifann not known who and what she was, he'd have offered her a job singing for her supper. She soon became something of a favorite at the Hare, once Steifann and the others had lost their awe of her lofty rank and title. Surely no one who was on such familiar terms with Corson could hold herself very high, they felt.

Steifann forgave Nyctasia for everything once she told him that Corson had never ceased talking about him, the whole while they were journeying together. And it was thanks to Nyctasia, after all, that Corson's work kept her in Chiastelm with him. He was disappointed that Nyctasia did not arrive in state, and that she usually ate in the kitchen, out of sight of his other customers, but she assured him that he could tell whom he liked that she frequented The Hare—after she'd returned to Rhostshyl.

Annin too was well disposed toward Nyctasia because she had promised to lodge an appeal with the Maritime Alliance on Destiver's behalf. As a mark of her particular favor, she took to scolding Nyctasia as freely as she did the others.

Destiver had been more heartened by this news than by anything she'd heard since Annin had brought her word of Hrawn brenn Thespaon's murder. If she was grateful for Nyctasia's help, however, her appreciation did not manifest itself in any noticeable way. "Who would have thought that bothersome little chit was a Rhaicime?" she remarked. "I should have charged her more."

Trask was enthralled at the unheard-of opportunity to ingratiate himself with a personage of such undoubted influence and eminence. He made even more of a nuisance of himself than usual, pestering Nyctasia to take him to court, where he declared he really belonged, among people of polish and breeding. Everyone had other suggestions as to where Trask really belonged, from a barn to a brothel, from the gutter to the gibbet, but Trask was not easily discouraged. Nyctasia was of the opinion that there was indeed a place for him at court—a deep dungeon far below the palace, which she offered to make available for him at any time.

Walden also approved of Corson's new friend, on the whole. She praised his cooking with obvious sincerity, and ate like a growing child whenever she came to the Hare, which was a sure way to Walden's good graces. "Only those who eat heartily can be trusted" was his motto, and it had never failed him yet. Nyctasia was too skinny, true, but no doubt she hadn't been properly fed. And she might be a Rhaicime, but that was probably not her fault. He did not hesitate to swat her with a wooden spoon when he caught her stealing raisins from the barrel in the kitchen.

All in all, Corson was well satisfied with the way matters stood, and it came as a bitter disappointment when Nyctasia told her that she'd soon be returning to Rhostshyl.

"Is it safe for you to go there yet?" Corson asked.

"Not at all. But it's time, you see. I've done all I can here—the nobility dare not defy me openly, now. I've seen to that. They fear uprisings in the city if it's known that they oppose my plans. They'll conspire against me, though." She gave a sudden cheerless laugh. "And they've not heard the worst of it yet! When they find out what more I have in mind, the screams of rage will be heard all the way to Tièrelon. Oh, no, it's not safe."

"I suppose you expect me to go with you, then."

Nyctasia appeared to hesitate. "Well, no, I think you needn't. Ioras can serve as my bodyguard at court."

"Ioras! I could worst him with one hand, and my right hand at that."

"I don't doubt it. Corson, I'm well aware that I'd be better protected by you, but, after all, do you want to call me 'my lady,' bow to me, walk a pace behind me, stand while I sit . . ."

"I'm cursed if I will!"

"Well, there we are." Nyctasia smiled, but her voice was serious. "I must command the respect of those around me, Corson, if I'm to work my will, in the days to come. You must see that I can't have a bodyguard who undermines my authority by speaking insolently to me before others. Folk will say, 'How is she to govern the city, when she can't even govern her own servants?' It would make me appear weak, and I cannot afford that. My people may not be your equal with a sword, but they know what behavior is expected of them at court."

"Do you think you're the first noble I've served? I know how to conduct myself in any household in the land—I'm not just out of the army! I can bow and grovel as well as another, when I choose."

Nyctasia looked doubtful. "Perhaps . . . but if you attend the ruler of the city, there's no choice about it. Formalities must be observed."

"Don't worry, I'll remember my place," Corson snapped. "I'll stay till you have matters in hand there, at least. You'd only get yourself killed, without me."

"Very likely," Nyctasia admitted. In fact, she had never had any intention of returning to Rhostshyl without Corson, but, noticing her reluctance, she had immediately resorted to the surest way to make Corson do anything—which was to suggest that she *couldn't* do it. "Well, if you insist on accompanying me, I don't suppose I can stop you," she said resignedly. "But you won't like it."

"I know," said Corson. Steifann wouldn't like it either, but at least Rhostshyl was within two days' ride of Chiastelm. Corson privately resolved that she'd make Nyctasia pay dearly for every humble bow and dutiful show of deference.

22

NYCTASIA MADE A ceremonial entry into Rhostshyl not long afterward, riding at the head of a cortege of her followers, surrounded by a troupe of guard. She had sent heralds ahead to proclaim her coming, and to make known that a distribution of meal and flour would take place at mid-day in the city square. Word spread quickly that well-guarded wagonloads of grain followed the procession, and cheers of welcome greeted Nyctasia on all sides. She was flanked by her brother and sister—in grim defiance of the matriarch—and Corson was not far behind.

The rest were dressed with splendor, as for a celebration, but Nyctasia wore mourning, her chain of office the only brightness about her. She sat straight, almost stiff, but she did not look proud to be returning to her city in triumph. Somber and unsmiling, she was every inch the earnest, careworn ruler. Even Corson was impressed with her regal dignity.

She did not ride straight to the palace of the Edonaris, but insisted on making her way through every part of the city, to learn for herself what Rhostshyl and its people had suffered. The destruction was perhaps less extensive than she had feared, but it was nonetheless pitiful to see, and to one who loved the city as Nyctasia did, it was nothing less than heartbreak. The poorer sections of the city had fared the worst, of course, but fire had not shown mercy to the more prosperous districts either. Nyctasia was met by throngs of the hungry and homeless, some holding out their ailing children to be healed by her magic. The guards kept back the crowds, but Nyctasia would not spare herself the sight of her needy subjects. She looked into the eyes of those she passed, and held out her hands toward them in a Vahnite gesture of benediction. Tales of miraculous cures would soon begin to spread through the city, she knew, not because she had any such power, but because folk wished to believe that she did. They themselves would work the sorcery, by means of a powerful and mysterious Influence that no mage or philosopher truly understood. To Nyctasia it was but another deception, to be numbered among many. By the time she had turned toward the aristocratic quarter of the city, she felt far older than her years, and deeply shamed.

She had dreamed that the city's great palaces lay in ruins, but now she found that they had in fact suffered least, being the best defended, and built of stone. Some roofs still gaped where wooden beams had fallen to fire, though the mansions of the victors had of course been set to rights. But Nyctasia was not comforted to see that the palace of the Edonaris stood whole again, in all its grandeur. She understood now that the fallen walls she had envisioned were emblematic of a more profound destruction, a loss that could not be repaired with timber and mortar. Her family's honor was in ruins, the proud heritage of the Edonaris, and she doubted that it could ever be restored.

With a heart burdened by such thoughts as these, Nyctasia ar'n Edonaris returned to her ancestral home.

Corson decided to speak to Nyctasia about her guards. They were not alert enough to suit her. They watched Nyctasia attentively, yes, but what was the good of that? Nyctasia wasn't a prisoner; it was not she who ought to be watched but those around her, any one of whom might be a deadly enemy. Corson looked everywhere, searching the crowd for any sign of danger, noticing every threatening glint of steel. Though she was satisfied that no one could approach Nyctasia, she also knew that she herself had never been prevented by mere distance from felling her intended prey. It was wisest to assume that anyone stalking Nyctasia was equally skillful, and Corson was not in the least surprised when she caught sight of a man crouching beside a chimney, with a knife poised to throw. She had pushed past Erikasten and caught the blade neatly on her shield before Nyctasia or her retinue realized what was happening. It was Corson who pointed out the culprit, who ordered the house surrounded before he could reach the ground and make an escape—and though she had no authority to give such commands, she was obeyed.

Nyctasia did not wait to see the capture. "A partisan of the Teiryn, no doubt," she said indifferently, adding in a lower tone, "It doesn't look like Mhairestri's work. Not at all subtle." Turning to Corson, she announced, "Henceforth the palace garrison will be answerable to you in all particulars."

Corson bowed. "As Your Ladyship wishes," she replied.

Nyctasia dismissed everyone but Corson, and barred the door behind them. Greymantle—who was groomed to a gleam and now wore a jeweled collar—she kept with her as a matter of course, having ignored all suggestions that he be sent to the kennels. She crossed to the balcony, but Corson made her wait while she pulled back the curtains and searched behind the tapestried arras for intruders. Then, leaving Greymantle to guard his mistress, she went through the rest of Nyctasia's apartments to see that all was secure. She had never been in rooms so spacious and splendid, lit by great traceried windows, bright with mirrors and crystal candelabra. Ornamental tiles adorned the fireplaces, and their pillars and mantles were carved with vine-leaves and faces and intricate scrollwork. The floors were carpeted, the walls hung with rich draperies, and even the ceilings plastered and painted with elaborate designs. Corson decided that she could best carry out her duties as the Rhaicime's bodyguard if she shared her quarters, instead of withdrawing to the warders' barracks at night. She now had the final word on all matters regarding Nyctasia's safety, after all. She only regretted that she couldn't show Steifann her magnificent lodgings.

"Gods! I've never seen such a bed," she said gleefully, when she returned to the first room. "It's as big as a hayfield. You've room for..." She stopped, but Nyctasia took no notice.

She still stood at the window, just as Corson had left her, gazing out at the ravaged city. To Corson she looked as white and rigid as a figure of marble. Greymantle pawed at her hand and whined.

"Nyc...?" said Corson uneasily. "Eh, Your Nycship, do you hear me?"

And Nyctasia turned to her at last, her eyes as grey as stone, the color of a leaden, sunless sky. "The walls are still standing," she said dully. "Why did I come back here?"

"Asye knows," said Corson, though she saw that Nyctasia did not expect an answer. "Nothing you do makes a rutting bit of sense to me. Maegor said you'd think it your duty to come back."

"My duty as an Edonaris and a Vahnite, yes. But a true Edonaris would not have gone, and a true Vahnite would not have returned. . . . I told Maegor I'd no right to call myself a Vahnite, and now I find I've no desire to call myself an Edonaris. What am I then?"

"You're a maundering half-wit!" Corson shook her, and the gold chain slipped off and struck the floor, where Greymantle sniffed it without interest.

Nyctasia let it lie. "Did you know that the chain of office signifies that the ruler is slave to the people? And that is fitting, for in Rhostshyl only the criminal are bound in service to the city."

"You're mistress of the city, fool—what does the rest matter? Stop carrying on like a stranded fish. I don't like talking to a half-dead hake."

Corson had thought to make her laugh, but instead she suddenly, helplessly, broke into tears. Her throat was torn with harsh, hoarse sobs, as if she did not know how to cry, and found it painful. Corson was bewildered, but relieved as well. She knew that Nyctasia rarely wept, but if she was grieved for her city, why shouldn't she cry, as anyone else would do? It was better than that deathly calm of hers. "At least I know you're alive," she said. "Only the living weep."

Startled, Nyctasia looked up at her through her tears. "What . . . what do you mean by that, Corson?"

"Asye, I don't know! I'm even beginning to sound like you now. Come along and rest—you're tired out, that's all that ails you. You're half-asleep on your feet." She picked Nyctasia up as if she were a child, and carried her into the bedchamber. "What you need's a nursemaid, not a bodyguard."

Nyctasia did not object. "I'd forgotten how exhausting it is to cry, rather like spellcasting," she sighed. "No wonder the Discipline forbids it." When Corson dropped her onto the high, wide bed, she gestured vaguely and mumbled, "boots," then fell at once into a deep, dreamless slumber.

"So now I'm to be your lady's maid as well, am I?" Corson said indignantly, but Nyctasia made no reply. She hardly stirred when Corson pulled off her boots for her, nor even when Greymantle scrambled up onto the bed and lay across her legs.

Corson took advantage of the opportunity to examine the rooms again, this time to satisfy her curiosity. She handled delicate ivory carvings, and toyed with a gameboard with pieces cut from jade and agate. She marveled at a gilded harp half as tall as Nyctasia. She opened chests and coffers and lidded bowls, dis-

covering now clothes, now books, rings or brooches, small clay
bottles or just fragrant dried flower petals. She tried on all the
jewelry she could find, and draped herself with silk scarves and
brocaded sashes. Then for a time she admired herself in a tall
mirror, its wooden frame supported between two slender twin
pillars like young trees.

This kept her amused for an hour, but finally, growing bored,
she left everything strewn about for a chambermaid to tidy away
later, and went to the door to summon a servant. "Her Ladyship's
not to be disturbed," she ordered, "but you can bring me something to eat and drink." She spoke confidently, but she half-expected to be refused, and she was prepared for an argument.
("I'm not to leave the Rhaicime—do you expect her to eat in the
kitchen with me? Do as you're told!")

But instead the man only bowed and said, "Will that be all,
mistress?"

Corson considered. Apparently, as Nyctasia's bodyguard, she
had privileges, and she meant to take full advantage of them. "I'll
have a bath now too," she decided. "Hot water, and plenty of it."
After all, if she was to attend the ruler of the city, she had to be
presentable. And besides, someone *else* would have to fetch in
the water.

When Nyctasia woke, she observed the disarray of the room,
yawned, and said, "I see you've been enjoying yourself. Or possibly a herd of wild swine strayed through here while I was
asleep . . . ?"

Corson grinned. "I think I could learn to like it here. The
servants are obliging, and the food's not bad at all."

"I'm glad you approve of my domestic arrangements. Tell
them I want a bath now, if you would."

"I've already ordered a bath for you, Lady Indolence. Hurry
up, or you'll be late for dinner."

"I can't be late," said Nyctasia, stretching. "They can't start
dinner without me, you see. Let them wait— they'll not go
hungry."

She lingered over her bath, and dressed in somber mourning-
clothes hardly more formal than those she'd worn to receive the
Saetarrin. After some searching, she discovered her chain of office around Greymantle's neck, where Corson had put it for safekeeping. By the time she went down to dinner, with Corson and
Greymantle at her heels, she was as composed and aloof as if

there were nothing whatsoever to distress her in all the city.

The company was indeed waiting for her, milling impatiently about the great hall, where tables had been readied along three walls. Only when Nyctasia took her place at the head of the highest table did the others move to their seats, murmuring greetings which she acknowledged with a nod. Corson stood behind her chair, satisfied that from this vantage point she could see everyone in the hall and watch for any suspicious movement. It was unlikely that an attack would be made on Nyctasia before all these people, but among her many enemies there might well be those crazy enough to try it.

Food was now set before them—platters of small roasted birds, joints of meat, whole baked fish brought live from the coast in barrels of brine—but Nyctasia's relations and guests touched nothing, still waiting for her to begin. She was testing them, Corson realized, deliberately flaunting her power, to remind them that she meant to use it as she chose. Now she only leaned back in her chair and regarded the choice viands with evident distaste. "We are well fed for people of a starving city," she said finally, to no one in particular.

The nobles stirred uneasily, some looking angry, some merely worried. Corson took note especially of those who exchanged furtive words or glances. "This banquet is laid in your honor, cousin," one of the men said, reprovingly, "therefore it behooves you to show the company more courtesy."

Nyctasia smiled graciously. "Forgive me, all, but after what I've seen in the streets of our fair city this day, I've little appetite for a feast. But in the name of courtesy, of course, let the meal commence." She picked up one of the roast birds and tossed it to Greymantle, then sipped from a goblet of water, but took nothing else. If she had told the company to their faces that she considered them no better than animals, the insult could not have been more plain. There was a tense silence, but then a few of Nyctasia's followers began to eat, and the rest soon joined them.

"She has the whip-hand of them now," Corson thought, "and they all know it."

Lord Therisain turned to Nyctasia with a look of triumph. "It is for you to propose the first toast," he reminded her.

"Surely," said Nyctasia. "But it is yet too soon. We are not all assembled."

Again an uncomfortable hush fell on the table. "The Lady

Mhairestri did not feel equal to such an occasion," someone offered hesitantly. "She has been unwell of late."

"Oh, I hardly expected the matriarch to honor us," Nyctasia said smoothly. "No doubt she sent her regrets. But what of Anseldon, and Lhejadis? Are they indisposed as well?"

"I believe they are bearing Mhairestri company," murmured Erikasten.

"How kind of them. But why do I not see my sister Rehal at table?" Nyctasia persisted.

Tiambria answered stiffly, "Rehal is confined to her apartments, under guard. She tried to leave the city secretly with her children."

"I was not aware," Nyctasia said, frowning, "that that was a crime."

"Rehal may go where she pleases, of course," an older woman said sharply. "But you know very well, Nyctasia, that she cannot be allowed to take Emeryc's heir with her."

Nyctasia sipped at her water again. "Not, perhaps, while he lived, Elissa," she agreed. "But once he was killed, his son was surely the next marked for death. I think it showed excellent judgment on her part to seek safety for him. And after all, a city at war is no place for children."

Tiambria shook her head. "No, it was only a fortnight ago that she tried to flee. We held the city, and the children were well protected. It was not our enemies but ourselves that she sought to escape."

"That, above all, shows her good sense," said Nyctasia drily. "Why have I not been told of this?"

"A fortnight ago, we first had certain news of your return—it is you Rehal fears," said Lady Elissa. Someone tried to silence her, but she continued in a furious whisper, "Rehal knows that the child will threaten your power one day, and you know it as well."

Nyctasia looked around the table at the faces of her kin, but most would not meet her eyes. "Oho," she said softly, "and so you have waited to know my wishes? I'm to be a child-killer now . . . ! Perhaps I could sacrifice young Leirven to demons, and so achieve two ends at once. Really, you begin to believe your own fancies about me. Why, if anyone's to murder the boy, look to 'Kasten here. He would stand to inherit Emeryc's title if Leirven were removed from the succession."

Erikasten turned on her with an oath. "You think that I'd—"

"Have you not thought the same of me?" said Nyctasia coldly. She turned to Tiambria. "But if I were to kill someone, surely it would be you, sister. In only a few years Lehannie's title will come to you, and you'll be in a position to challenge my authority. You pose a much more immediate threat to me than Emeryc's heir does."

"I have thought upon that," Tiambria said evenly.

Nyctasia suddenly laughed. "Then you have wronged me, upon my honor. I have other plans for you—not death, but something you'll like far less." Though she sounded amused, Corson did not think she was joking. "And I have plans for my niece and nephew as well," she continued, addressing all of them, but looking at Lady Elissa. "Plans which I shall discuss first with their mother." She stood. "I must go to her at once and attempt to reassure her. She is not to be kept under guard, nor is her son to be forfeit to my ambition. I trust that that is now understood." She made a formal bow to the company. "Friends, family, a good appetite to all."

Corson followed a pace behind her until they were out of sight and hearing of the rest, then fell into step beside her. "Nyc, I thought you had only the one sister," she said, puzzled.

"Yes, Rehal is my brother's widow, my sister by marriage."

"Oh. Well, why hasn't she the right to take her children where she likes?"

Nyctasia sighed. "She has no rights in this household, Corson. She's a commoner, you see. She was only a laborer on one of our estates before Emeryc took a fancy to her."

"Do you mean to say that a brother of yours married a peasant woman!"

"He insisted upon it, in order to legitimize his children by her. She'd been his mistress for some years, but when she bore him a son who could succeed to his title, he wanted to make the boy his heir by law."

"And your family *let* him?"

"On the contrary, they forbade it. But Emeryc was of age, and willful, as we all are. Mhairestri gave way when she saw how determined he was, lest she lose her influence over him by thwarting him in this. And she wanted the children too. We Edonaris aren't as prolific as we once were—folk say that if we didn't bear twins so often, our enemies would soon outnumber us. Mhairestri worries that the dynasty will come to an end within a few generations. She didn't want Rehal, of course, but she reasoned that a mere farm woman could be easily set aside when the time came to establish an advantageous marriage-alliance for Emeryc. It would have been different if he'd sought to make an unsuitable match with a girl of good family, whose kin could demand that her rights be respected. . . ." Nyctasia's voice grew bitter, and Corson knew that she was thinking of her own bond with Erystalben ar'n Shiastred, a bond her family had succeeded in breaking.

"Rehal didn't want the marriage either," Nyctasia continued. "She's no fool—she knew she'd never be accepted at court. But she agreed for her children's sake, so that they could be raised as nobles."

She fell silent as they approached the guarded passage to the widow Rehal's chambers, and Corson dropped behind her again, the patient, impassive bodyguard. Dismissing the sentry, Nyctasia unlocked the door and pushed it open herself.

Rehal was coaxing her little boy to eat his dinner, but at the sight of Nyctasia and Corson she gasped and caught the child up in her arms. "Deirdras, go into the other room, quickly," she whispered to the older child, a girl of perhaps nine years, but her daughter made no move to obey her. Quietly setting down her spoon, she only sat and glared at Nyctasia as if daring her to come farther into the room. Her little brother, alarmed by his mother's fear, began to whimper and wriggle.

"My lady, have mercy," pleaded Rehal. "They're only children! I'll take them away—they will forget that they are Edonaris." Though she spoke to Nyctasia, she stared in terror at Corson, sure that she was there to carry out the sentence of death.

"Corson, wait for me outside," Nyctasia said calmly. "You alarm the Lady Rehal to no purpose. I shan't need you." Corson bowed and withdrew.

Nyctasia shook her head in gentle reproof. "Rehal, sister, you should know me better. I mean no harm to you or your children. You are under my protection here."

Still clutching her son, Rehal sank to her knees, and Greymantle—taking this for an invitation—joined them, wagging his tail and snuffling curiously at Leirven. "Don't be afraid, he won't bite the boy," said Nyctasia, smiling, "and neither shall I, you'll find."

Leirven, having forgotten his fright, was trying to escape his mother's arms and embrace Greymantle. "Want to *play*," he insisted, crowing with delight as the dog licked his face thoroughly, washing off a good deal of the dinner which he had managed to smear over himself.

Nyctasia approached Rehal, offering her hand, to help her to her feet. "I've told you before, my dear, that you're not to kneel to me."

But at this, the other child suddenly shrieked, "Liar! Don't touch him! Don't touch my brother, or I'll kill you!" She seized one of the table knives and threw herself between Nyctasia and the others, holding the knife high, ready to attack.

Nyctasia fell back a pace. "Well! I see I dismissed my body-guard too soon," she said mildly.

"Deirdras, stop that!" cried Rehal. "The Lady Nyctasia will help us—"

"You don't understand, Mother. You're not an Edonaris," said the child scornfully. "She's come to kill Raven, and me too. I know all about her."

"Don't speak to your mother in that way," Nyctasia repri-manded her, "and don't speak of me in that way either, bratling. You know nothing. Why should I kill Leirven? I'd only have Erikasten to deal with then—and he'll come of age much sooner than your brother."

"'Kasten's weak," Deirdras said promptly. "You think you'll be able to control him."

Nyctasia was taken aback. "I see . . . ! And why should I kill you, then? You're not important."

As if repeating a lesson, Deirdras responded, "Because you know I'd avenge my brother. And you're afraid of me—if *you* died, I'd be Rhaicime!"

"Sweet *vahn*, the child is a true Edonaris," sighed Nyctasia. "Come, we'll declare a truce, shall we? Lay down your arms and I shall do the same." She loosed her sword-belt and let her weapons slide from it to the floor, but Deirdras only gripped her knife tighter as Nyctasia took a step toward her. "Very well," said Nyctasia, "look to your guard, then." As she spoke, she flicked the belt toward the girl's face.

Startled, Deirdras struck out wildly, and Nyctasia seized her by the wrist, forcing the knife from her hand. "Let me go!" she shouted, outraged at the trick, but Nyctasia picked her up and kissed her, in spite of her struggles.

"This is no way to greet your aunt," she laughed, holding her close. "I swear I don't want to kill you, Derry, but I might give you a good beating if you don't mend your manners in the future.

A lady is always respectful to her elders." She set the girl on her feet again, holding her firmly by the shoulders. "And you don't know how to wield a knife, either. Always hold it low and strike upward. I'll teach you one day."

Deirdras tried to break free, beating at her with small, fierce fists. "You hate me," she shrilled. "You were my father's enemy, and you're my enemy—Mhairestri told me—"

Nyctasia's face darkened. "I thought as much. The matriarch has taught you well. You've learned to hate the Teiryn, haven't you? And to fear me, and to disdain your mother. Hate and bitterness and pride are all that Mhairestri has learned in her long life, and all that she has to teach." She gripped Deirdras more tightly. "Do you want a life like that for yourself, child? Do you want to be like her? *Do you?*"

Deirdras stared at her, wide-eyed, but to such a question as this she had no answer ready. Her chin began to tremble, and she seemed to grow limp in Nyctasia's grasp.

"I'm sorry," Nyctasia said gently. "I'm not angry with you. You're brave and strong, Derry, and I'm proud of you. I shall rely on you to protect your family, remember." She let the girl go, and Deirdras ran to her mother's lap, sobbing in confusion.

Rehal gathered both children to her, and led them back to the table. "Finish your dinner now," she said, "and let me talk to Her Ladyship. Deirdras, watch your brother." Deirdras began to eat her soup slowly, watching her aunt more than her brother. Leirven was too excited to eat, but he enjoyed feeding most of his dinner to Greymantle.

Nyctasia dropped onto a couch and gestured for Rehal to join her. "I remember now," she said, taking Rehal's hand, "I never could persuade you to address me by name. Rehal, it was Mhairestri who told you I'd have the children killed, was it not?"

Rehal dropped her eyes. "My lady . . . Nyctasia . . . I . . ."

"And warned you not to say so, of course. She saw to it that you were frightened enough to flee, then had you watched and caught when you fled. Oh yes, you may be sure that your capture was her doing. She only needed some such reason to convince the others that the children shouldn't be left to your care. She has no intention of letting them forget that they are Edonaris, I assure you."

The bewildered Rehal had no way of knowing whom to trust. Her husband had been of the matriarch's faction, but she knew that Mhairestri had opposed the marriage—while Nyctasia had been one of the few people at court to show her much kindness. Most had simply taken no notice of her and she had thought to continue being safely ignored, but after Emeryc's death she had learned that she had enemies. She was not afraid for herself, but how could she possibly protect her children? "We should never have come here," she said helplessly. "Please—I only want to take them away. Let us go."

"But that is just what I want you to do, my dear. There *is* danger for them here—not from me or my followers, but from the enemies of the Edonaris. There are still those at large who will seek to destroy them because they are of Edonaris blood, and will one day be among the rightful rulers of Rhostshyl. Until there is true reconciliation in the city, I want the children kept out of harm's way. You're to take them into the Midlands, to an estate in the valley, where I have friends who'll make you welcome." She rose and began to pace back and forth, laying her plans. "It will be best if you tell no one of this, lest you be followed, but I'll send my most trusted people to safeguard you on the way. Will you do this, Rehal?"

For all that Rehal knew, Nyctasia might be sending them to their deaths, but she had no choice save to obey, and both women knew it. "If you think it best, Rhaicime."

"I would do the same if they were my own," Nyctasia said seriously. "I know you mistrust me, and the *vahn* knows I cannot blame you, but think on this, Rehal. . . . You and your children are in my power. If I wished them harm, I could just give my orders and have done with it—there is no one to stop me. Why then should I take the trouble to tell you lies? I've no need to deceive you, and nothing to gain by it, do you see? Their death is no part of my design. They are vital to my plans." She broke off to look over at Deirdras, who was staring solemnly at her over a cup of milk. "Their lives are as precious to me as if they were in truth my own children. I care only for the future of this city, and they are the future of this House. I need them. Why, Deirdras is my heir."

Rehal wanted desperately to believe her. Much of what Nyctasia said made sense, but she ventured to ask a question, feeling that she had to know the worst. "You may have children yourself one day, my lady—what then?"

Nyctasia had made sacrifices of which she rarely spoke. Now she said only, "You forget that I'm a witch, Rehal. My brother's daughter will inherit the Rhaicimate from me." She retrieved her

sword and dagger, and put them on, then kissed Rehal and said,
"I'll leave you now. You are not under guard, but if you wish to
leave the palace, take an escort with you, for the *vahn*'s sake.
The city's not safe, believe me."

She called to Greymantle, and Leirven clambered down from
his stool and followed, dismayed at the prospect of losing his
new friend. "Doggie," he explained earnestly to his mother and
the lady with the shiny gold chain in her hair, "he *likes* him."

"He means that the dog likes him," Deirdras translated shyly.
She stood a little to one side, now, watching Nyctasia warily lest
she should suddenly decide to stab Leirven. When Nyctasia
picked him up, she started forward, alarmed, but the bloodthirsty
Rhaicime only set her little brother astride the great dog, much to
the boy's delight.

Nyctasia winked at Deirdras. "You seem quite agreeable when
you're not threatening one with cutlery," she remarked, then
asked Leirven, "Would you like to live in the country, and learn
to swim, and have a whelp of your own?"

The child considered this seriously. "Big one?" he asked hope-
fully.

"The pick of the litter," said Nyctasia.

Leirven gave a yell and kicked his heels into Greymantle's
sides. "Derdis, look at *me*," he demanded. Greymantle, who was
a patient animal, and used to children, simply settled back on his
haunches and let his rider slide to the floor. Deirdras caught him.

"I wish I could keep them with me," Nyctasia said to Rehal,
her voice filled with longing. "Not long ago, I asked myself why
I had come back to this *vahn*-forsaken city, but when I look upon
them, I remember." She knelt and kissed Leirven. "Goodnight,
little one. Time you were abed."

Deirdras submitted stiffly to her embrace. "Daughter," said
Nyctasia, "this family has another matriarch, and you shall meet
her soon, if all goes well. Learn what you can from her." She
kissed Deirdras quickly and hurried away.

Nyctasia always claimed in later years that she had known,
when she sent her brother's widow to the Edonaris of Vale, that
she was sending them a bride for Raphistain. But if she knew, she
said nothing about it at the time.

23

"UNBIND HIM!" NYCTASIA ordered curtly. "Do you think I cannot defend myself against an unarmed youth? Leave us." The guards obeyed, and Corson too retired, at a nod from Nyctasia.

Lord Jehamias ar'n Teiryn, son of Rhavor ar'n Teiryn, and principal heir of the House of Teiryn, looked around him uncertainly, trying to decide what to do. He ought to attack the Rhaicime, of course, but she could recall her guards in an instant, and she herself was armed with a sword. He could not possibly accomplish anything, except perhaps his own death. Still, he would undoubtedly be killed before long, so perhaps he should try to die heroically. . . .

Nyctasia was sitting at the window, watching him closely. "Don't be a fool," she advised him. "Sit down."

Jehamias sat. He might as well hear what she had to say, though he thought he knew what to expect. If it were merely a matter of his execution, as an enemy of the ruling house, he would not have been brought before the Rhaicime. She did not need to see him to arrange that. It could only be information that she wanted from him, but though he might not be a hero, he was not a traitor either. When she discovered that he wouldn't willingly tell her what she wished to know, she'd surely order other means to be employed. Jehamias sometimes thought that he'd be able to stand up to torture, and at other times he was sure that he couldn't. He'd had more than enough time to think over such things as he sat in his small stone cell and waited to learn what the Edonaris would do with him. Now, at last, he was about to find out.

It seemed to him a long time before Nyctasia spoke again, and then she said only, "You favor your father, Jehame."

Stung at her use of the familiar form of his name, he said angrily, "It ill becomes the victor to taunt the vanquished. I expected better, even from an Edonaris." He was appalled at his own boldness, but then what had he to lose?

Lady Nyctasia looked genuinely surprised. "What do you— oh, I see—but I didn't mean to mock you, upon my word. I took the liberty of addressing you thus because I was a friend of your father's. But of course you didn't know that."

"They say you killed my father."

Nyctasia sighed. "And do you believe that?" she asked with weary disgust.

"I've never known what to believe about you," Jehamias said carefully. "My father always spoke well of you himself, but he was the only one who did. The others all claimed that you'd cursed him—except for my father's servant-boy, Randal. He'd sworn to have vengeance on you and when he disappeared they said you'd killed him too." He shook his head in confusion. "But then he came back and told people that you were innocent after all, or so I heard. Of course he was sent away in disgrace. I was never allowed to listen to his story."

"He was devoted to your father. He tried quite sincerely to kill me, I assure you—he just wasn't very good at that sort of thing. But there were several professional murderers after my blood at that time, and they fared no better, so perhaps it wasn't his fault."

Jehamias half smiled. "My father once said that you were the only Edonaris with a sense of humor."

Nyctasia laughed, but she felt a stab of sorrow for her old friend. "I loved him, Jehame," she said simply. "Here, we'll have a toast to his memory. That would have amused him—I who always warned him against drink. But you look as if you could do with a little wine." She went to the table and filled two small goblets, mixing her own till it was half water.

Jehamias had never in his life wanted a drink as he did then, but he refused the goblet Nyctasia held out to him. She had not touched her own. "Oh, come, use your sense," she said. "If I intended to kill you, you'd have been dead days ago."

It was not poison Jehamias feared, but a drug to loosen his tongue. All the talk of his father must have been meant to put him off his guard. "Why would you let me live?" he countered.

"Does this city need another corpse?" Nyctasia demanded. She sipped from his goblet herself, then offered it to him again. This time he accepted it. "Jehame, you could be very useful to me, alive."

"Why should I be useful to you? If you think I'll betray—"

"Not to me, then," Nyctasia said impatiently. "Not to the House of Edonaris. To Rhostshyl! You can help me to save the city if you choose. Or you can go forth and gather the remnants of the people still loyal to your House, and lead them against me. They'll be killed, of course, probably you'll be killed, most likely more innocent people will be killed, but if that's what you want I'll see that you have the chance. And then I'll destroy you, with a free conscience and clean hands. 'They left me no choice,' I'll declare. 'I offered them peace, but they demanded the sword.' Will that satisfy you?"

Jehamias sat with his head bowed, looking at the floor. "No," he said softly, "I don't want more war in the city. We couldn't win it, I know that, and even if we could, I'd not be the one to declare it. But I will not help you hunt down those of our people who've escaped, or give you the names of those still loyal to us—not even in the name of peace. Nor do I think that you can force me to it." His jaw shook slightly, and he clenched his teeth to hide it.

But Nyctasia merely dismissed his words with a wave of her hand. "Oh, I could, you know," she said indifferently, "if I had any use for such information. But you mistake me, my friend. I have a much crueler fate in store for you. I want you to marry my sister Tiambria."

Jehamias could only stare.

"She's a vixen, I admit, but perhaps time will mellow her temper. Think of it as a sacrifice of your personal peace in the interests of municipal peace," she suggested.

Jehamias found his voice at last. "But—but—" he gasped, "marriage between a Teiryn and an Edonaris! It's impossible, you're mad—"

"You know what they say, Jehame—all the Edonaris are mad, and all the Teiryn are stupid. I may be mad, but I don't think you're stupid. Are you? Are you too stupid to see what such a marriage-alliance could mean? Think of it—true peace, not this worrisome waiting for the next blow to fall, and the next act of vengeance. You'll be head of the House of Teiryn when you come of age, and Tiambria too will serve on the Rhaicimate. If you both declare that our two families are united, who is to withstand you?"

"That's all very well, lady, but nothing would make my elders consent to this, even though it might be the last hope of our House. They'd die rather."

"I know. The Teiryn aren't the only fools in the city. My own kin will oppose the plan just as blindly. The matriarch Mhairestri will never forgive me."

"The Edonaris have the advantage. Surely you can't expect them to give it up?"

"I *demand* that they do so! This is no time to consider the advantage of our House. Only the good of the city matters now. I have the authority to overrule your kin and act on your behalf myself, in the name of the Rhaicimate. Tiambria is already my ward, by law, and the others have no say in the matter. It's your consent that concerns me."

Jehamias looked more wretched than ever. "I *can't*, Rhaicime. It's not that I scorn to wed an Edonaris, but if I did it I'd become an outcast, I'd be nameless, a ghost. . . . My family would disown me, and yours would despise me."

"I know what I ask of you, believe me. I too have been called a traitor. One grows accustomed to it, however."

"Worse, lady, I'd be called a coward. Folk would say I did it only to save my life."

Nyctasia nodded. "You're right, I'm afraid. It will be hard, yes, but duty generally is."

"And if I refuse?"

"Oh, you'll not be put to death—nothing so merciful. If you won't help to save the city, you will have to live to see it die."

"It's true, then, that you mean to issue a general pardon?"

So the rumors had somehow reached even to the prisoners of war. That was well. "There is precedent for it," Nyctasia pointed out, "on occasions of extraordinary celebration—such as this wedding will be." She paused, letting Jehamias realize the weight of his own responsibility. "At the ceremony, you and Tiambria will declare a number of pardons, with my authority, and later—perhaps at the birth of your first child—certain others will be freed. By then perhaps they'll be resigned to the union of our Houses, and at least the affairs of the city will be more settled. Once order has been established it will be more difficult for them to make mischief."

"And so the fate of my kin rests with me," he said, his voice accusing.

Nyctasia shrugged. "Yes, in a way. I'll not tell you that the general pardon will only be granted if you fall in with my plans, but it will take place much sooner if you do. And if you don't . . . then I fear that the pardons will be in vain. Unless a bond is first forged between the ruling families, those who are spared will only turn to the attack again, and be crushed—you know it well. If your kinsmen and their followers were at liberty now, they would seek to avenge themselves on the Edonaris before the day was out. Can you deny it?"

Jehamias couldn't, and didn't try. "But do you believe that this marriage can prevent that?"

"I believe that nothing *else* can prevent it," Nyctasia said slowly. "Mhairestri and her party would solve the problem by killing all of you, and"—she paused in her pacing and fixed Jehamias with her grey gaze—"it may yet come to that. But we can try first to establish a marriage-alliance, a dynasty that shares Edonaris and Teiryn blood. If the next generation of heirs to the Rhaicimate belong to both Houses, there is at least a chance that both Houses will accept their rule."

"And a chance that neither will."

"Yes, curse you! But a chance is better than certain doom. I'm afraid, Jehame. Afraid that if I'm forced to put down a rebellion now the city will be crippled beyond recovery. Let us give Rhostshyl this chance—if it fails, we shall be no worse off than we are. All who are willing to let the past lie will be permitted to take part in the city's future. I know there will be those on both sides who will continue to foster the feud, but I have hopes that they will be too few to prevail, and I shall take no steps against them unless I must. But if they threaten the peace..." She shrugged again. "Perhaps they could be sent into exile, but I expect they'll eventually force me to kill them. Rhostshyl has suffered enough for our families' pride, and I'll have no more of it. You too, Jehamias, may have to condemn your own people for the good of the city. I hide nothing from you. You will be cursed by your kin, as I have been, but one day they will see that you were right, I swear it." Jehamias wiped sweat from his face, but still said nothing. Nyctasia drew a long breath. "And it would have been your father's wish that you do as I bid."

At this he looked up, seeming almost hopeful. "How do you know that?"

"You will not believe me, I daresay, but I was nearly your stepmother. For years I sought to persuade Rhavor to marry me, and at the end he saw that there was no other way. Had he lived, I believe we would have married."

"I do believe you," Jehamias said unsteadily. He was like a man suddenly wakened from sleep. "Do you believe in dreams, lady?"

Nyctasia did not find the question strange. "You've dreamt of your father?"

He nodded. "He said, 'Greet your sister for me. It seems she's to have her way at last.' And he laughed. I have no sister, lady. But if you're to have your way, then that message is for you."

"He laughed at everything," said Nyctasia, smiling.

"He'd have thought it a fine joke to marry an Edonaris. He'd not have cared what the whole city thought of him. Why did he refuse, then?"

"Because he cared what the whole city thought of me. He wished to spare me the sacrifices—and the dangers—that I shall bring upon you, his son, and upon my own sister. And I would spare you both if I could, but there's no time for such scruples now. There is only time to act, and act without hesitation, before it's too late."

Jehamias's sigh was almost a groan. "I wish I had your faith that it is not already too late, my lady."

Nyctasia was sure of him now, but she offered her final argument nevertheless. "You ask if I believe in dreams," she began, "and that is a matter that does not admit of certainty. But I can tell you this: I dreamed of this marriage before the idea had ever occurred to me. I saw a wedding-procession wend through the scarred streets of Rhostshyl, and it seemed to me that Rhavor and I were the newlyweds, though I knew that this could never be. Only long afterward did I begin to see the truth of it. You were the groom I took for Rhavor as a youth; the bride I took for myself as a girl was Tiambria. And, Jehame, wherever they passed, stone walls stood as if they had never fallen, and wooden walls were as if they had never burned."

Jehamias listened, spellbound.

"You understand, then," Nyctasia concluded, "that I will do anything I must, to make that dream a reality. . . . But I needn't threaten you, I think."

"No," said Jehamias, with a rueful grin much like his father's, "you needn't send for the thumbscrews, Rhaicime. I shall be honored to accept the Lady Tiambria's hand, if she'll have me."

"Well, my sister has not yet given her consent, not altogether," Nyctasia admitted. "But she will."

"I won't! Nothing could make me marry a Teiryn! I'll not oppose you over the pardon, 'Tasia, but I'll never agree to *this*, never! Why, it might have been he who killed Emeryc, for all that we know."

"That is not at all likely," Nyctasia said quietly. "Jehamias fought bravely, they say, but by all accounts Emeryc was set upon by several at once. It is of no consequence, however, whether he did or not. War is war. Emeryc would certainly have killed him, given the chance."

"That Emeryc would have killed him hardly seems a reason for me to marry him!"

As Nyctasia had expected, her sister was proving far more difficult to deal with than Jehamias ar'n Teiryn had been. After all, it was in many ways to his advantage to accept the alliance, but Tiambria could only lose prestige by marrying a vanquished enemy. Nyctasia would willingly have locked her in a tower and kept her on crusts and water, had she not known—being an Edonaris herself—that such treatment would only make Tiambria more stubborn. The only way to influence her would be to harness that Edonaris pride in the service of duty.

"This is my own fault, Briar, I suppose," Nyctasia sighed, deliberately using her sister's childhood nickname. "I spoiled you when you were a child. Before Mhairestri turned you against me. You and 'Kasten were always afraid of her, and you still are. You may have defied her to side with me, but you're afraid to break with her completely, aren't you? You know that if you take this step there'll be no appeasing her, no getting back into her favor."

"I see now that I was wrong to defy her at all. But even Mhairestri never dreamed you'd betray your own blood like this. If I'd known, I never would have taken your part."

"Of course not, my dear. That's why I didn't mention it before. But I am head of this family now, and ruler of the Rhaicimate, and it's my displeasure you should fear, not the matriarch's. You'll obey me or suffer the consequences, I warn you."

But Tiambria paid no attention to her threats. "It's past belief that even *you*, 'Tasia, could expect us to enter into kinship with the Teiryn. The very idea's degrading. It's indecent."

"Briar, I am aware that you were raised to regard the Teiryn as a breed of detestable vermin. So was I. But you're no longer a child. You're of an age now to understand that we were taught a great deal of malicious nonsense. The Teiryn line is as old and noble as our own—you may consult the City History if you doubt my word. I grant you that there are fools among them, but every family has its share of fools. And I don't propose to marry you to Lord Ettasuan or to any other who's unworthy of you. Jehamias Rhavor is not only your equal in rank, but your superior in good sense and good breeding. You could do far worse."

Corson was bored with the argument, which she'd heard so often of late that she could recite it almost as well as Nyctasia. She secured the doors, bowed, and went into the next room, where she could at least sit down without committing a breach of court etiquette. She pulled a bench over to the curtained doorway and settled down to wait out the dispute.

Nyctasia had been arguing for days, with everyone from Teiryn prisoners to her own closest allies, but she had so far avoided confronting Tiambria directly, preferring to wait for the girl to come to her. Corson could well understand her reluctance to face Tiambria. If anyone was a match for Nyctasia, will for will and word for word, it was her young sister.

Corson was growing bored even with the luxurious life of the court. She trailed after Nyctasia all day, rarely letting her out of her sight, and regarding nearly everyone as a potential assassin. But except when Ettasuan ar'n Teiryn attacked Nyctasia with his bare hands, there had not been much for Corson to do. She occasionally caught people lurking about the grounds who couldn't account for themselves to her satisfaction, and these, if they were armed, she turned over to the guards. Those who tried to bribe her met with the same fate. She never heard any more about them afterward.

Nyctasia was always hard at work and had little time for Corson, though she was always with her. When she wasn't defending her plans, she was dictating letters, receiving petitioners, settling disputes, or studying reports on the spring sowing or the repairs to the city walls. She often rode into the city to inspect conditions in various quarters for herself, and to see that her orders were being carried out. When Corson tried to persuade her to go to Chiastelm for a few days' rest, she said grimly that there would be no occasion for rest till after the wedding.

The only diversion she allowed herself was to go out now and then with the hunters who scoured the countryside for game, to help feed the city. Hunting was not one of Corson's favorite pastimes, but it made for a change from the court, at least, and she dared not let Nyctasia go without her. She'd not be the first of the nobility to meet with a stray arrow in a hunting accident. Corson insisted that she wear a shirt of fine chain mail beneath her jacket. Nyctasia complained that it hindered her bow-arm, but she brought down her share of game nonetheless.

The hunting-parties had so far been peaceful. Indeed, there had been far less trouble since her return than Nyctasia had anticipated. "People have begun to believe that I bear a charmed life, that I can't be killed," she told Corson, "and that my enemies inevitably perish. It's a most expedient reputation to have. I encourage it." Corson had begun to think about traveling up the coast for a while. She wasn't needed here now.

Greymantle jumped noisily down from the bed and came to join her, nudging her hand with his nose. Corson scratched his head and muttered, "You're restless too, aren't you, Grey? You're no palace lap-dog. You need room to run." Grey laid his head on her knee and dozed contentedly. If he was dissatisfied with court life, he never gave any sign of it.

"You yourself refused to be married against your will!" Corson heard Tiambria shout. "You renounced Thierran, and yet you expect me to marry a Teiryn!"

Corson peered out at them from behind the curtains. The little she-wolf might try to push Nyctasia off the balcony, after all.

"I was willing to marry a Teiryn myself," Nyctasia was saying. "One reason—one among many—that I refused Thierran was that I hoped to establish a marriage-alliance with Lord Rhavor before he died. I failed, but I tell you, you and Jehamias are destined to succeed." Earnestly, she related her dream of the joyous wedding-procession.

But Tiambria was scornful of her visions. "Dreams show us what we wish to see," she said with a sneer.

"Briar, in that dream I saw Emeryc and Lehannie among the dead, with Thierran and Mescrisdan and Brethald. I was far away in the Midlands then. I'd had no news of them." (And in that dream she had seen Erystalben among the living, but of this she did not speak.)

Tiambria frowned. "You're lying."

"No, my dear. If I were lying you'd believe me without question. Rhavor too appeared to me, and said that it was not too late for our marriage-vows. That can mean only one thing."

"Very well then, *you* marry his wretched son."

"That wouldn't do, I'm afraid," Nyctasia said, sounding amused. "Jehamias is an appealing young man, certainly, and no doubt he'd make a pleasing consort. It is I who am unfit for this union, sister. I am barren. This marriage-alliance must provide heirs to both Houses—I believe that the future of the city depends upon it."

"If the future of the city depends upon my bearing brats of Teiryn blood, then let the city perish!" Tiambria cried, and for a moment the two stood face to face, both white with anger, grey eyes blazing. Their features were much alike.

Then Nyctasia turned away to the window, looking just as she had when she'd stood there like a statue on the first evening of her return. "There speaks an Edonaris," she said in a low, harsh tone. "Let our honor be abandoned, let our duty be undone, as long as our name is inviolate, our power unchallenged. Look!" She pulled Tiambria to the window. "Look out there! It was no stray lightning-bolt or careless lamplighter that burned half the city. We did it ourselves. We, who are charged with the welfare of the people."

"No," said Tiambria. "It wasn't our doing. Blame the Teiryn —they began the feud."

"They did, but we sustained it, Briar. We saw what they failed to see, that we were too strong for them, that they would never overthrow us. And so we refused peace whenever it was offered —oh, yes, the city records will bear me out. Your forebears and mine would have no terms of peace. They knew they had the upper hand. They forced the Teiryn to carry on the feud."

"What they did is no fault of mine. Why should I be the one to pay for their pride?"

"All your life you've enjoyed the privileges they won for you, and never questioned your right to them. This war too is your heritage, never doubt it. And were you not of the matriarch's party? Did you not agree when she called for the destruction of the Teiryn?"

"Of the Teiryn, yes! I didn't know it would mean the destruction of so many others, of so much—"

Nyctasia looked almost pitying. "You didn't know? Do you suppose it is of any comfort to the suffering, to the bereaved, that you didn't *know*? Do you think it makes you any the less accountable for your actions? It's time you learned that an Edonaris has obligations as well as rights, and you yourself have much to answer for. Now go! And keep your face from my sight until you're ready to do your duty. I'm ashamed to call you sister!"

Tiambria stood her ground. "You looked exactly like Mhairestri when you said that," she spat.

Nyctasia's hand flew up to slap her, and she was prevented

only by the sudden realization that this was precisely what Mhairestri would have done. Meeting Tiambria's defiant stare, she slowly lowered her arm, saying, "And you, my dear, look very like Deirdras just now. Send for your cloak—you're to come for a short ride with me. The view from the palace windows is none too clear."

Corson rejoined them at once, frowning to herself. Though a change was always welcome, she considered Nyctasia's visits to the heart of the city as an unnecessary risk. The Lady Tiambria too would be a target for the enemies of the Edonaris. They'd have to bring extra guards, and that would make them even more conspicuous. Nyctasia usually knew what she was doing, Corson thought, but since she'd returned to Rhostshyl she'd seemed to be courting danger. And if she cared nothing for her own life, no bodyguard could defend her.

They left the palace compound by a back gate, accompanied by two other guards and a groom, with Corson bringing up the rear as she watched to make certain that they weren't followed. The farther they rode from the palace, the poorer and more crowded the streets became. Some folk scattered at the sight of armed guards, but most had lost fear along with hope, and only stopped to stare at the riders, bowing as they passed. Few seemed to have any idea who they were.

At the mouth of a narrow alley, they left their horses with the groom, and he handed Nyctasia the heavy satchel he carried. The houses in this quarter had been gutted by fire, and the smell of charred timber was still thick in the air. As Nyctasia led the way through the litter of refuse and debris, Tiambria saw to her astonishment that there were people still living in these wretched, half-fallen dwellings.

Here Nyctasia was known, and when news of her arrival spread she was quickly surrounded by a knot of the city's most destitute and desperate. They dared not press close to the Lady Tiambria, but she had a far better look at Rhostshyl's poorest than she was accustomed to. A ragged beggar-child grasped at Nyctasia's sleeve, and she took his hand, stepping aside to let Tiambria see him. "Explain to this one that you didn't know what war would bring," she murmured. Half the child's face was hideously scarred by fire, one eye sealed shut forever. Tiambria turned away, sickened at the sight. "Perhaps we should take him back with us, make a page of him," Nyctasia suggested, "and have him before our eyes every day, lest we forget what we now know." Tiambria made no reply.

They visited several of the ruined houses, where people lay on the floor, injured or sick, and hungry children huddled in corners. Tiambria watched, silent, as Nyctasia changed the dressings on wounds and treated savage burns with salves and unguents. At each place she left medicines or bandages, money to buy food or to pay the gravediggers. Finally Tiambria too stripped off her costly rings and bracelets and gave them to those who appealed to her for alms. She spread her cloak over a woman who lay shivering with fever and whispering wordlessly to herself.

Nyctasia said nothing more to her for some time, and only when they were ready to depart did she seem to remember her sister's presence. "Do you know, it's the strangest thing, Briar," she remarked, "but none of these folk has ever asked me, 'Why should I be the one to pay?'"

"But . . . even if I marry the heir of the Teiryn, 'Tasia"—it was the first time she had admitted the possibility—"it won't undo the harm that's been done."

"No, but you'll have done your part to see that it doesn't happen again. That's all you can do, now, and it's little enough to ask of you. You can never pay what you owe."

"I hate you," Tiambria whispered, her voice choking.

Nyctasia gave her a tired smile. "I love you," she said.

24

NYCTASIA HAD SENT her respects to the Lady Mhairestri as soon as she first arrived in Rhostshyl, but she had received no reply and had not expected one. But when the day appointed for the wedding was only a fortnight away, she was suddenly summoned to present herself to the matriarch.

It was evening, and Nyctasia had already retired to her apartments, with only Corson and Greymantle in attendance. Corson was practicing her penmanship by writing a long letter to Steifann about the opulence of the court and the importance of her own position. When she stopped to rest her hand, she listened with pleasure as Nyctasia played the gilded harp and sang an old ballad. Nyctasia had been more at her ease of late, since preparations for the wedding ceremony had been set under way, and Corson had found her better company.

But when she had dismissed Mhairestri's messenger, she leaned her head on her hands and said resignedly, "I might have known that matters were progressing too smoothly. I taunted Tiambria for her fear of Mhairestri, but in truth I still fear her myself. Well, it won't do to keep her waiting. You may as well stay here, Corson. I can't appear before the matriarch with an armed escort."

"Why not?"

"It wouldn't be respectful. It would look as though I didn't trust her."

"You *don't* trust her," Corson pointed out. "She's tried to have you killed before."

"Oh, of course everyone knows that I don't trust her, but you see, it would be discourteous of me to *show* it. Don't worry, she'd not send for me in order to make an attempt on my life. She wouldn't put me on my guard first."

"Discourteous! I should have thought it more discourteous to try to have people murdered," Corson rejoined. "Take Greymantle with you at least."

* * *

There was nothing welcoming in the matriarch's manner when she received Nyctasia. She remained as straight and stiff as the hard, narrow chair she sat in, and no word or gesture of hers acknowledged Nyctasia's presence.

Nyctasia dropped to one knee before her, in the proper attitude of formal humility, and reverently kissed her hand. "Madame," she said, "you do me honor. I hope I find you well."

The old woman pushed her away, looking down at her coldly. "So you have come to complete the destruction of this House, Nyctasia Selescq."

Nyctasia stood, but remained facing the Lady Mhairestri. "I am sorry that I cannot please you, Madame, but I will allow no further bloodshed in this city, not Teiryn blood, nor that of the innocent. There is nothing to be gained."

"No, to you our name is nothing!"

"It will be to the honor of our name to show mercy to a fallen enemy, to allow peace to return to the city."

"Peace! Can you not see that the only way to bring peace to Rhostshyl is to destroy the enemy while they are in our power? If the Teiryn are not crushed nòw, they will rise against us again, and more will die on both sides."

Nyctasia was silent. It was the one argument which held any weight with her. Mhairestri pressed her advantage, becoming persuasive, almost cajoling. Nyctasia was struck afresh by her resemblance to the Lady Nocharis. "I've lived long . . . long, Nyctasia . . . and I know that some things never change. I've seen your kind before. You are young, you believe that things which have never happened before may yet come to pass at your bidding, that words may do the work of swords, that two bulls may graze in one field. It must be so because you would have it so." She shook her head, unassailable in her certainty. "I tell you, *one* house must rule. As long as there are two, war will be inevitable."

Nyctasia leaned against the mantle, her hands pressed to her temples. "I am no longer so young," she said. "I know that you may be right—that is my greatest fear." (*Only remember that you are a healer.*) "But the future is always uncertain. I will not murder the survivors of this battle to prevent an uprising that may never come. I cannot." (*Let nothing persuade you to forget that.*)

"Then do not speak to me of the welfare of the city! It is the welfare of your own spirit that concerns you."

"Perhaps," said Nyctasia, more to herself than to Mhairestri, "but if that were so, why would I have returned here?"

"You are weak, weak! Now, when this house needs a strong hand to guide it! Fool, ah—" the old woman leaned back in her chair, breathless, weak with passion, and there was a long silence in the chamber. "That I should live to see the end of this family . . . !" she said at last.

"I mean to unite the family—"

"Traitor! You mean to unite the family to our enemies!"

"You have said that one house must rule—very well, I shall make one house of the two. And, Mhairestri, I believe that that house will be the House of Edonaris. The Teiryn will become part of us—we shall devour them as surely as the she-spider devours her mate. Edonaris blood will tell, you know it is so. And I—I have reason to believe that many generations will not suffice to change that. If we continue to intermarry with the Teiryn, in time there will be no Teiryn."

"And no Edonaris! You will have us a bastard breed, our line polluted by Teiryn blood, all so that you may say you were not guilty of shedding that blood. You have ever been a dreamer, a madwoman. It is useless to reason with you."

"Certainly this discussion is useless, Madame," said Nyctasia, her courtesy unwavering. "I weary you to no purpose. I shall take my leave of you, with your permission."

The matriarch pierced her with an angry stare. "Do you love your House, Nyctasia Selescq?"

Nyctasia hesitated. "I love this city."

"Answer me!"

It was pointless to lie. "I do not, Madame. I did once."

"Get out of my sight," said Mhairestri with surprising calm.

Nyctasia made one final effort, though she felt little hope of success. "Mhairestri—Mother—" she pleaded. "You must love this House for both of us. I know that you want what is best for the Edonaris, as I want what is best for Rhostshyl, but the family and the city cannot be divided—surely our wishes must often be the same. Would it not be to the benefit of both if we should at least appear to be unified? Only let me report that you withhold judgment on my plans, not that you approve or support them, but at least—that way—"

"I see. Thus, it shall not appear that I was simply powerless to prevent you. My dignity will be spared," Mhairestri said disdainfully.

Nyctasia spread her hands. "Yes," she admitted. "And if I succeed in bringing about a truce, you will be honored for your

farsightedness. If I fail, you have reserved the right to condemn
my actions. Only permit me . . ." her voice trailed off to silence
as she regarded the matriarch's face.

The old woman gripped the arms of her chair. "You are Rhaicime," she hissed. "Do as you will—but not with my blessing! If
I cannot save the honor of this House, I must look to my own. I
have told you once to leave me—go! Get out! Get out of here!"

Nyctasia bowed low and said, "Give you a good night, Madame." She backed out the door without once turning her back to
the Lady Mhairestri, a mark of respect usually reserved for roy-
alty, and requiring considerable skill to perform with grace.

Corson sat on the edge of the bed, brushing her hair, and
wishing she had the courage to summon one of Nyctasia's maids
to brush it for her. Most of the servants accepted Corson as a
person of some authority, but the lady's maids clearly thought it
unsuitable that an ill-bred mercenary should share their mistress's
chambers. They seemed to regard Corson and Greymantle's presence there with equal disfavor, and behaved as far as possible as
if neither of them existed.

Nyctasia had explained that a few of them were Mhairestri's
spies, and others simply jealous that a mere guard was on terms
of greater intimacy with the Rhaicime than they were themselves.
Indeed, they might well feel slighted, for Nyctasia demanded
little attendance, and rather neglected them. She preferred pri-
vacy to being waited upon; she rarely wore clothes that were
difficult to put on or take off unassisted, and her close-cropped
hair required little attention.

"I need a maid more than she does," Corson thought, "but I
don't suppose the haughty little chits would lower themselves to
wait on me. Nyc would brush my hair for me, but not her rutting
proud maids-in-waiting. . . ."

Corson brooded on the paradox of the aristocracy, then
yawned and lay back on the bed, stretching. She removed her
leather vest and chain mail and tossed them on the floor, leaving
only her comfortable loose linen shirt.

But not until Nyctasia came in and barred the door behind her
did Corson take off her sword-belt. She hung it carefully over the
head-board of the bed, where her weapons would be near at hand
should she need them in the night. "Nyc," she said, "if I told one
of your lady's maids to brush my hair, would she?"

"Yes, I believe so. They'll ignore you if they can, but they'd be afraid to offend you outright, because they think I make a favorite of you. But I'd rather you didn't call for a maid just yet. I don't want any of my people to see that Mhairestri's upset me." Nyctasia found Corson a welcome sight, lolling lazily on the bed with her long hair flowing about her. She looked warm and inviting after the company of the harsh, forbidding Lady Mhairestri. Nyctasia was drawn to her as to a comforting hearthfire on an icy winter night.

"You do look like a hind harried by hounds," Corson observed. "What did the revered matriarch do to you?"

"Nothing—yet. But she means to do something soon, and I don't know what. Now I'll not sleep tonight for thinking about it."

"Ah, I've told you time and again, you think too much. And stop that pacing, you make me giddy." She reached out her long legs and caught Nyctasia between them. "If I can't have a lady's maid, you'll have to do. Here, you can take off my boots for a change."

"Is that any way for a common swordswoman to address a Rhaicime?" Nyctasia chided, but she obeyed, kneeling before Corson as she had before Mhairestri, and tugging at her heavy boots.

Corson grinned down at her. "If you don't like my manners, you can get yourself another bodyguard," she suggested.

Nyctasia sat back on her heels and regarded her with a wry smile. "I should," she agreed, "but where would I find another so fetching? Raphe called you the Goddess of Danger and Desire."

"Mmm, he did?" Corson said appreciatively. She'd be sure to tell Steifann that. "That one knew something about lovemaking —did you ever have him?"

Nyctasia laughed and shook her head. "We couldn't, Raphe and I. We'd flirt, but—well, he looked so like my brothers . . . and of course he couldn't see me without thinking of 'Deisha. It was impossible."

"Well, in the dark what's the difference? You should have kept your eyes closed. When Raphe stops talking, he's very fine indeed. On my oath, you Edonaris can talk till the stars fall." She nudged Nyctasia with one foot. "I'll wager the *true* hindrance twixt you and Raphe was that neither of you could keep quiet long enough to—no! Stop that, you—"

Nyctasia had grabbed Corson's ankle, and was mercilessly tickling the sole of her foot. Corson, who was unbearably ticklish, writhed and cursed, pummeling Nyctasia with her free foot, and laughing helplessly. "Grey," Nyctasia called, "you're not to let people kick me! Help!" Greymantle barked and wagged his tail helpfully. Nyctasia surrendered, released Corson's ankle, and fell over on the floor, holding her side and groaning dramatically. "Half my ribs are broken," she complained. "I could have you hanged for treason."

"Yes, and you probably would too, nasty little bitch," Corson grumbled, rubbing her tingling foot. "That's the thanks I get for saving your life—first I'm tickled, then executed!" Both women started to giggle. "Next time someone tries to assassinate you, you ungrateful wretch, I'll—"

"That—ooph—reminds me," said Nyctasia, sitting up. "Corson, how would you like to be a Desthene?"

Corson forgot what she was saying. She's done it again, she thought. Nyctasia's gifts always took her by surprise. But, a *title*? Was it possible?

". . . was originally a military rank, you know," Nyctasia was explaining, "so it seems most appropriate for you. It meant 'commander,' or something of that sort. You'd not get the proceeds of the estate, mind you—not for some years, at least. The deaths in the city have left me with a number of titles at my disposal, but all those who receive them will have to agree to turn the revenues over to the City Treasury until Rhostshyl has returned to its former prosperity. But you'd be entitled to style yourself 'lady,' and have lodgings befitting a noblewoman whenever you're at court, and there are some other minor prerogatives. What say you?"

"Nyc, do you mean it? Can you give a title to anyone you choose? I thought the other nobles had to agree. They'd never accept the likes of me among them."

"I couldn't legitimately ennoble anyone I wished, no, not on a mere whim. But you have shown yourself worthy of the distinction, you see, in accordance with established custom. You've performed noble deeds—heroic deeds—in the defense of the Rhaicimate, and it is no more than my duty to reward such service as it deserves. Corson, I *am* the Rhaicimate, and you've saved my life more than once—before the whole city, on one occasion. My peers may think it extravagant of me to invest you with a title, but they cannot deny that I am well within my rights to do so." She smiled at Corson's obvious delight. Kneeling before her again, she took both Corson's hands between her own. "Corson, my valorous and faithful servant," she recited, "do you accept the authority, appurtenances, dues, duties, obligations, rights and perquisites pertaining to the dignity of the Desthenate of the City of Rhostshyl?"

Laughing, Corson seized Nyctasia by the wrists, pulled her up onto the bed and kissed her ardently, holding her in a crushing embrace. "Will there be a ceremony?" she demanded.

Nyctasia settled comfortably against her, pillowing her head on Corson's shoulder and stroking her thick, tawny hair. "Indeed, yes. As part of the wedding celebration, I'll be conferring pardons on my enemies and titles on my allies. You'll be one of many honored."

"Can I invite Steifann to see it?"

"You may invite anyone you like," Nyctasia promised. "Even the odious Trask."

Corson chuckled. "They won't believe it—*me*, a lady of title and influence, just like that fortuneteller predicted, the night I first met you." Nyctasia's doublet soon joined Corson's vest on the floor. "I *did* give you a bruise!" Corson exclaimed. "What delicate skin you must have."

Nyctasia smiled. "But you know I heal quickly, love."

Corson gently kissed the dark mark below Nyctasia's breast. "Sorry," she said contritely.

"Oh, all right, I won't have you hanged," Nyctasia teased, nuzzling her neck. "It *would* be a shame, when milady has such a lovely throat." She continued to caress Corson's hair, letting her fingers follow its long waves to where they spilled over her ripe, full breasts.

Corson drew Nyctasia's hand beneath her open shirt. "Lady Corson," she murmured contentedly.

Nyctasia raised her head and kissed Corson lightly on the lips. "Lady Corisonde," she corrected, kissing her again. "For the occasion of the formal investiture, we'll use the Old Eswraine form. You'll be the Lady Corisonde"—another kiss, soft and clinging—"Desthene li'Rhostshyl"—a harder kiss, now— "brenn Torisk."

"I like the sound of that," Corson whispered. "Tell it to me again." She took Nyctasia by the hips and pressed her closer, kneading her thighs.

Nyctasia had no difficulty falling asleep that night, after all.

In the morning she was wakened with the news that the matriarch Mhairestri had died during the night, after taking poison.

25

NYCTASIA BREAKFASTED ALONE with Corson, having given orders that no one else was to be told of Lady Mhairestri's death. "Curse her! She did it so that folk would say I'd poisoned her," she told Corson.

"Did you?" Corson asked, tossing a piece of cheese to Greymantle.

Nyctasia half smiled, and shook her head. "No. I'd have waited till after the wedding, you see. She thinks—thought—that I'd have to postpone the festivities, in order to observe the traditional period of mourning. But I'll not play her game. This is no time to respect the proprieties." She rose and began to pace about, chewing a honey-roll and frowning. "The wedding will be held sooner instead," she decided, gesturing with the pastry as she spoke. "It shall take place in a week's time, before news of Mhairestri's death has had a chance to spread. There will be a grand state funeral some days afterward, and I shall declare that it was the matriarch's dying wish that it be so."

"Will anyone believe that?" Corson asked doubtfully.

"Certainly not. But it will show a certain courtesy to her memory, to say it." Nyctasia sat down again, and went on with her breakfast quite calmly. "She will not stand in the way of my dream, Corson. She cannot. Her too I saw among the dead."

The days passed quickly with the hurried preparations for the wedding celebration. Corson was fitted for an elegant gown, and trained assiduously for her part in the ceremony of investiture. She would have to descend a staircase and cross the great hall with all eyes upon her, then perform an elaborate obeisance before the assembled nobles and kneel to receive Nyctasia's formal commendation.

"It's only a few phrases of Old Eswraine, meaning that you're exceedingly brave and loyal and worthy," Nyctasia explained. "Then I shall take your hand and raise you up, and all the rest of it, and you've only to stand aside and wait. It's really very simple."

Corson was beginning to have serious misgivings about the whole affair. "But I *can't* walk down stairs wearing that dress, Nyc," she said desperately. "Or kneel! I can't even *move*. The bodice is so tight I can't bend, and the hem falls all over my feet, and the *train*—it's worse than full armor! I'll make a fool of myself."

"Nonsense," Nyctasia said soothingly, "the gown fits perfectly, and you look magnificent in it. You'll be the most admired person in the company."

This appeal to Corson's vanity had its effect, but she still sought further reassurance. "It looks well enough, if I stand still and don't stir a muscle, but if I move one arm I'll tear it to shreds."

"There will be no occasion for you to swing a sword. You're to hold your hands so, and keep your back straight, just as I showed you. You've plenty of time to practice, if you like, but you already do the curtsey beautifully, Corson. I've seen you."

"Oh yes, in an old robe, in front of the mirror. But before a lot of strangers, in that miserable gown! I'll fall on my—"

"You'll do nothing of the sort," Nyctasia said firmly. "You've only to put one foot before the other, and the whole ordeal will be over in a moment. I know that court ceremony is strange to you, but you've nothing whatever to fear." She chose her words deliberately. "Still, if you truly feel unequal to it . . ."

As ever, Corson's resolve stiffened at the suggestion that she was afraid. "It's not that," she grumbled. "It's your position I'm thinking of. You said you must command the respect of those about you, but if I don't acquit myself well, your people will find fault with you for trying to make a lady of a lout." She shrugged. "If you don't care for appearances, I surely don't. You've only yourself to blame if I disgrace you. And I'll kill anyone who laughs at me, so I warn you!"

"Fortunately, no one would be so ill-bred as to laugh. And a lady, Corson, would simply take no notice if they did. It would be a mistake to dignify such behavior with death."

"I'll try to remember that. Well, and what then—after I fall at your feet and you pick me up?"

"Very little, since you'll be the last. The trumpets will sound, and everyone will come flocking to be presented to you. They'll kiss your hand and congratulate you and bow, but you needn't curtsey."

Corson immediately forgot her bravado. "But what am I to say to them?" she wailed.

"Just thank them politely," Nyctasia said patiently. "Do stop fretting. If you remember that you're a lady and as good as any of them, they'll be charmed by anything you say, I promise you."

Corson nodded thoughtfully. "It's true that folk already treat me differently here. The lady's maids are as respectful as you please. And even Lady Elissa deigned to address me directly today."

"Did she now! What did she want of you?"

"Your brat sister'd told her about the sights of the city you showed her, and Her Ladyship asked me whether you'd visited other parts of Rhostshyl as well."

"Oho. And did you tell her the truth?"

Corson looked pleased with herself. "Well, I exaggerated a bit, perhaps. I said there was no part of Rhostshyl where you weren't well known. Then I told her, 'If she should be overthrown, half the people of the city would rise up and storm the palace.'"

Nyctasia hugged her, laughing. "My dear Corson, you haven't a thing to worry about. A courtier born and bred couldn't have answered her better."

"Is that what they do, then—spread rumors?"

"That, and carry tales. Upon my word, you do learn quickly, Corson."

"Corisonde, you mean," said Corson, with a grin.

EPILOGUE

ONCE AGAIN A messenger had arrived at The Jugged Hare with a letter from Corson, and as usual Steifann did not regard its contents as the exact unvarnished truth. In fact, he believed very little of it, and it was only with difficulty that the courier succeeded in convincing him that he and his people were indeed invited to witness the investiture of Corson brenn Torisk with the title and rank of Desthene, at the court of the Edonaris in Rhostshyl, upon the occasion of the solemnities attending the marriage-alliance between the noble Houses of Edonaris and Teiryn.

And Steifann still found it hard to believe, a few days later, when he stood in the great hall of the palace among the distinguished citizenry and aristocracy of Rhostshyl, watching Corson's pert little friend Nyc confer honors and dignities upon those who knelt before her. She had somehow taken on the manner and mien of an empress, and it seemed impossible that she could ever have been a familiar visitor at his own tavern. Steifann felt that he must have dreamed it all, and that he was dreaming still.

He had always before refused to leave the Hare for more than a day, no matter how Corson had urged him to go off with her somewhere. This jaunt would take nearly a week in all, but it was not one of Corson's fool escapades, after all. This was an important event that would never come again. How could he fail her at such a time? In the end, he had determined not only to go but to do the thing handsomely—this once, he would close the Hare and give everyone a rest, to celebrate Corson's good fortune. Walden had declined to join him, but Annin had accepted, curious to see the pageantry. And Trask had given him no peace till he'd agreed to take him along as well.

Everything had been arranged for them, at Nyctasia's personal order. Her courier had escorted them to Rhostshyl, and seen to their lodgings. A page was assigned to look after their needs and serve as their guide at court. They had even been provided with suitable clothes for the occasion. But Steifann felt out of place and awkward nevertheless. He was uncomfortable with his fine, stiff new clothes and with the refined, stiff courtesy of those around him. He was too tall to go unnoticed in any crowd, and he was sure that these elegant gentlefolk were all staring at him, calling him a clumsy, mannerless oaf. And why hadn't he had any sign from Corson since he'd arrived in Rhostshyl? When wine was offered to the company, Steifann partook of it very freely, and often.

Annin was indifferent to the behavior or the opinions of her fellow guests, but now that her curiosity had been satisfied she was beginning to grow bored with the spectacle. She wished that Nyc would get *on* with it, for the Hlann's sake, so that she could be off to keep an assignation she'd made with a handsome steward for a tryst when the morning's festivities were over. "It's a shame Corson's the last," she complained. "We'll have to wait through the whole lot, to see her."

"It's a place of honor," Trask informed her, with the air of one who had long been thoroughly familiar with court procedure. He was already learning to mimic the manners of the nobles around him, and he felt neither uneasy nor restless in their society. He had exhausted Nyctasia's page with his questions, then patronizingly promised to commend him to the Rhaicime, who, he explained, was an intimate friend of his household. The bewildered page had no idea what to make of Trask and his companions. They were clearly common working people, yet they were here as guests of the Lady Nyctasia herself, and they referred to her as "Nyc," speaking of her with the most shocking familiarity. It would seem that at least some of the strange stories about the Rhaicime must be true. . . .

Corson would have been on hand to welcome Steifann herself had she not been a prisoner, all that morning, of a formidable array of maids and seamstresses who were intent on making scores of final preparations to her apparel and her person. Corson was bathed, scented, powdered and fussed over endlessly before she was permitted to dress in the precious gown of brittle cloth-of-gold and ivory lace. Her hair alone took hours to wash and arrange to her handmaids' satisfaction. Corson would have braided it and pinned it up, but instead they somehow gathered much of it into an intricate net of pearls at the back of her head, and let the rest fall over her back, entwined with long skeins and loops of pearls. Another fillet of pearls circled her brow, and strands of them adorned her gown as well, fastened at each shoulder with an ivory clasp and falling gracefully across her breast just above the low-cut bodice.

Corson had been draped in layers of frothy undergarments that made the skirts of her gown stand out stiffly around her, like the wings of a golden pavilion. Then the long, trailing sleeves were stitched into place at last, making Corson feel more than ever like a ship in full rigging, becalmed by dead seas. She could not be expected to carry herself down a flight of stairs, not like this! It was impossible. It must be some mistake.

But then it was time to present herself to the assembly waiting in the hall below.

Nyctasia had anticipated the sensation Corson's appearance would make on the company, and she was not disappointed. Those who had disapproved of her raising her bodyguard to the rank of Desthene would never again question her judgment, she thought with satisfaction.

The sun was high in the sky, filling the tall windows with light, and Corson was bathed in a golden radiance as she began very slowly to descend the marble staircase. Her bearing was straight and graceful, her beauty undimmed by the splendor of her garments. She seemed to drift down the steps, holding up her billowing skirts slightly before her, with her long hands bent elegantly at the wrist, exactly as she'd been taught.

"The Lady Corisonde Desthene li'Rhostshyl brenn Torisk," announced the herald.

An absolute silence fell on the hall at first, but it gave way almost at once to an excited murmur of admiration and speculation. Few of those present recognized this statuesque beauty as the sullen, suspicious guard who had been following Nyctasia for weeks like a grim shadow. Even Trask forgot himself so far as to clutch Steifann's sleeve and gasp, "Asye's teeth! Look at Corson!"

"Don't be an idiot," said Steifann. "That's not—"

But, to his horror, it was.

Steifann had expected Corson to be preened and prettified for the celebration, in a fancy dress, but he had not been prepared to see her looking not only so breathtakingly beautiful, but so cold, so distant, so regal. . . . She seemed to belong in this palace with its noble lords and ladies, not in an ale-house with a common taverner. He'd laughed at her when she'd insisted, "I could better myself if I chose!" But now she seemed to have chosen, and chosen the life of a lady, and a stranger. When she passed almost within arm's reach of where he stood, she did not so much as spare him a glance, but glided past him like a proud young queen. Steifann felt as if he'd been kicked in the chest by a horse and forgotten to fall.

It was not pride of place, however, that lent Corson this air of majestic dignity—it was simply that she was rigid with terror. Fear of snarling her feet in her heavy hem made her move with a measured, stately tread, and dread of tearing the seams of her tight bodice kept her back stiff and unyielding. She held her head high and perfectly still, not daring to look to the left or right lest the pearls fall from her hair and clatter to the floor. Unthinking, unseeing, almost numb, Corson moved through the great hall like a puppet on strings, keeping her eyes fixed strictly on Nyctasia, in hopes that she could thus somehow cross the immeasurable distance between them and reach her without mishap. When she found herself kneeling at last before the dais where Nyctasia stood, she could hardly remember how she'd come there, and she was not at all sure whether she'd just performed her ritual curtsey or forgotten it entirely. But she must surely have done it, for Nyctasia was smiling as she took her by the hand and bade her rise.

Nyctasia had finally abandoned her mourning-clothes, and now wore a velvet doublet of purest white, crossed with a gold sash from shoulder to hip, and fitted with golden trimmings. Her hose were of a spotless white as well, and her boots of white kid with golden buckles. A cape of white ermine was fastened at her throat with a golden clasp, and she was crowned, as usual, with her heavy gold chain of office.

"I shall look as sallow as a stirred egg," she had complained to Corson, at the last fitting of these dazzling garments. "But vanity must be sacrificed to tradition on such an occasion, I suppose."

And certainly she did look even more starkly pale than usual, but she tipped a wink at Corson as she took the golden medallion and chain from a white velvet cushion held by a page in white silk. After kissing Corson ceremoniously on both cheeks, Nyctasia slipped the medallion around her neck, whispering in her ear as she did so, "Now aren't you glad you didn't kill me?"

Corson blushed and bit back a laugh, remembering when Nyctasia had first asked her that question. But then trumpets were sounding, and she realized suddenly that the formalities were over. She had done her part. She was a lady, a Desthene . . . ! In a

moment she was surrounded by a throng of well-wishers and
flattering courtiers, all lavishing extravagant compliments and
congratulations upon her. If *this* was what it was like to be a lady,
Corson thought, she would be well able to bear the burden.

Seeing Corson receiving the attentions of the nobility with
seeming ease, Steifann felt more desolate and heartsick than before. He couldn't get near her through the crowd that pressed
around her; Annin had disappeared, and Trask was busy explaining to someone how very well indeed he knew the Lady Corisonde. Steifann went in search of more wine, and found a great
deal of it. By the time Corson had escaped from the circle of her
admirers and sought him out, he was drunker than she'd ever
seen him.

Trask and the page between them had managed to convey him
to a small, empty antechamber, where they left him sprawled on
a couch, senseless and snoring. When they led Corson to him an
hour later, he hadn't moved a muscle.

She shook him indignantly. "Steifann, you rutting pig—where
have you been? You're the only one I wanted to see, you bastard,
and I couldn't even find you! You could have stayed in Chiastelm
to get drunk and sleep all morning!"

Steifann opened his eyes on a vision of a golden goddess
bending over him and cursing at him in a decidedly unladylike
tone. "Corson," he said thickly, "thank the Hlann—!"

Reaching for her, he tried to rise, misjudged the whereabouts
of the floor, and fell heavily against her, nearly knocking her
over.

Corson pushed him off. "Let go, curse you! You'll tear the
sleeve."

Steifann sank to his knees and embraced her clumsily.
"You're so rutting beautiful, Corson," he said brokenly, almost
sobbing.

Corson's resentment suddenly lost much of its force. Steifann
had never said anything of the sort to her before, and his rather
inelegant compliment was more welcome than all the polished
praises of the courtiers. But she didn't mean to let him off so
easily as that. Not yet. "Well, why didn't you come to congratulate me, eh?" she demanded, giving a spiteful tug at his hair.
"Everyone else did, and they don't even know me. *They* weren't
off somewhere getting stinking drunk while their friends were
being presented at court."

But Steifann wasn't listening to her tirade. "Every time you go away, I'm so afraid you won't come back," he mumbled, burying his face in her skirts. ". . . so afraid . . . I thought I'd lost you to those lordly folk. You're my treasure, Corson, you're my jewel . . ."

Corson's bodice seemed somehow to have grown even tighter. Her heart was so filled with joy and gratitude that for a moment she couldn't breathe or speak. Steifann would probably deny it all when he was sober, she thought, but she would remember every single word. Forgetting to be careful of her costly gown, she leaned down and helped Steifann to his feet. "Up you get, you sotted swine," she said cheerfully. "You can't lie about here all day—it wouldn't be seemly. You smell like you fell into the wine-press at harvest time."

Steifann looked around the unfamiliar room, which seemed to be turning and moving away from him. "Where are we?" he asked suspiciously, swaying.

"Asye—!" Corson held him around the waist and pulled his arm over her shoulders. "You're worse than Nyc when she was drunk in Hlasven, and tried to raise a demon. And you're a deal heavier, that's certain. Come along, then, we'll take the back stairs. I've rooms of my own here now—you'd not believe how grand."

Steifann leaned against her all the way, keeping his eyes closed much of the time, because of the unpleasant way the stairs were shifting. He trod on Corson's train several times, nearly tripping her, but somehow she dragged him up the narrow stairway and reached her own bedchamber with only one strand of pearls broken. "Look!" she said proudly. "All this space just for me. I have plenty of room for you. Did you ever see such a bed? Nyc's is even bigger."

Steifann muttered something disrespectful about Nyctasia's personal habits, adding sanctimoniously that everyone knew the aristocracy were nothing but a pack of brazen wantons and whore-mongers. Then he collapsed on the bed, pulling Corson down with him.

Corson chuckled and kissed him. "They *sewed* this gown onto me—I don't know how to get the thing off. But maybe you can help me, hmm?"

Steifann's only answer was a thunderous snore.

He didn't wake when Corson pulled off his boots and

breeches, unlaced his shirt, and drew the bedclothes over him, laughing to herself. "Sleep well, love," she said, kissing him again, and closed the curtains about the bed. Then she summoned a maid to set her gown to rights again, and went back downstairs to the celebration for a while, to garner more flattery and admiration.